Leap
of
faith

Julia Regul Singh worked as an urban planner and urban designer in Germany and the US before turning to writing. She holds a Bachelor of Geography from the University of Bayreuth (Germany) and has a master's degree in Urban Planning and Urban Design from the Technical University Hamburg-Harburg (Germany). She is also the author of *Boris the Bench*, a children's book.

Julia resides in New Delhi with her husband, bringing up their three children Punjabi-style and working on her Hindi.

leap of faith

JULIA REGUL SINGH

RUPA

Published by
Rupa Publications India Pvt. Ltd 2015
7/16, Ansari Road, Daryaganj
New Delhi 110002

Sales centres:
Allahabad Bengaluru Chennai
Hyderabad Jaipur Kathmandu
Kolkata Mumbai

ISBN: 978-81-291-2480-7

First impression 2015
10 9 8 7 6 5 4 3 2 1

The moral right of the author has been asserted.

Typeset by Saanvi Graphics, Noida

Printed at Gopsons Papers Ltd, Noida

For my in-laws and parents,
and for Harjiv

Part 1

Autumn in New York

Chapter 1

Andalip Singh starts his five-mile run around the Central Park Reservoir every morning way before most people in New York City wake up. Today turns out to be an unusually cold September morning. The sun is just starting to rise above the East River, its rays shining through the high-rises along 5th Avenue, throwing shadows over the artificial lake. No matter how late it gets the night before, Andalip never misses this sight for anything. Amongst the morning mist, the trees are glowing in the most glorious autumn colours, ranging from yellow and orange to dark red and brown. He zips up his long-sleeved jacket and picks up the pace. Still his legs feel like ice sticks in his running shorts. Like most mornings, he heads south towards Columbus Circle to pick up a hot cup of coffee at his favourite corner news-stand along with *The New York Times*, *The Wall Street Journal* and a couple of magazines. He glances at the bridal magazines, wanting to pick one up for his fiancée Christina, but decides against it. She won't need a white dress for their upcoming wedding in New Delhi. He places some dollars on the counter, nods goodbye and dashes across Central Park South. Instead of heading home this morning like he usually does, Andalip moves towards a small diner a few blocks south. The sun is fully out now. Just before he enters the Lucky Diner, the bright neon light above the entrance is switched off. Just like at the news-stand, he is greeted by a fellow Indian. A tall Sikh gentleman with a pink turban welcomes him with a hard but friendly pat on the back and a loud 'Good Morning, Beta, *kya hal hai*?' The man reminds him of his many uncles back home with his broad shoulders, proud light eyes and beard tied up. Andalip feels right at home, grabs a bar stool, places his papers and coffee onto the counter and starts chatting in broken Punjabi.

'I am absolutely fine, Iqbalji. How are you? How is the family? How is the village in Punjab? Looks like business is going good! Not even seven yet and you've got a full house here.' Andalip scans the crowd of early morning breakfast-eaters, a pretty good mix of young and old from all around the globe. He had discovered this place a few years ago when he was returning home after a late night out with friends. It was the only diner close to his apartment that promised to serve some hot food 24/7. He didn't expect much when he had opened the door of the pretty run-down looking corner shop for the first time, but he was surprised by the clean, bright interior, the larger-than-life posters of the local Manhattan tourist sites as well as the Golden Temple of Amritsar and the Taj Mahal of Agra, and the smell of incense. The food turned out to be surprisingly good too. Iqbal had made a name for himself by serving the usual American favourites of grilled cheese sandwiches, milkshakes and burgers but also managed to introduce some of his Punjabi breakfast classics like *anda bhurji, aloo puri* and all varieties of *paranthas*. Andalip was craving for the latter.

'Son of a ..., you can say that again. These foreigners just love Punjabi cooking, any time of the day. But you haven't come to talk business, have you son? What can I do for you today? I see you've already bought your coffee from some other place. Throw that away, it can't be good. Do you want some *aloo paranthas* with that? I got some *hari mirch* and *dhania* this morning that will make it taste like your mother's cooking.' Iqbal keeps punching Andalip in his biceps. To an outsider this must look like abuse, Andalip thinks. For him it is a reminder of how his various relatives back home would express their love for him—in a loud, rough and very personal way but still full of affection and kindness, which he so often misses in America.

'Thank you Iqbalji, I will take the coffee, but I have to pass on the *parantha* at this time of the day.' Oh so tempting, he thinks, but not after this morning's run. 'Can you organize an egg and cheese sandwich for my fiancée though, on brown bread, with fresh tomatoes and lots of *dhania*. And don't forget the mint *chutney* on the side! She is crazy about it.' Andalip chuckles at the thought of Christina—a German—enjoying Indian food so much that she started adding coriander and *chutney* to almost everything these days. He opens *The Wall Street Journal* and enjoys his second cup of coffee. Iqbal leaves him with another pat on the back, starts bossing his staff and welcomes other guests. Ten minutes later, the sandwich arrives in a little brown bag, followed by a larger-than-life dinner plate with two oversized *aloo paranthas*, onions and extra chillies on it. Iqbal pinches Andalip's cheeks and loudly says, 'Beta, you have to eat. All this running-shunning is no good if you don't eat. I hope this little fiancée of yours knows how to feed a Punjabi man? If not, I will send my darling daughter Chotu over to make some butter chicken for you.' Iqbal laughs heartily, but then he turns a little more serious. He puts his strong, hairy arm around Andalip, lowers his voice and stares into Andalip's eyes: 'By the way, I am still looking for a suitable husband for Chotu. You know who I am talking about. The pretty one back there who just prepared your breakfast. Let me know when you are ready to settle down and we can talk man to man.'

Andalip gulps down the coffee. He has many answers to his friend's comment: *I am taken, my man, I am taken! You sound like my Dadi, trying to hook me up with a proper Sikh girl…*or maybe a plain *Thank you ji, will talk to my dad about it.* He decides to laugh instead and stuffs the *parantha* into his mouth to avoid further conversation. There goes his pre-wedding diet, he thinks. As soon as Iqbal lets go of him, Andalip jumps up with a glance at his watch, trying to look rushed. 'Oh, so late already! Thanks Iqbalji, I've got to run. I will see you later', grabs the sandwich and rushes out before Iqbal has time to further discuss his daughter's future.

On the way up to the apartment, he picks up the mail. It's been a week since he has done that and he struggles to balance the papers, the sandwich bag and a big pile of letters while pressing the elevator button. He starts thinking about what Iqbal had said and he realizes that it bothers him. Why do people always have to assume Christina is just an adventure for him and not his fiancée? Why shouldn't he get married to a non-Indian? He has been in NY for over 20 years now, dating girls from all over the world, so why should he marry somebody from back home. He would have, if he had met somebody he liked, that was not even the question. His thoughts are interrupted by the loud BING that announces the arrival of his floor. He rushes through the half-open elevator door and runs down the long hallway, clumsily searching for his keys and dropping half the mail in the process.

When he opens the door he is welcomed by the aroma of his favourite Harlem Blend coffee and a voice from the bathroom. '*Schatz*, is that you?' His mood lightens. He loves it when Christina addresses him as *schatz*, literally meaning 'treasure' in German but used for 'darling' or 'dear'. For a moment the smell of coffee takes him back to the day he saw Christina for the first time at his favourite bookshop-cum-cafe in the West Village. It was a few days before his final MBA exams at NYU and Andalip was daydreaming about his future career as an investment banker when Christina walked in. His friends still tease him about how he got up and bought her a cup of coffee, right there and then. 'Maybe if that finance textbook would have been more gripping, you would have missed her that day!' he remembers his classmates joking when Andalip started dating Christina a few weeks later.

Since that day almost five years ago Andalip can't imagine his life without her. It just felt right although Christina was and still isn't very affectionate. It used to bother him and he kept telling her to look after him better, kiss him more, hold hands or cook some tasty food for him. He remembered her reply clearly: 'What's your problem? I thought it is forbidden to kiss in public where you come from. I am German after all, I cannot sing and dance with you around a tree to show you that I love you. My love for you is right there in all the little things I do for you, like picking up your dirty laundry and making your coffee in the morning.' He knows exactly what she means but he still loves to tease her. He keeps telling her that back home, his family has help to do that for him. He enjoys watching her getting mad, frowning in disgust and usually changing the subject to avoid further confrontation. He still teases her every time she makes coffee for him by saying 'Wouldn't it have been easier to just kiss me or tell me you love me instead of going through the trouble of making coffee for me?' 'I love you too,' he jokingly says to the coffeemaker and pours himself another cup of coffee. He laughs at himself for acting like a teenager in love rather than the successful investment banker he is today. Then remembers the mail and his papers, and before sitting down at the kitchen table to enjoy his coffee, he heads back into the hallway.

'Your mom called. She asked whether we have received the wedding invitation yet.' Christina pops her head through the bedroom door, wrapped with towels from head to toe, reminding him of a very badly tied turban and *sari*. 'Cute. That's what you are going to wear for the wedding?' he jokes. Christina doesn't seem too amused. She briefly replies: 'Why don't you answer when I talk to you? Did you hear what I said? Your mom has been calling. More than once by the way on all the numbers. Did you see the wedding invitation in the mail?' Andalip pulls out the big pile of letters from the shelf in front of him: 'I was just looking for it!' 'Good, let me know. I am just getting ready for work. Oh, and by the way: THIS is what I am going to wear for the wedding.'

Christina turns around, drops the towels on the floor and shows off her milky-white bottom, before she walks back into the bathroom. 'Now we are talking, baby!' Andalip chuckles, calling after her with a fake German accent: 'That's why I asked you to marry me, Fräulein Christina von Hoisdorf!'

He returns to the kitchen, throws the pile of mail onto the table and sorts through it. Junk, junk, and more junk mail followed by last month's bills and more junk, he thinks. Still, in the middle of it all Andalip finds a large bulky letter-sized envelope and a smaller rectangular letter from India. Latter one is his monthly greeting from his grandma, who without fail, has written to him ever since he left Delhi for college in the US. She has been using the same off-white envelope for years, he smiles. Usually she updates him on what is happening on the family front as well as some suggestions on which Bollywood movies to watch. Recently, she had started adding photos and details of women she thought suitable for Andalip to marry. She had told him once on his last trip home that she thought Christina was a very lovely girl, polite and pretty, but that he should consider keeping her as a girlfriend rather than a wife. He tried not to take it too personally. She is getting old and reading too many gossip magazines, his sisters joked with him after he had mentioned her comment to them. At the end of his trip he sat with her again for a long time and waited for her to bring the topic up again, but she didn't. Before he left for the airport, he kissed her on the forehead and told her as politely as he could: 'Dadi, I know you have different plans for my future and the future of this family. But as you know too well, sometimes things just don't work out the way we plan it. I don't intend to hurt anybody, especially you. But, I have fallen in love with Christina and I have made my choice for a life partner. I hope you will be able to understand and over time and accept my decision.' He remembers his words like he had spoken them yesterday. He also cannot forget his grandmother's look as she just stared blankly for a few seconds before she turned to him, held his cheeks with both hands, and she replied: 'If that is how you feel, Beta.' Just that one sentence, that's it, he thought. He had expected her to fight him on the issue but the conversation was over at that point. She let go of his face, smiled and hugged him farewell. The moment had passed quickly, interrupted by relatives coming into the room wanting to see him off. Andalip figured that was it and forgot about the conversation as soon as he left his parents' house that evening. After his return to NYC, the wedding proposals started to arrive and he wondered about his grandma's reaction once again.

Christina comes out of the bedroom, this time fully dressed. She wears a light blue linen suit that they had bought together in Delhi last winter. 'You are going to freeze in that. It is colder outside than it looks. I almost lost my legs out there. Seriously, go change!' Besides being worried about her actually being cold, he also enjoys stressing her about her wardrobe. The frown on her forehead appears again and he watches her returning to the bedroom, mumbling something in German. He yells after her: 'No, it looks great but it is really cold out there. Come, feel my legs!' Andalip drops his grandma's letter back on the pile of bills. He picks up the brown paper bag with the sandwich. 'Hurry, I got you your favourite sandwich from Iqbal. He says hello and sends his regards for the wedding!' Christina appears wearing another suit, spins around and asks: 'Better, *meri jaan?*' 'Perfect, now sit down and look at this.' He kisses her on the cheek and then shows her the larger of the two envelopes from India. 'Here, this must be it. Just smell it. The smell reminds me of this bookshop I used to hang out in as a teenager. They used to burn so much incense our eyes would burn when we entered the store. Still a lot better than the dusty smell of old paper. The place is still there at Khan Market, I will take you next time. You will love it too.' He holds the envelope right under her nose. She smells it and laughs: 'More like the polluted air you smell when you step out of the airport in Delhi. You open it, I don't want green *chutney* all over this precious thing.' She sits down at the kitchen table opposite Andalip and looks at a bright red booklet that he pulls out of the envelope.

Andalip can tell by the look on her face that she is disappointed. Christina pushes away the sandwich, wipes her fingers before she pulls the card out of his hand. He watches her flip through the different-sized cards inside the large, heavily decorated envelope. He stops counting after five. 'Just look at this. Didn't we decide to keep it a small wedding?' She waves the cards in front of his face. 'And I don't like the design at all. It is nothing like we have discussed with your sister. What are all these beads and funky stones in the front of the card? I thought we wanted some classic Sikh symbol, not kitsch. One can hardly read the awful golden lettering on this shade of red. Do you think we can still change that? Can't this whole thing be a little simpler? What happened to the idea of an Indo-German fusion wedding theme? This is totally way over-the-top Punjabi now.'

Andalip just nods, then shrugs. He knows that to Christina the term 'over-the-top Punjabi' is often used for anything that, as he would describe it, a rather traditional Indian way usually with some semi-precious stones and gold. Or as his youngest sister likes to call it: 'Bling, baby, bling!'

On Christina's first trip to Delhi she would constantly use her newly-coined phrase to describe oversized wedding rings, golden Gucci bags, shiny high heels or the newly built shopping malls onthe outskirts of Delhi. For her, good taste was defined by straight lines, plain colours and simple patterns. At first he had agreed with her and felt like she had with that phrase captured the style of India's newly rich who defined themselves through money and designer brands rather than family names or business skills. Crystal candle-stands, golden vases and imported cars that had become the new standard at his old school friends' houses annoyed him more than they impressed him. He also agrees with her that Indian gods and goddesses look great on modern wedding invitations, simplified in black and white. But India is a colourful place that challenges one's senses all the time, he thinks and pictures his mother's kitchen and the girls working there, as the first example that comes to mind to underline his point. At any given morning in his childhood, he was greeted by two or three girls in the brightest *salwar kameezes* running around in his mother's red kitchen while he rushed by in his bright yellow and blue school uniform to catch the bus. Of course that gets translated into very colourful wedding invitations, he reasons. Where do you draw the line between somebody's taste or a country's traditions and religious beliefs? In India, he thinks with amusement, gold might as well be just another colour in the rainbow, tracing the gold writing on the wedding card with his finger.

'As a sociologist, I thought you would know better not to generalize. I am sure most Indians find that western wedding cards look cheap and boring. You would have killed me if I had said that about your cousin's obviously home-made wedding invitation. Just looking at it, I thought somebody had died,' he tries to joke with her but knows that as soon as he had opened his mouth, he just made it worse. 'So you like this…this thing? This book? You really want a card like this? I hope you didn't give your mom the green light to print this.' She tries to catch her breath. The card lands in front of him with a loud thump on the glass table. Christina takes another bite of the sandwich, but pushes the rest of it aside, shaking her head: 'You know, I cannot believe you sometimes. I thought we have the same taste.' And with that she gets up and busies herself with getting ready for her day at New York University.

This time he decides to stay quiet and picks up the paper. That is why he didn't want to get involved in the wedding planning in the first place. Not only will he hear complaints from Christina, but also from a bunch of female relatives in Delhi, who have taken on this wedding as their new hobby. 'Andy, we are not done discussing this. I've got to go. Let's decide something tonight, OK?' Before she rushes out of the house, she comes over, kisses him on the forehead and pleads with him: 'Just don't mention it to your mom when she calls. Say I haven't seen it yet. Love you, bye!'

By the time Christina slams the door behind her, Andalip is already on his third cup of coffee, finishing off the rest of the sandwich—definitely killing the pre-wedding diet with that—and is back to reading the newspaper. Within the next 10 minutes, the phone rings at least three times. Twice it is his mother, once Christina, but both times he ignores it and decides that *The New York Times* is more important.

After getting ready for work, he takes a quick look at the wedding invitation again before he reads his grandmother's letter. He is not surprised by either of them. To him the wedding card looks like many of the invitations he has received over the years and which he has spent less than a minute looking at. The cards list the typical events of a Sikh wedding from prayers, ceremonies and functions to lunches, teas and dinners. Spread over a week and hosted by different members of the family at different locations all over Delhi. The key event is the wedding ceremony which will be held at the local gurudwara. All the other events, even though written in gold, could still change. The card is just a formality in his eyes. He checks inside the envelope again, just to make sure he is not missing any sweets or treats that his mom might put with the invitation cards. It's just a card, he grimaces. Christina has been to many Indian weddings with him, so she should have known what it means to agree to a wedding in Delhi. The card is just a small piece in this big wedding puzzle. Wasn't a Delhi wedding her idea after all?

As for the letter, Dadi sent her usual update on Delhi's weather, family gossip and a gentle reminder to send his feedback on the last minute few marriage suggestions. He smiles since his mom has already briefed him on all of the above during her weekend phone call. Except for the suggestion for a better bride! For a moment he considers taking the wedding invitation and mailing it to his grandmother, just to remind her that he is done with looking for a suitable bride. His BlackBerry vibrates and he forgets about everything and everybody that instant and switches into work mode for the rest of the day.

Chapter 2

By the time Christina reaches the street, she has already thought through at least 20 different ways of dealing with the wedding invitation. Ignore or not to ignore? Maybe she could come up with her own design and email it to Andalip's sisters and act like she has not seen this red monster card yet? Red is fine, but she had imagined more of a wine colour with white lettering. No stones and just the minimum info on it. A black and white photo of the two of them instead of the Sikh symbol in front would look just so much better, she feels. Maybe she should just get her own version done for her German relatives and claim that the Indian postal service has lost the original invitations? It would not be the first time, she smiles. Or she could just be honest and say that she hated this invitation. At the end, none seems satisfying since she knows exactly how Andalip will react if she dares to bring it up again with him at dinner: 'You agreed to get married in India. I told you my mom and sisters will take over. You are not even in Delhi to help with the preparations so just lean back and suck it up.' She dials his number. No answer. Christina smiles to herself, picturing Andalip already engrossed in his newspapers. He couldn't care less about the invite, she knows, but hopes he will at least try to understand her a little bit. For her, the topic is not done yet.

She realizes that she is early for her class at New York University. This semester she ended up teaching a condensed workshop instead of the entire lecture series since she would be taking a break for the wedding in a few weeks anyway. Only ten students had signed up for this month's session on German immigrants to New York after World War II. Her seminars are usually packed, and at first she was annoyed by the low attendance, but now she is glad because there is no way she could handle situations like this morning's wedding card disaster and a jam-packed classroom.

She decides to pass the next subway stop and walk a bit to make some phone calls. The sky above her is a clear bright blue. She admires it for a minute, knowing that only in New York can one finds such blue skies. September in Germany is already grey and rainy and she has never been to Delhi at this time of the year. So far she has only seen foggy December days or the sweltering heat in May. Both times she was sure that pollution was hiding the true colours of both sky and sun. November is supposed to be nice. She dials her friend's number, lets it ring once then changes her mind. No way P — short for Purnima — is up at this early hour. Her new best friend from Delhi, married to a banker from Delhi, had moved to NYC right after her honeymoon. P had quickly established herself as Christina's constant relationship adviser who could give a female perspective on being married to an Indian. She had met her last summer at a NYU teachers' conference. One of P's favourite things is to sleep late into the morning. She is the only teacher Christina knows who manages to only teach the afternoon seminars. Maybe it is better to discuss the wedding invite with her over a cup of coffee after lunch. Or better yet, once her seminar is done tonight at Happy Hour! This way she can vent and have her thoughts all sorted out before talking to Andalip about it again later tonight.

She calls her mom instead. Germany is six hours ahead and her mom must be already home from her early morning rounds of shopping and tennis. '*Von Hoisdorf!*' her mom picks up the phone after two rings. '*Ja, Mama, ich bin's...*' Christina doesn't get to finish her sentence. 'Oh, *schatz*, I am so glad you called. I was just thinking of you. Guess what we got in the mail today?' Her voice sounds eerily chirpy. 'What?' It can't be the wedding invitation since that is just a draft, right? She stops and closes her eyes, hoping this is just a joke.

'Your wedding invitation! Oh my, it is so gorgeous. I have already shown it to my friends at the club. They were so impressed. Such eye for detail, I especially like the stonework on top. And I tell you, it must be hand-made paper, such quality. I am just a little confused about all the cards inside and names of the functions. Me-hen-di, San-geet, Mil-ni, Baarat...' Her mom is trying to read through the cards. 'I found one card that had our name on it, but they spelled my name wrong. Did you see that? Bärbel...it's Bärbel! Add at least the "ae", Baerbel is fine too. Will you make sure of that? ... Christina, *schatz*, can you hear me?' Christina cannot believe her ears. Her mind is spinning. They've got the wedding invitation already. The unfinished draft! The draft that she has not approved of yet, the draft that she hates. Unbelievable! She hangs up the phone and sits down on the step beside her.

A minute later her mom calls her back. Christina presses the reject button. Of course, Bärbel tries again. She is tempted to throw her phone into the dustbin right next to her, but just pretends to do so, opening her mouth wide for a soundless scream. Christina picks up, 'Sorry, must be a bad line. I am about to go into the subway, on my way to work. I just wanted to check how everybody is doing.' She tries to sound normal.

'No, we are absolutely fine. I just told you, not sure if you heard me, that we got the wedding invitation. We absolutely love it. These people really did a great job. I know we had our arguments about the wedding, but I am starting to feel this is really going to be nice.' Christina nods: 'Sure Mama.'

Her mom continues, 'I just have some suggestions. I found some typos. And I am not so sure about all these functions. I told your sister to look them up on the Internet for me, but you know how she is. Frauke is still mad that she has to come to India for this. Berndt still doesn't want to go and is very clear that the kids shouldn't go either. All he says when I try to talk to him is 'Malaria and pollution. I don't think so, Ma.' Why don't you talk to her again? Tell her about all the pretty outfits we will be wearing. Should I try a *sari* or do you think that is silly?' Christina cannot believe her ears. She is really worried about what to wear now? 'Sure, Mama, you can wear whatever you wan't. I am sure everybody will be more than happy to see you in a *sari*. Although, I am not sure a *sari* is really what people wear at a Punjabi wedding...they have these other outfits called...' Christina's sentence is interrupted by another round of questions. She rolls her eyes in irritation, rests her head in one hand while she holds the phone up in the air to avoid the rush of 'when, what and how?' that she predicts to follow. Christina has just spoken to her mom a few days ago to explain to her the programme for the wedding week in Delhi. She knows that for everybody this wedding will be a new experience and not at all like the typical Christian church wedding. Both she and Andalip have spent many hours on the phone going over what to expect but still her family and friends seem more than confused.

Andalip calls it typical German behaviour, Christina calls it organized: the need for Christina's family to plan events or vacations several months in advance. As soon as the engagement was announced, Christina's father had rushed over to the computer to look up flights to India. Andalip told him that they hadn't discussed dates yet. 'The wedding will be some time in the winter when the weather is nice in Delhi, but we have not even decided on a month yet. I promise, you will be the first one to know,' Andalip had told him. Michael looked disappointed: 'Let's just hope we will find a good deal and all of us find tickets for the same flight.' Christina had teased her dad: 'We haven't even discussed the year yet. You will have enough time to do this later. Let's enjoy this moment first and then we worry about what comes next.' That was almost two years ago. All of a sudden last summer they had decided to finally go ahead with the wedding and the planning had taken off. Both families quickly agreed on a wedding in late November. A week was blocked for everybody to keep free by July. Details would need to be worked out later. Michael booked flights for the first round of friends and family, who within a day had decided to take the same flight to New Delhi and attend the wedding.

After that, Christina had decided to keep her family out of the planning as much as possible. She suffered mild heart attacks every time Andalip announced a different programme for the wedding week. Or worse, a different week for the wedding. Andalip soon decided to keep the phone calls with his sisters to himself and assured his fiancée that in the end, the wedding will take place the same week that everyone had decided upon in July. When she saw the draft of the invitation this morning, Christina had noticed that all events did fall within that week. Planned or coincidence, she was not sure.

She can still hear her mother. 'And Christina, please make sure you send us the details on the hotels as soon as possible. People have been asking, you know. We will be arriving in less than two months and we still don't know where we will be sleeping, *schatz*. I keep joking about it and tell them that this is how things are in India. You know, like you said, everything happens last minute. You know I don't really care but between you and me, please get this done and tell Andy that these things cannot be pushed off until the last minute. Can you also remind him about the list of vaccinations we should be getting? Are you working on an itinerary yet? You know, for the days when there are no wedding obligations. I told you, people want to see something of Delhi too, sightseeing and getting some shopping done. Nobody wants to just sit around a wedding for an entire week.'

Bärbel is quiet for a moment. Christina puts the phone to her ear again. 'Sure, Mama, I am on it. Got to rush now, getting late for work. Can we continue this on Saturday?' Even though her mother could not see her, she quickly gets up, collects her bag and starts walking again.

'Of course, go on. But you know you work too much. Enjoy this time. This might as well be your only wedding! Love you, bye!' She hangs up but calls back within seconds: 'Oh, by the way, what about white at the wedding, can I wear white?'

'No, you can't Mama, unless it is decorated and has some colour in it. It is the colour for funerals and widows, remember I told you? BYE now.' Christina hangs up before her mother gets another chance to reply. She switches off her phone, just in case, and starts walking back to the last subway stop. She does not feel like talking on the phone anymore and she is definitely done with her stroll through Manhattan.

This morning did not turn out as planned, she thinks while pushing by people on the platform. She is mad at Andalip—or Andy as her entire family calls him now—for not getting involved in the wedding planning at all. The day she met him he had told her that he wanted to spend the rest of his life with her. For the first three years she thought he was joking, but she always loved his charming ways and happily fell for him. After three years they decided to make their relationship more official and on a trip to Germany and India told their parents and families about their decision to get married. She loved him even more when he stood up to both families and their arguments against their union. He used to assure her that he would do anything to make her happy and he was ready to run off to Vegas with her and get married any second. She thought he would be happy when they finally decided on a wedding back in India. She still likes the idea of a colourful Punjabi wedding, but shouldn't Andalip be a bit understanding about what it involves? She hates it when he just says, 'I told you I will marry you and I will be there for you all my life, but the wedding, that is a woman's job. Call Mom or Jazz or better all my sisters and let them tell you how this works. I really don't know. You will be the expert by the end of it, you will see. Just have fun, it's all about having fun!'

She is mad at whoever decided the card was ready without consulting her. But at this point she doesn't even know who in Andalip's large extended family is in charge of the card. Christina has been emailing back and forth on wedding outfits and venues with his three younger sisters. Simran, just a year younger than Andalip, lives in Singapore with her husband and daughter. From the beginning she wholeheartedly supported the wedding, but has been too far away to really help out. Jazz, or better Jasneet, exactly Christina's age, officially took over the organization of the event. She and her family live just minutes away from the large Singh home in Central Delhi. Even though she has two sons and is pregnant, she manages to run not only her house but also a successful baking and catering business out of her kitchen. She loves organizing birthdays and family functions as a hobby and was the first one to agree to be on top of everything wedding related. Preeti, the 'baby' of the house being nine years younger to Andalip, works in advertising and volunteered to overview the design of everything from outfits, venues and, of course, the wedding invitation.

Last time Christina talked to Preeti on the phone a few weeks ago, they had agreed on a fusion theme for the wedding. Christina imagined something that would combine elements from India and Germany in both the outfits as well as the overall party design. Christina loves Preets (as she started to call her), and admires her style and the ease with which she managed to navigate western and eastern settings. She thinks the world of this confident 30-year-old newly-wed, and is often impressed by how she moved to Mumbai with her husband and re-invented her career in advertising. She trusted that Preets would understand what she wanted for her wedding theme. Christina was convinced that Preets would have never chosen this hideous card. If she did, Christina was comfortable enough to tell her that she hated it. If it was anybody else, most likely Mom or Dadi, maybe Jazz, then this card was set in stone. Well, now that her mom had shown the card to the entire Hamburg North Tennis Club and it was publicly approved of, as her mom said, Christina was starting to believe that there was nothing else she could do about it now.

When she gets off at West 4th Street, she decides to try Andalip one more time and talk to him on his way to the campus. This time he picks up. 'What's up?' he sounds cheerful. Christina is happy to get him on the line and says: 'Hey. Sorry about this morning. I thought about the card on the subway ride down here and you can tell your mom that it's fine. I don't really like it but at least it is done in time and I guess it is just a card after all. It will be fine.'

'Oh good, I've already told her that it is great. She kept calling and I figured the same. It's just a card! What else is going on? I got a meeting in two minutes. We'll talk tonight, OK?' He finishes his call with a kiss, which she thinks is so tacky. What would his colleagues say, an almost 40-year-old guy kissing into the phone? Then it hits her. Why would he tell his mom that the card is fine after the way she, and says: reacted this morning? She is annoyed again, but tries to play cool: 'I love you too, Andy. By the way, I might be late tonight. I want to meet P for drinks after I am done here. Bye.'

She puts the phone away and enters the campus. She is mad at herself for once again losing control over anything that is related to Andalip. Maybe love really blinds you, like they say in Germany. Maybe her mom was right and relationships are always hard work, even within your own culture, forget marrying somebody from across the world? Maybe she is just nervous about the wedding? Or maybe she just woke up on the wrong side of the bed this morning? She will have to discuss this with P tonight.

Chapter 3

'Are you excited about your move to Delhi?' P asks Christina, who is sitting across from her in a small narrow Lower East Side cafe, which is packed with hipsters in their mid-20s. P is sure she recognizes a few of them from her classroom. P hates coming here for exactly that reason but Christina had lured her with the delicious cake selection and the perfect cappuccinos, that Christina was worried she wouldn't find in Delhi. P didn't want to refuse her wish, since this was her friend's last week in the city.

Both women had been trying to get together for almost two weeks now. P had been down with the flu for a few days and then Christina got busy with her wedding preparations. Christina did not even get a chance to fill her in on the invitation disaster. Christina's travel schedule had been discussed with P and then finalized weeks ago, like anything her straightforward German friend plans and does in life. This was Christina's last official weekend in NYC before she was going to hop on a plane eastwards. First she stops in Germany for almost a month to spend some quality time with her family. Andalip's plan on the other hand, as P can't stop musing, is as unpredictable as life itself with possible weekend trips between NYC and Hamburg or sudden work commitments around the world. But God willing, Andalip will collect his future bride in time to reach Delhi hopefully before the rest of the German family arrives in India and with enough time to spare to get his wedding suit tailored.

'Hey, Doctor von Hoisdorf, are you listening to me?' P smiles. She loves addressing her friend by her last name. When they first met, she thought Christina was from an aristocratic family in Germany or something blue-blooded like that. She was disappointed when Christina gave her a long lecture on family names in Germany. P learned that her friend was not an aristocrat at all, but that the family name indicated that her family came from a small town north of Hamburg. 'Well, centuries ago, but now we are big city folks,' she remembers Christina making a point. P had joked with her that Hamburg is not a big city with its 1. 9 million people and that at least that many people live in her Delhi neighbourhood of GKII. She had told her: 'Once you move to India, you can call yourself a big city girl. Ok, New York is not bad for a start. Until then, just claim you are the daughter of some baron. In Delhi you will get away with it.'

P taps her friend on the arm to wake her up from her daydream. She watches Christina adjust her blonde curly hair into an untidy ponytail. She misses her short bob which she thought was Christina's trademark when they first met on campus. She knows that Christina had made an effort of letting her hair grow for the wedding. Not that anybody had asked her too, Christina had told P, but she wanted to make an effort of 'fitting in somehow' at a Sikh wedding as she had called it. All her sisters-in-law had beautiful long thick hair, following Sikh traditions of not cutting it.

'I am sorry. I keep making lists in my head on what all I need to do before I head out. Andy will still come back to NYC a few times for work, so I don't really have to pack up the apartment. I am sure at the end of it Andy will be too lazy and he will have packers do the job. Let them figure that one out. My stuff is all sorted in boxes and clearly labelled, that should be OK. So besides packing my personal things, I just want to explore more of the city. I just have been so busy with work the last two years. There is so much more I want to see and do before I fly out. You know India is not just a day-trip away. Who knows when I can come back next? Now, what did you ask?' Christina uses a spoon to scoop the foam off her cappuccino. Then she reaches over the table and holds her friend's hand: 'Oh, I will miss you P. I will miss this. I hope they have good cappuccinos in Delhi.'

'Well, you can't get rid of me. I still have to come to Delhi once a year to see my family and the in-laws. I will find some time to sneak out of the house and come to see you. And I will make you a long list of all my favourite restaurants and coffee places for you to check out. Please, Chrissie, promise me not to jump right into work again. Take some time off, make some babies and enjoy the good life with lots of servants and endless socializing. Honestly, I would do it! There is still time for you to be a famous sociologist when you are old and ugly.' P giggles. She's still having a hard time picturing her dear friend as a professor. 'You are just way too fun and too pretty to end up behind some dusty college desk at Delhi University. Have you considered Bollywood as a career?'

Christina laughs. She knows P means well. As a colleague, she has seen first-hand how hard Christina has worked to be at this point in her career. One of the youngest tenured professors at NYU in her field with a PhD from Germany and the US, several books under her belt and several offers as guest lecturer at universities all over the US, she is not ready to retire just yet to enjoy the 'good life' as P calls it. She has already spoken to some friends of P at Delhi University and was hoping to start a new teaching position next semester. At NYU she had just been granted a sabbatical for at least a year, extendable for another year if necessary. She wanted to have something just in case she couldn't live in India and wanted to return to the States. P knew about this but Christina had not gotten a chance to discuss this with Andalip yet. He seemed so excited about the move back to Delhi. He had managed to land a one-year consulting job with his company there which allowed him to move back and forth between Delhi and NYC for a while.

In the meantime, he was planning to finally join his dad in the family business. Christina just could not picture Andy in his dad's auto part factory in Noida after leading the exciting life of an investment banker, always telling clients what to do, taking them out for fancy dinners, and constantly chasing after planes. Yes, his work hours would be less, which both of them were looking forward to, but was he really ready to sacrifice his sky-rocketing career in NYC and work for his dad? Well, she knew for herself that she wasn't ready to be a full-time mom yet, so she doubted Andy was ready to put his career on ice either.

'You know P, I think the move will be good.' She nods and continues, more to convince herself: 'It will add a new spin to my research. And you are absolutely right. I should start a family sooner rather than later. I am 35 years old, the biological clock is ticking. I need all the help I can get to manage kids and stay on top of my career. NYC is fun and all but I am ready for something new.' She points at P: 'You said it yourself in one of your lectures— all kinds of people are moving to India these days. It's the new frontier, the Promised Land, full of opportunity, right? America is the old world now, India the new. I definitely want to be part of that. You should hear Andy when he talks about going back. He seems really excited. He is at that age now when the family is getting more important to him. It will be good for everybody, I think.' Christina drinks a bit of her coffee before she continues. 'Oh, before I forget, look at these,' and with that, Christina pulls out a folder from her bag. 'Preeti sent those. A bunch of clippings of outfits she thinks appropriate for the wedding. I am not so sure. What do you think? You are from Delhi, you had an Indian wedding and you know better what is OK and what's not.'

She spreads out the clippings on the coffee table between them, moves a little closer to P and starts sorting them by cuts and colours. Her soon to be sister-in-law had emailed her a wide selection of Indian bridal outfits, from the typical Punjabi *salwar-*

kameezes to *lehengas* to *saris* and some Indo-western mixes. She recognizes some of the models to be famous Bollywood actresses and knows that Preeti had consulted some of her favourite movies for outfit ideas. She likes most of them, but was not sure if she could wear them too. 'I think Preeti forgets that I am not your typical Indian bride. On top of that I am blonde and really pale. I would look horrible in these colours.' She picks up a yellow and pink outfit. 'Look at the cut. Who wears this? It would end right under my boobs. Not that I am afraid to show skin, but I think Andy's mom and grandma would not be happy about that. And with that colour I don't think some of the aunties will be able to tell where my belly starts and hair ends…' she giggles.

P shakes her head. 'You are selling yourself all wrong here. You are not blonde. Your hair is a beautiful golden colour and your skin a perfect porcelain. Fair is beautiful, that is your biggest plus in India. And people are not as prudish as you think. Have you seen any Bollywood movies recently and noticed what girls wear these days? You don't want to lag behind your sisters-in-law or nieces in style, now do you?'

P flips through the clippings. Then she stops and looks at Christina until she notices her stare. 'Are you sure about all this? Do you really seriously want to get married Punjabi style? It might look fun in the movies, but it is a lot of work, honey. Even a Delhi girl like me found it hard to so without a breakdown. How will you handle all this, Chrissie?' P knows Christina has made up her mind and she will go through with it, no matter what. She will not start backtracking now and change plans at the last minute. Instead of waiting for a reply, P picks out three outfits: an old-pink *sari* with rich but modern embroidery; a heavy-looking, golden *lehenga* fit for a royal wedding and one long black Indo-western coat fit for the runway in either Milan or Mumbai. Her friend will look stunning in all three of them, she knows. 'Perfect for a small wedding at home, a fancy fusion wedding or grand Punjabi family affair, you should wear something like these. They are a good mix for a traditional wedding as well as a modern high-society party. I can't wait to see you all dressed up at the wedding. It will be fabulous!'

The embroidery on the *sari* reminds Christina that she has forgotten to tell P about the invitation. And that the small family affair with both western and Indian elements now turns out to be a week-long traditional full-fledged Punjabi wedding. There are only going to be five official ceremonies or parties, but Preeti had written in her email that Christina will need at least ten outfits tailored: 'What about the dinner invitations and first official parties which you guys will have to attend after the wedding?' With her career in advertising, having travelled the world and living in the film and fashion capital of India, Mumbai, Christina knows that within the Singh family Preeti comes closest to knowing what would suit her. At least that is what she thought until the wedding invitation arrived. She still isn't sure who ultimately chose the final invitation design but to be on the safe side and to avoid the same mistake with her wedding outfits Christina is happy to have P to discuss this before she leaves NYC. P is watching her friend skim through the many clippings. Like teenage girls they go on discussing the many choices, wondering if Christina's sister-in-law knows her well enough to make the right choices for her. P muses that Christina is not the type to wear such low-cut blouses or belly free tops, knowing how tom-boying she looks at home. Her 5 foot 10, rather athletic figure looks too tall and flat-chested for these cuts. Christina checked with Andalip, but as with the invitation he refused to get involved when it came to picking her wedding clothes. 'You will look great in anything!' he assured her over and over again. Christina figures she might mix them up with some of her dresses or suits, but was getting confused. Thank God she likes to wear Indian clothes so she assumes at the end of it all, it will be fun to dress up for this special occasion. She picks up a few more clippings and adds them to P's selection. 'We are talking about a week-long wedding now and God knows how many functions. Preets said to decide on ten outfits. Do you think that is too much? In Germany, the bride usually wears only one wedding dress, the typical white one, and might change into something more comfortable for the evening party, but that's about it. I really don't know how to choose 10 outfits!' With that she drops her head on the table and plays dead.

P pulls Christina's ponytail. 'Honestly Christina, are you messing with me? You are going to do ten outfits? If you pull this off, you are definitely ready to move to Delhi! Well, I didn't have a Punjabi wedding and I don't remember how many outfits I wore during my wedding, but ten sounds a…LOT.' P moves even closer to Christina. 'But darling, go for it. If your family gets them done for you…' With that she picks up the clippings and lets them rain into Christina's lap and laughs loudly: 'This is your wedding and the best time to bring in the clothes, the jewellery and the money, my dear.' P leans over to her friend and hugs her: 'Sounds like you are moving into Delhi's high society as we are speaking. Live it up, babes. Like I said, you will be busy socializing and producing babies.'

'Oh stop it, P. Just help me choose some cuts and colours. And make sure you will get time off for the wedding. I will need your help wearing all this.' Christina is tired of all this talk about clothes and wedding. Suddenly she is in the mood to enjoy the time with P. 'Let's go over to Rosa's and have some frozen margaritas. Let's pretend we are 27 and let's go dancing without the boys tonight. I'll just choose the clothes later. Let's get out of here!'

Chapter 4

As Christina and P are starting their girls' night out in the Lower East Side, Andalip receives a call from his dad in his midtown Manhattan office. Andalip is sitting on the 15th floor looking south on 6th Avenue. He picks up the phone and realizes that it is getting dark. The lights of Times Square are starting to fill the sky. 'Dad, what's up? Isn't it a little early in Delhi to be calling?' Andalip checks his watch: 7. 30 pm in New York, about 10 am in Delhi.

'Don't panic, Beta, but something's happened. We thought Dadi had had a heart attack but the doctors at the hospital think it was just a panic attack. I wanted to let you know since she was asking for you! Maybe she's getting worried about the upcoming wedding?' Andalip can tell that his dad is trying to sound normal but he knows his father is shaken up.

The last time his then 80-year-old grandmother ended up in the hospital was four years ago when his grandfather passed away. She had announced that she was ready to join her husband in the next life and stopped eating. Luckily she had changed her mind soon after. A few months later Andalip came to know that Dadi had seen her beloved in a dream who told her to look after unfinished family business. Since then she'd been after Andalip to get married and produce an heir for the family empire, an auto parts plant that his late grandfather Zorawar had started out of a small workshop that he created 'out of nothing' after Partition. She constantly reminded her grandchildren of the hardships that their grandparents had faced and managed to overcome when Pakistan and the Republic of India were 'born' in 1947 and they—amongst many—were forced to leave their old lives and belongings in Lahore behind and find a new home in Delhi. She kept telling him that as the oldest son, it was up to him to continue the family's tradition and run the family business one day.

Andalip had spent many nights with his parents on the phone to discuss his grandmother's state of mind and her future plans for him. Neither mom nor dad ever pushed him to get married or return to India to run the family business. Andalip's younger cousin, his *bua's* (father's sister) son, Anhad, was more than happy to fill that role. Andalip however knew that his mom especially was more worried that he was almost 40 and still unsettled, than his joining dad at the plant. Dad was proud of him for having gone his own way and 'making it big abroad', as he would overhear him telling friends and family, usually after a few drinks at the club. Dad had taken him aside only once—was it his 30th birthday, he couldn't remember?—and told him, they were hoping that he would marry within their religion and community. Ever since Andalip had talked about Christina, his parents were really welcoming and warm to her and did not say anything else about it again.

When he had brought Christina to their family home in Golf Links, to announce their engagement, Mom had cried and asked him if he was sure he was doing the right thing. She said she was worried about him. In the long run, he might not be happy marrying an outsider and his life ahead would be so much harder than what she always wanted for him. He was certain this was just part of her mother-son drama that she felt she had to stage to show how much she loves him and only wants the best for him. As soon as he told her that they were planning to move back to India one day, she seemed to be happy with his choice and had been very supportive ever since. He knew that once his family would get to know Christina better, they would love her as much as he does.

A few months ago, Dadi got involved with the wedding planning as well. Andalip figured that since he wasn't marrying a girl of her choice, she had decided that she might as well make sure that the wedding would be conducted in the right way, and, at the same time, give Christina a few tips about her new culture and family traditions. At first he was a little concerned about how Christina would handle the whole affair, but from what he could tell over the last few weeks, she was really getting into the idea of a traditional Indian wedding and was enjoying the extra attention. If anything, Christina would take it as one of her sociology case studies and write a research paper about it later. At the end, he thought, this might work out well for everybody.

Maybe Dadi got carried away and ventured out to Old Delhi to do the wedding shopping. He knew his sisters, Simmi, Jazz and Preets, were doing most of the legwork but doubted Dadi would listen to them either. He pictured Dadi working her way through the maze of narrow lanes in Chandni Chowk, on a cycle rickshaw, haggling with shopkeepers over the best prices for her purchases. Just like she used to when he was a little boy, he thought sentimentally. Till today he admires his strong-willed grandma for always getting the best deals at any market and spoiling him with forbidden deep-fried treats that his mother would never have allowed him to eat right off the street. I should apply some of her bargaining tactics in my finance career, he constantly jokes.

His worry lessened with the certainty that at least ten members of his family were sprawled out in her hospital room right now, not leaving Dadi's side until she was discharged. He was looking forward to moving back to Delhi so that his children would not miss out on the love and affection of a large joint family, especially in situations like these. He wants his kids to grow up amongst cousins and so many relatives that counting them would be difficult at any given family get-together. After living in the West he had learned to enjoy being alone and spending time on his own instead of worrying about being abandoned. He remembered noticing the pity in his mother's voice when her son had to go to the movies alone. That same pity he had noticed in Christina's eyes when he had told her about spending a weekend with lots of unannounced visitors from India, who had camped out in his small apartment. Happy in both worlds, he still feels nothing can beat the feeling of having a room jam-packed to the ceiling with people who love you in a crisis like this.

'Dadi is sleeping right now. Talk to your sister, she has been with us all night.' Andalip can hear his father talking to some people in the room and suddenly felt a bit homesick. Be real Andy, he pulls himself up and thinking out loud, how can anybody sleep with that many people around?

'Andalip, it's me, Jasneet. Don't worry, we got it all under control. I told Dad not to call you. She will be out of here in no time! But Dad just wants to include his son in everything—you know how it is!' Andalip is glad to hear his sister's voice. He knows that she is right and they do have everything under control. She should have been the son, he often jokes with her. She is always there for the family and always there to help his parents with everything while looking after her husband, her two kids and in-laws at the same time. Thanks to her Andalip never felt too guilty about following his dream of making it big in the West. He knew Jazz would be there covering his back.

'How is Christina doing? Have you guys packed your boxes yet, ready to move to Delhi? Really, don't worry about Dadi. Like all of us, I think she is just really excited about your wedding and the fact that her oldest grandson is finally coming home. Mom caught her practicing the bhangra in front of her bedroom mirror for an item number at your wedding. Of course she will have heart issues doing that.' Jazz laughs wholeheartedly at her own joke. Andy giggles, trying to picture his Dadi as the star of a Bollywood dance scene.

After the phone makes the rounds in the hospital room, Andalip finally hangs up with the promise from his family to call him when Dadi gets up. Suddenly he feels tired and alone and decides to track down Christina to take her out for dinner. When she does not pick up the phone, he leaves the office and starts walking across Manhattan soaking in the lights, the smells and the energy of the city that he has been calling home the last 20-odd years. Is it really time to leave all this behind and return to a home that he had left half a lifetime ago? Is he prepared to step up and be the grandson, son, brother, uncle—roles that he had ignored all this time? How can he add husband and one day father to that extensive list? He spots an old neighbourhood bar where he used to hang out in with his college friends when he had first arrived in New York City. He suddenly longs for those long lost days full of adventure and new beginnings, free as a bird with no responsibilities but to himself. One cold beer for the way, he smiles and enters the bar. Dinner can wait until tomorrow. We have an entire life ahead of us, he thinks. He opens the door, welcomed by loud laughter and music. He greets the crowd with a loud 'Cheers to that, cheers to that!' and forgets about the present and the future, hanging on to his past for just a little bit longer.

Part 2

Nostalgia in Germany

Chapter 5

Christina's plane arrives three hours late at Hamburg's Fuhlsbüttel airport. It's grey and rainy outside, typical October weather in Northern Germany. It already feels like it is getting dark but it's not even two o'clock yet. Christina had left New York last night at around 10 pm on a flight to Frankfurt and had an early connection to Hamburg this morning. What was supposed to be a two-hour layover turned out to be five at the end, due to some technical problems with the local commuter plane. Christina hates when this happens since she is sure she could have easily made it home in less time if she had just hopped on a train. Maybe not today, she thinks, looking down at the two large suitcases next to her and her oversized hand baggage, including a carry-on roller bag, laptop bag and her handbag, of course. She is glad Andalip had booked her in business class, since there is no way she would have been able to take so much luggage with her in economy class. Again she looks down at the bags beside her and feels like crying. This is pretty much my life right here packed up in these suitcases, she thinks sadly.

She sits down on one of the bigger suitcases and switches on her BlackBerry. She had talked to her sister from Frankfurt a few hours ago. Frauke had already been to the airport once this morning but decided to drive home to wait for Christina there. Both her and their parents' house were just 20 minutes away from the airport and the sisters decided it was best for Christina to call once she gets to the airport. Somebody would drive over and get her instead of everybody spending the day at Fuhlsbüttel. Christina had called right after touchdown, but had switched her phone off again while going through customs. Until now nobody has returned for her, no familiar face is waiting for her in the arrival hall. Christina checks for missed calls and messages. Nothing! She is tempted to just catch a taxi home. Once more she decides against it due to the mountains of bags she is carrying.

Andalip drove her to the airport in the middle of rush hour yesterday evening but they still had reached JFK almost four hours before take-off. Christina was packed and ready to go since lunch and after just hanging out all afternoon at the apartment, she convinced Andy that it was time to leave. 'Let's just grab coffee or dinner at the airport and hang out there until I have to board the plane. It's making me sad to sit here and think that I won't see this apartment again,' Christina had told him. They had rented the two-bedroom apartment on Broadway and 63rd Street less than two years ago when Christina started to work full-time at the New York University. Theoretically one could see both Central Park and the Hudson River, if it wasn't for the high-rises around them. But they had a fantastic view along Broadway looking south. The plan was that Andalip would hand over the place once he returns to NYC in January. Christina was convinced they would never have such a fantastic view again. Besides, this was the first apartment that they had rented together, besides visiting each other in either Andalip's bachelor pads—as she used to refer to Andy's apartments in NYC—or Christina's student housing in Hamburg.

They have a small apartment waiting for them in Andalip's parents' house in Golf Links which his parents had renovated for them. It's on the second floor overlooking the service lane at the back of the house. Officially the unit has a separate entrance but the house was built in such a way that it still works as a large family home. Christina and Andy would be living under one roof with eight other family members: Andalip's parents, his grandmother, his *bua* and her son, Anhad, and his wife, Maya, and their two kids. Andy's *chacha* and *chachi* own the house next door, adding at least two more daily visitors. Andy's sisters are all married and have moved out. Still his sister Jasneet manages to visit her parents several times a week, since the Sikh family she married into lives just a short drive away.

Christina's thoughts are interrupted by her sister's voice. 'Hi baby sister. Sorry to let you wait so long. I had to drop Fiona at a friend's house on the way.' Fiona is Christina's 14-year-old niece, who was supposed to come to the airport with Frauke to pick her up. Christina and Fiona recently became friends on Facebook. Christina woke up a few days ago to find a post on her Wall from Fiona that told the Facebook world how excited everybody in Hamburg is to have Christina come home and that Fiona was planning to wait for her at the airport. Christina thought this to be very cute and looked forward to it. Especially since she felt that she didn't really know her sister's children that well. Christina was shocked at how grown-up her little niece looked online and what a social life she seemed to have, constantly posting photos of outings to cafes along the Elbe, school parties and weekend trips with her friends from the stable. Fiona rides ponies for tournaments and is quite good at it, her sister had proudly told her. When she saw both Fiona and her little brother Ben in Germany last summer, they were 13 and 9 years old respectively and not very interested in their aunt who lived in New York. At that age, Christina remembered, it was more fun being with friends outside the house than hanging around with the oldies.

Christina gets up and hugs her sister. 'It's so good to see you, Frauke. I didn't wait that long, it took me a while to make it until here with all my bags. I didn't have euros on me so I couldn't get a cart. Where have you parked? Do you think we can make it without a cart or should I try to get one now?'

Frauke looks through her purse and hands her sister a euro. 'Honestly Christina, how do you survive in a place like New York? Why didn't you just ask somebody for help? They have carts over there. Just pick one up and I'll watch your bags.' Christina does as she is told. While walking over to get the cart, she shakes her head in disbelief. She's has just landed in Hamburg, yet Frauke manages to make her feel like she's the little sister again in an instant. Forgotten are her doctorate, her career and her international travels. Now her sister, who is five years older, will tell her once again how things are done. She tries to ignore her annoyance, following Andy's advice on enjoying her family instead of fighting with them. Maybe I better get used to other people telling me what to do, she muses, realizing that from now on, she will be sharing her life with the man she loves and his entire extended family.

She returns with the cart and both women load it with the suitcases and smaller bags. 'Here, let me push that. You must be exhausted from the long flight. What happened in Frankfurt? Couldn't they put you on a different plane? We were all getting worried that you might get stuck down there for another day or so. Berndt told me about a colleague of his who was stuck because of a flight controller's strike last week and did not make it out of the airport for almost two days. From all I hear these days, Lufthansa is just not what it used to be.' Frauke sounds seriously upset. Christina looks at her sister while they are navigating their way to the airport towards the parking lot. Both women share the same Nordic features and definitely look like sisters, both tall and slim with blonde hair and blue eyes. Christina always thinks that Frauke resembles their mother more. She admires both for their impeccable style and taste in clothes, keeping their hair in neat ponytails and always on top of every situation. 'How is Mama?' Christina asks to avoid another lecture about things that her sister sees as problems but which really aren't.

'Fine. You will see her in a minute. She wanted to clean up the house one more time before you arrive, so I told her to stay home,' Frauke replies. Then she smiles: 'I left Ben to help. Can you believe it, a 10-year-old would rather hang out with *Oma* and help her around the house, than be with his father? Berndt has to work today—on a Saturday, I am so mad—but I told him to take Ben to the office and make him help out a bit. I am sure they have some little tasks for him. Remember, how Papa would take us to the office sometimes and make us stuff envelopes? I thought that was fun. Plus we got some extra father-daughter time! That's so important but I don't think Berndt gets that.' Frauke pauses. 'Not that I am complaining about Berndt, he is a good guy. A good dad! He just does things differently from Papa. You know what I mean, right?'

'Absolutely!' Christina replies, but thinks to herself, I have no idea what you are talking about. Just leave the poor guy alone for a day and let him enjoy some quiet time at the office. If that's where he went, Christina wants to add but keeps it to herself. She'd known Berndt for as long as she can remember. Frauke and he were high school sweethearts and grew up just a few streets away from each other. He was a constant guest in the house. Nobody was surprised when they got married at twenty-five. Christina remembers joking with Frauke when they were teenagers that her sister would probably marry Berndt as soon as she would turn eighteen. But both of them—super responsible and happy to please their parents in any way—had finished their education first. Berndt became a tax accountant and took over his father's practice a few years ago. Frauke decided against college but finished her formal training at a local bank, where she has worked ever since. A year after they got married, Fiona was born and five years later Ben. They managed to buy a house in the same street as Mom and Dad to be close to one set of grandparents in case they needed help with the kids. Berndt's parents live only 30 minutes away by car.

They had moved out of the city after his dad retired. They wanted to be closer to the coast and spend more time on their sailboat.

Christina often envies her sister for her life. It all seems so easy and straightforward and everybody seems so content. She, on the other hand, keeps chasing after bigger and better assignments and challenges and still hasn't found a place yet that she can truly call home. 'Here we go, that's it. My car!' Frauke stops in front of a silver Mercedes, A class. She opens the trunk and starts dragging the suitcases towards it. 'You did not tell me you got a new car?' Christina is surprised. Frauke has been a true defender of her white VW Golf that Papa had gifted her when she started working at the bank. She remembered her big sister teaching her how to drive when she turned eighteen. 'An early 40th birthday gift from Berndt. Can you believe it? Me in a Mercedes? I feel like Mom now!' Their mother has been a big fan of German luxury cars since they can remember and refuses to drive anything else but a Mercedes or a BMW. Frauke laughs. Her birthday is coming up next week. Her parents had been trying to plan a surprise dinner for her next weekend, but Frauke had spoiled her plan by organizing a big party for herself on Saturday.

'Wow, Frauke, this is a nice car. Business must be going well then?' Christina comments while getting into the passenger seat. The interior is a light grey colour, the leather feels smooth and the car still has that distinct new car smell. The car bears no signs of kids, no toys, no clutter, no cookie crumbs in sight. Christina watches her sister turn on the radio, sets the A/C and then, to her surprise activates the navigation system. 'Here, look at this. He got me a navi too. I will never need a map again! It covers all of Germany and you can add Europe as well. I love it!' Frauke sounds excited. Christina wonders why her sister would need a navigation system between here and her house but does not get a chance to ask her about it. As soon as Frauke pulls out of the parking spot, she continues: 'I just love how the voice tells me where to go. You wouldn't believe how many new routes I have discovered lately.' She heads out of the garage onto the airport ring road. Everything still looks the same, Christina thinks.

'Enough of my car! Now you tell me how you are feeling. How are all the wedding preparations going? You must be more than nervous about all this. Weddings are nerve-racking enough but I can only imagine how stressful the preparations must be when you are trying to do all that from a few thousand kilometres away.' Frauke gets interrupted by the voice of the navi: 'At the next light, turn right.' Frauke laughs: 'See what I mean? Isn't this fun?'

Christina giggles. Honestly, who is the baby sister here, she muses. 'Yes, great car, great gadgets.' Christina does not really care about the car but she replies to buy some time. She knows that the next few weeks will be all about her upcoming wedding, the trip to India and the decision to move to Delhi. When Andy and she had planned the move, they had decided it would be best for Christina to spend some time with her family before flying to India. This way she could prepare the Germans about the festivities and all that would come with it: lots of Indian relatives, lots of eating and drinking, lots of noise! Andy also thought it was important for Christina to get a chance to bond with her family alone without him before the wedding. Christina was not convinced she would need four weeks for that. At the end, it seemed to be her only option. She was done with NYC but not ready for Delhi yet. 'If anything,' Andy had joked, 'after a few weeks with your family, you will be waiting for me to whisk you away to India.' When he said that, Christina got mad at him, since she loves her family more than anything and often feels sad that they are so far away. After spending 15 minutes in the car with her sister, she wonders if Andy was right. She loves being back in Hamburg, but she hates the fact that her sister made her feel like a teenager once again in such a short time.

When they pull into her parents' driveway, Frauke blows the horn. In less than a minute, her parents Michael and Bärbel rush out of the front door, followed by Ben. Her mother is dressed up in a grey skirt and white blouse, complete with pearl necklace and earrings, while her father is wearing his typical Saturday outfit: jeans and Polo shirt. They could not be more different, Christina thinks, but it seems to work for them. After 43 years of marriage they still look very happy together.

While her mother is greeting her with hugs and kisses, her dad is already taking the luggage inside. Ben is helping too and Christina watches him nervously, as he tries to handle her roller bag and laptop case. What feels like seconds later, she finds herself in the middle of her parents' living room. As long as she can remember, her mother has kept it in the same way. Dark wooden floors, white walls, furniture in a light beige — modern design tastefully mixed with a few antique dressers and shelves that they had inherited from Michael's mother when she had passed away almost 20 years ago. Christina walks through the room and soaks in images of her childhood: the corner glass table with at least 20 silver frames of all shapes and sizes with family photos, mainly in black and white, from the last 45 years; her dad's book collection neatly kept away behind glass shelves in one corner of the living room; her mother's antique secretary desk that nowadays shows off her laptop and stores her mother's extensive correspondence with several clubs, such as her tennis club, book club and Rotary Club, of which she is an active member. As always her mother had made sure that the house would be filled with fresh flowers. Everything is in its place, just like in the *Homes & Gardens* magazine that her mother has been a fan of for as long as she can remember.

Michael returns and gives his daughter a big hug: 'Christina, welcome home! We have missed you.' His beard tickles her cheeks. She notices how grey it has gotten over the last few years, the dark brown hair on his head and face looks like a mixture of salt and pepper nowadays. He is still tall and slim but since selling his furniture business and design firm last year, he has gotten a small beer belly protruding from under his T-shirt. 'You look good Papa. I have missed all of you. It feels great to be back home!' and with that she sits down in one corner of the large fluffy couch overlooking the terrace and backyard. Impeccably kept, just like the interior, Christina admires her mother's hand for design. Even though she never went to college, she started helping out in the family business and created a niche for herself as an interior designer, mainly decorating the homes of the rich and famous in Hamburg. Not Broadway, she smiles to herself, but not bad either. She pops up her legs on the little footrest in front of her and finally relaxes.

Christina spends the rest of the day in pretty much the exact spot. Her mother spoils her with home-made cheesecake and freshly brewed cups of cappuccinos. When Berndt arrives later in the afternoon with Fiona, Bärbel decides to end the rounds of coffee and brings out rolls with cheese and cold cuts and Michael opens a bottle of champagne. 'This calls for a celebration,' Michael announces. 'It's been a long time since the entire family has been together in one room. Here's to that!' Michael raises his glass. Everybody follows his lead. Even the kids raise their glasses filled with Apfelschorle. Christina watches her sister and brother-in-law kiss. Fiona rolls her eyes, but does not move from her mother's side. Ben sprawls out on the floor and gets busy with his video game. The perfect German family, just out of a commercial, Christina thinks.

Christina remembers her brother-in-law as a senior at her school. Even then he was always dressed up in a shirt and wearing something more dressy than jeans she used to tease him a lot about his hair, since she thought it was funny that a 17-year-old boy could use so much gel to keep his hair in place. Berndt had not changed much since those days 23 years ago—still dressed up in a suit after a morning in the office, with a pair of round horn-framed glasses and the same blonde gelled-back hairstyle. Today he looks tired though and she notices that Berndt was getting a beer belly just like Papa.

Fiona starts telling her mom about her visit to her friend's house. Berndt joins Christina on the sofa. 'Rough morning, I heard, but looks like you made it OK. Looking good for somebody just flying over the Atlantic,' Berndt jokes with her. 'Well, you don't look too bad either after going into the office on a Saturday,' Christina replies. Berndt helps himself to the cheese rolls and offers one to Christina. She is still full after the cake and shakes her head. 'No, thank you.' Berndt laughs: 'Don't tell me you are on some pre-wedding diet? I thought Indians like their women a little fat around the hips.' Christina notices Frauke's stare across the room but the moment passes quickly. Berndt keeps up his small talk. They gossip about the weather, common friends and the economy for a while. Berndt does not like to travel as much as Christina does and the topics revolve mainly around Germany. He has never once asked her about life in New York, her work or her upcoming move to India. He's in his own little world Christina had realized years ago and does not care much about what goes on in other people's lives.

'Did you see my wife's new car? What a beauty, right? I was tempted to keep it myself, but Frauke really deserves this one. A beautiful mother of two, her little career at the bank and me working long hours these days. I wanted to get her something special just for herself!' Oh, you are so full of yourself, Christina thinks but keeps it to herself. Especially when she sees her sister smile at them across the room. After all these years, she still looks up to him like she did in high school, Christina cannot believe it.

Suddenly Christina feels the urge to bring up the fact about Berndt refusing to join them in Delhi for the wedding. Bärbel had told her a few times over the phone, that he does not want

Fiona and Ben to join Frauke on the trip. Frauke seemed fine with that and defended Berndt, saying that he was kind enough to let her go. Christina had decided on the plane that she will try to be cool about it and let Frauke deal with her husband. But after his conversation and hearing him act as the generous husband, she has a hard time controlling herself. 'So Mama said you aren't joining us in Delhi for the wedding? How come? Too expensive for a family of four?' She laughs and slaps him on his knee. Berndt's smile disappears. He puts his plate down on the coffee table in front of him and turns towards Christina. 'You couldn't wait to bring that up, ha? Nice try getting me with that reverse psychology, like I would go all out and buy four business class tickets for my family to prove you wrong? I know you have discussed this with everybody already, but let me break it down for you one more time. I like you and Andy a lot and I am happy for you that you're finally getting married. If you would have decided to get married here, I would definitely have attended the wedding, but how can you except everybody to come to India for this? I have done my research and I have been talking to people and I don't think it is a safe place to travel, especially with kids. What if they fall sick? Will you take the responsibility for that? Because you know if they do, I will hold you responsible for it.' The room falls silent. Everybody is watching Berndt and Christina on the sofa, even Ben has stopped his game.

'Listen Berndt, no need to get all worked up. I didn't mean to sound snappy. But you can't be serious about this. We are going to Delhi, a big city not some village. One just has to be a little careful about the water and maybe carry some mosquito repellent, but it's really not that bad. You have been to Spain in the 1970s. It's a little bit like that, just don't take ice in your drink, avoid salads and go with the flow. You will be spending more time in five-star hotels and people's houses than on the streets or the slums that you might be picturing. And God forbid something happens, Delhi has some of the best doctors and hospitals in the world to take care of you. I bet you have read about all these medical tourists who fly to India to get treated for all types of problems. I would not talk my family and friends into coming to Delhi if I thought I would put them in any kind of danger. It will be a great experience for everybody, you will see!' Christina is looking around for support. Michael is the only one who seems to agree with her. He nods at both of them, but does not add anything to what his daughter just said.

Bärbel isn't getting involved either, which Christina reads as a sign of support for Berndt. The last few times they had discussed a trip to India, her mother had sounded much like Berndt. Many dinners had ended with either mother or daughter leaving the room in tears. Christina had tried to educate her mother about India through movies and books, but at the end she thought her mother just gave in and figured it was not worth the fight with her younger daughter. Since some of her friends at the Rotary Club showed keen interest in Christina's wedding and a few of them even wondered if they could come along, Bärbel seemed more open to the idea now. Recently she even seemed a little excited about the trip. Christina does not expect her mother to stand up for her, but she is glad she is staying out of it. Frauke is avoiding her sister's stare. She is probably agreeing with Berndt, Christina thinks, but is caught between showing support for her husband and looking after her little sister's interests.

'Honestly Christina, it's your choice to marry an *ausländer*. You cannot expect everybody to be happy about that and, on top of it all, to be quiet about it. I am totally supportive of you getting married to Andy and I have been telling everybody what a fine guy he is. But don't give me a lecture on India, just because you've visited it a few times. Dating somebody from India doesn't make you an expert about it yet. You should be happy I am letting Frauke go with you.' Berndt gets up, but before he excuses himself to go home, he turns around once more and addresses Christina: 'And don't think that I'm the only one who thinks that way. Just because I'm the one saying it out loud don't turn me into the bad guy here! Anyway, welcome home and maybe you should get some rest before you start discussing this wedding again.' He says a quick goodbye and thank you to Michael and Bärbel, reminds Frauke about their dinner plans and tells her to meet him at their house later. Once again, Christina watches Fiona roll her eyes and Ben looking up from his game.

Frauke gets up and follows Berndt into the hall. Christina can hear them arguing but trying to keep it down. Michael gets busy with refilling the glasses. Bärbel sends Fiona to the kitchen for more snacks and then comes over to Christina. 'Maybe Berndt is right, why don't you get some rest. Do you have to pick a fight with him just hours into your visit? You better talk to Frauke. She must be very upset. I told you she is already anxious about the whole thing. Couldn't you be a little more sensitive?' Her mother gets up and starts cleaning up the living room, not waiting for Christina to respond. When Frauke returns, Christina gets up and tries to talk to her sister.

'Oh stop it Christina, I think you have done enough talking for today. I'm not in the mood to discuss this now. I have to get the kids over to the house and get them ready for the babysitter to take over. Berndt and I have plans tonight and I don't want to get late and spoil his mood further.' Frauke just walks pass her sister and pulls Ben's T-shirt. 'Time to go, buddy. Say bye to Tante Christina and get your sister out of the kitchen.'

Christina feels tired and just gives up. 'All right then. Thanks for picking me up from the airport. When do I see you again? Are you working this week?' Christina hugs her sister. Frauke returns her hug and forces a smile: 'Of course, I'll come and pick you up. Anytime, even though you can be very irritating. And of course, I have to work this week. How else do you expect me to take a week off next month for your wedding? Let's make plans for lunch this week and maybe you can help me out with some party preparations for next weekend. Remember, my 40th is coming up.' Ben and Fiona arrive back at her side, jackets on and backpacks over their shoulders, ready to go. 'Bye, Tante Christina!' Christina watches her sister and kids leave.

Michael hands her another glass of champagne. 'Here, drink that, you will feel better. Don't think too much about it, it will all work out at the end. Family functions always bring out the worst in people. It will pass and nobody will remember it at the end. Like I always say, it is still best to keep family out of things that are important to you in life. Makes things so much easier! You should rest now and I will help your mom in the kitchen.' With that Michael gets up, kisses his daughter on the forehead and disappears into the kitchen.

It all feels very familiar to Christina but sitting in the quiet living room, she feels like she is just an observer in her own life. Who are these people? Suddenly she starts feeling tired and misses Andalip miserably. Without saying goodnight she heads upstairs to her bedroom. Let's hope tomorrow will be a little better, she thinks. She curls up on her bed which pretty much looks like it did the day she left for college. Her mom had tried to make it look more like a guest room but she had left Christina's books and photos on the shelves. She notices a large silver vase on her desk, filled with pink roses. 'Thanks Mom, I love you too,' she whispers before she falls asleep, fully dressed in her travel clothes with her luggage untouched.

Chapter 6

The week after Christina's arrival passes fast. She manages to enjoy herself and she is happy to be back home. The argument with Berndt on her arrival has passed and the topic has not been brought up again. Christina has been trying to listen to Andalip's advice to just have fun with her family and that things would fall into place. His advice seems to work and she spends lots of quality time with her family. She has been lucky with the weather, too, whiling away most of the nice sunny autumn week along Lake Alster and River Elbe, discovering new restaurants and sharing delicious meals with family and friends. One day she actually took her bike out and explored the city and its parks just like she did before she could drive. At times she feels like a teenager again.

So far she has not managed to meet up or talk to everybody who is joining them in Delhi for the wedding. She is so used to dealing with her German friends online that she is having a hard time just picking up the phone, making plans to meet up in person. Besides her parents and Frauke, Christina only has three other relatives who will come along for the wedding. Her father's first cousin's family who used to be very close to their family when they all grew up together in Hamburg. Although both her parents are single children, her father's grandmother had four siblings, whose seven children were as close to her dad as brothers and sisters when they were growing up. In that sense, she remembers telling

Andy once that her dad kind of grew up in an extended family just like the Singhs. Michael and four of them were close in age and even went to school together. Christina used to be jealous of his childhood stories of how he and his cousins used to terrorize their neighbourhood. When she and Frauke were young, her dad would make it a point to invite his cousins over for Christmas. Over time these occasions were less frequent, with people moving all over Germany and only one of the cousins, Karl, remaining in Hamburg.

Onkel Karl used to be dad's business partner for a few years. They both shared a passion for design and had created some beautiful furniture together. This worked well for many years but after some silly fight over how to deal with a client, they went their separate ways. Michael and Karl still talk but the relationship is not the same anymore. Till today Christina is still very close to Onkel Karl's three children, all between 30 and 40 years of age. His two oldest sons, Olaf and Karl Jr, are both married. Christina likes their wives, Bettina and Ute respectively, and when in Hamburg, they all would go out together. Andy and she took a long weekend off to come for Olaf and Bettina's wedding last year. It was a one-day affair, a small reception followed by a church wedding held on one of Germany's islands, Langeoog, in the North Sea. Although it was Andy's first church wedding and first trip to the Baltic Sea, he had felt right at home and mixed well with family and friends. Both were looking forward to meeting them again after a long time in Delhi. The youngest of Onkel Karl's children is her cousin Anna who just turned thirty. She reminds Christina a lot of herself. Anna had just returned from a one-year college exchange programme in Mexico, during which time she managed to visit Christina and Andy for a week in NYC last April. That's when they met Anna's new Mexican boyfriend Juan, who was planning to fly to Delhi for the wedding as well. Even with these six cousins and their partners, Christina had less than 10 relatives on her side who would attend the wedding. No match for the Indians, as Andy loves to joke with her.

Christina didn't feel like inviting many of her friends. The Internet and social networking sites like Facebook kept her in touch with many people from her past and present, but when it came down to whom she really wanted to be there at her wedding, she came up with just a handful of good friends, spread all over the world. It was pretty clear that only a few of them would be able to attend the wedding due to distances, work obligations or family restrictions. P would be there, of course, but without her husband, who hadn't been able to get time off from work. One friend from elementary school really wanted to travel to India and was one of the first to accept the invitation. She and her husband had left for India a month ago. Both had put their job on hold and taken a few months off to explore India. Christina was really surprised to hear that and was a little envious that she had never gotten a chance to do the same herself. She complained to Andy one night about how little she has seen of India and that her friends would be the experts before her. Just yesterday she had gotten an email from Amritsar, where Julia and Markus had spent the weekend visiting the Golden Temple.

At the end, Christina felt that her parents should invite some of their friends to the wedding too. She had no aunts and uncles on her side and she felt under-represented considering the number of Andy's relatives attending the wedding. She knows she cannot compete with the 300 people that her mother-in-law considers close family who have been invited for most of the functions, and she's really scared to face the 700 people invited for the reception. She told Andy that she wants some non-Indian support from her side as well. Either way, Andy does not seem to care how many people are coming from abroad. He keeps telling Christina not to worry too much about formalities and that she soon will be apart of his large extended family and there will be no 'my side or your side of the family' anymore.

Christina still thinks more Germans are needed. So Dad's friend Wolf and his wife will be there plus two couples from mom's Rotary Club, who she has never met. Bärbel has arranged a dinner at the house next week for everybody to meet and have the opportunity to ask Christina some questions before the trip. Bärbel's main concern seems to be what to wear, but her friends will want to know about costumes and traditions that seem to confuse her mother. 'Elisabeth wants to know if you really will have to change your first name after the wedding to a Sikh first name. She said you will have to convert. You never told me that Christina. I hope you know what you are getting into?' Bärbel had asked her last week over lunch. Christina found all these questions a little silly and felt like telling her mom to start reading up on the topic and inform her friends as well. She knows that would just make things worse so at the end she agreed to sit through a 'question-and-answer' session one night. Maybe Bärbel will get more excited about the trip and maybe Berndt might change his mind and want to join in the fun as well.

Christina is thrilled that her best friend Günther is coming for the wedding after all. Günther studied sociology with her in Hamburg and they had started teaching around the same time. Originally from Bavaria, Günther came to the north to be with his true love, a decision that cost him his family. His parents had disowned him when they discovered that the chosen life partner was another man and not a woman as they had assumed. Christina simply adored Günther and his boyfriend Daniel and when she lived in Hamburg, she was always at their beautiful flat overlooking the harbour. For a long time, Bärbel was not convinced that Günther liked men and was always telling her daughter how charming she found him and what a great couple the two of them—Günther and Christina—would make. Andy liked Günther and had accepted their special relationship. When Christina had told him that she wanted Günther and Daniel to come for the wedding he was fine with it, but hoped that they would not live out their relationship in public. She remembers their conversations clearly—Andy being firm about it, reiterating the fact that to be gay is not accepted culturally and that his family will not understand. 'You know I like Günther but in this case it is not about what I want, Christina,' Andy had said and decisively ended the topic. She felt really irritated at first and did not know what to say to Günther about it. When he had told her that they wouldn't be able to attend the wedding, she was relieved in a way but sad that he would miss it. This wedding was really bringing out the best and worst in people, she thought, and was hoping it was just a phase and things would return to normal afterwards.

But when Christina reached Hamburg, she learnt that Günther could come to Delhi after all but without Daniel. He had connected with P via Facebook and the two of them had planned to be each other's dates since both were travelling alone. Günther had joked that he was looking forward to shocking everybody when they saw the other German-Indian couple at the wedding. Little did he know Christina thought, that this was the least shocking of all the scenarios she had pictured for his arrival in Delhi.

Chapter 7

Andy enters Christina's room. 'Are you ready for the party?' Christina turns around. She is standing in front of her closet and cannot decide what to wear for her sister's party. Jeans and a black top or an Indian *kurti* over leggings? Christina holds both up and looks at Andy: 'Or a skirt?' Andy comes over and hugs her: 'Don't ask me. You never listen to my suggestions anyway. But whatever you decide, quickly get out of your track pants! Here, let me help you.' He tickles her, takes the hangers from her hands, throws them on the floor and pushes her on the bed. To his surprise, she does not object when he pulls her T-shirt up, caressing her flat, perfectly shaped stomach. Like a kitten, she snuggles against him and he knows that she is enjoying his hands exploring her curves. He knows 'she has to get into the mood' first and for a few minutes he just soaks up her scent, watching her take pleasure in his gentle touch.

Andalip arrived in Hamburg this morning. It is exactly a week since they had been together but he wants her as if it has been an eternity. He was supposed to arrive later this month so that they could fly to Delhi together and have a full week to sort out their wedding clothes and last-minute things before the Germans arrive. But as it often happens, plans had changed at the last minute and Andy will have to work in NYC until just before the wedding to finish a proposal for a new project. Of course, his new flight isn't booked yet, but the company had assured him that they will get him to India in time for the big day. Christina had been furious when he told her on the phone, wondering why he didn't stand up to his boss. Andy didn't think it was such a big deal and there would be enough time for him to get to Delhi. Still, he felt the need to see Christina and make up in person–secretly he finds her super sexy when she is mad at him. So on Thursday he couldn't wait to be with her and impulsively decided to take a Friday and Monday off before the new assignment begins and show up in Hamburg in time for his soon-to-be sister-in-law's 40th birthday bash. He wanted the visit to be a surprise—maybe to make Christina feel a little guilty about being so mad at him—and told Michael to keep his secret safe.

Andy had slept in late on Friday morning and leisurely went out shopping to get some last-minute gifts for his future in-laws and family. He hates shopping but wanted to make a good impression. He ended up buying more for himself but was happy about the gift he had bought Frauke for her birthday. He had found a blue and gold Espresso set decorated with paintings by her favourite artist Gustav Klimt. That should get me some brownie points, he had thought, proud of himself for this addition to Frauke's designer kitchen. Michael had picked him up from the airport. They arrived just before lunch. Christina was out shopping so he was able to spend some time with Bärbel and Michael alone. He was glad since he wanted to talk to them about the upcoming wedding without Christina interfering.

'I just want you to know that Christina and I are very happy that you are travelling all the way to Delhi for our wedding. I know that you had pictured something different for your daughter's wedding. I will try to help out in any way I can to make you feel at home and enjoy your week in Delhi to the fullest.' Even though their English was quite good, he was not sure if they totally understood him. Bärbel got emotional and hugged him. She said that, of course, they are happy that they are getting married and not to worry about them. Michael got all serious and told Andy

that he was hoping that he would take good care of his daughter
and he made him promise not to hurt his baby girl. He believed
he heard Bärbel say something like 'If not, I will cut off your 'you-
know-what'…hahaha' but she had addressed him in German and
he decided not to ask her to repeat it. Quickly he shook hands
with both and smiled sheepishly. It seemed as if everybody was a
little awkward about discussing the wedding any further. Bärbel
changed the topic and asked Andy about his work.

Christina walkes in just before lunch is served. She looks very
German with her dark skinny jeans, long grey coat and matching
leather boots, he chuckles. Although her face is hidden under the
sporty baseball cap that she likes to wear when biking around the
citys, he knows that she is truly surprised to see him. She quickly
walks across the kitchen and hugs him tightly burying her face in
his neck, hiding the tears which he could feel. Instead of kissing
her firmly as he had dreamed of on his journey across the ocean,
Andalip gently dries her tears with his lips. He cannot help but
wonder if his surprise visit is as successful as planned or if he is
the one getting surprised. Though full of love for his soon-to-be-
bride, Andalip is shocked to see her so emotional. He had seen
her irritated and moody but the times he had seen Christina cry
were few. Maybe never, he tries to remember.

After that, lunch turned out to be a casual affair. The rest of
the afternoon had sped by with Andy taking a nap to be fit for the
evening's party and Christina going over to Frauke's house to help
with last-minute preparations. They had spent the last hour sitting
with Christina's parents over the traditional *Kaffee und Kuchen*—
coffee and cake—typical for a weekend afternoon. Christina had
excused herself half an hour ago to change for the party but never
returned, so Andy followed her upstairs ostensibly to change but
hoping for a chance to finally satisfy his lust.

When Christina does not react to his caresses, he decides to
change his warming-up strategy and his fingers work their way up

and around her back, playing with the hook of her bra. She opens her eyes. 'Finally alone,' Andy whispers into Christina's ear. He pulls her closer and tries to kiss her but Christina pulls back. She complains about her sister and her usual worries about lack of privacy. He feels her relax, then she returns his kiss. 'Sweet caramel kisses,' he whispers longingly. Christina laughs: 'Show me what you've got, *schatz!*' Finally, he thinks, rolling on top of her. 'But quickly, I am telling you, somebody or the other will look for us pretty soon!' he hears her whisper.

Andalip feels a bucket of cold water has been dumped over his head, 'I have not seen you for a week! I think your mom understands that and I seriously doubt that she will come up.' He kisses her once more but his excitement has passed. He knows Christina won't let him come much closer than this. He sits up and looks at her. 'So tell me, why were you crying when I saw you at lunch? Did anything happen last week that I should know of? Or are you really that sad to see me?' Andalip honestly wants to know. He has been trying to figure it out all afternoon, but the moment had passed so quickly that he couldn't find any more clues.

Christina waves her hand. 'Honestly, Andy, I don't know myself. I am happy to see you, but I am also extremely mad and disappointed at you. It's our wedding, Andy, and you are leaving me and your family to do all the last-minute work and decisions. Why can't you pull some all-nighters and finish your work early? Or work from Delhi—it's the 21st century—and finish this off via email and Skype! I really thought we both should be in Delhi that last week before everybody arrives. I just don't understand why work has to be so important all of a sudden since you are planning to quit in a few months' time and join your dad.' Christina pauses, but when he keeps quiet she continues: 'What's done is done and I will handle it alone. I guess I would do the same if it was my work. Guys are just lucky they always get away with it.'Andalip had expected this speech. Instead of trying to argue with her, he takes her hand and kisses it. He does not want to apologize for his decision to take on the project. He knows she will forgive him.

Christina had also told him about the fight with Berndt. Other than that, she had not mentioned any other arguments with her family when they talked on the phone. Andalip studies his fiancée's face, framed by wild blonde curls. He gently strokes them back behind her ears and looks into her eyes. He is perplexed to see that her tears seem to have turned her blue eyes even darker–like a beautiful ocean, he finds himself thinking. His passion for her has turned into true love and concern for her. Maybe she is just getting nervous about getting married? Isn't that what usually happens with people right before the big day? So far he was not feeling nervous or anxious at all, but maybe women were just different after all. 'So what else is bothering you then?' he forces himself to ask her, pulling himself away from her mesmerizing eyes.

'After such a long speech from me, that is your comeback? Thanks Andy, great start to our marriage.' She pulls her hand away and tries to get up. Andy holds her back. 'Come on, Christina, what do you expect me to say? I know you are mad, but as you said, what's done is done and it was a work decision and had nothing to do with the wedding. It's just a few days and there will be enough time for things to get done by enough people for sure. Trust me on this one! If you want, I can re-book your flight as well and we just get there a little late.'

He can tell that Christina is tempted to take him up on the offer but knows better not to do so. Andy's mom and sister are waiting for her to get there and help out with the last-minute planning and preparations. 'You know I can't do that. I will be fine, don't worry.' She sounds less angry but Andy notices that she looks sad again.

Christina adds gently: 'It's just been a hard week, *schatz*. Actually, it's been fun. At moments I felt like I had never left Hamburg. Worse, it felt like I had never left home and was a kid again in my parents' house. Besides that first afternoon, we have not really talked about anything wedding-related. Nobody has asked me about work and the fact that I had just left a great career behind to get married in India. And I had a lot of time alone, walking and riding around Hamburg, which gave me lots of time to think.'

Christina gets up from the bed and starts walking up and down in front of him. He smiles and wonders if this is how she speaks in front of her class. Christina is underlining each sentence with several hand movements and her entire body seems to be part of her lecture. He feels the urge to sit up and pay closer attention to her. That's what I call German authority, he muses but dares not speak up.

When she stops talking, he replies: 'But that sounds as if you had a good week then? Right? Bonding with your family, spending time at home.'

Christina pulls in a deep breath. 'Yes and no. Of course I am happy to be here. The only problem is that I've realized that I am not the same person everybody thinks I am. They just treat me like the daughter, sister, aunt or friend that I was years ago. But I'm not, I've changed. I have met you, I moved to New York, I have evolved professionally, I have developed as a person, but my folks don't seem to realize that. At first I took it personally but then I thought maybe it is because everybody else and everything else is still the same and nothing has changed. I want to feel at home but I don't. I feel like I don't fit in anymore.' She pauses and stops in front of him. 'And now I have invited all these people to our wedding and feel that those who are coming to Delhi are the ones who don't understand me. I thought it would be great for everybody to see what my new life will be like, but now I feel like I've just forced people into doing something they don't want.' With that Christina sits down next to Andy on the edge of the bed and puts her head on his shoulder.

Andalip puts his arm around her. 'Not people, baby, family. They are your family and it is OK if they don't always understand you. My family doesn't always understand me, but they love me and they want to be part of my life. Our life now! Don't think too much about it and keep doing what you have been doing last week. Just enjoy your time here and it will all work out at the end. You will see!' Andy hugs her and loosens her ponytail, still looking for an opportunity to finally be close to her. There is a knock on the door making them both grimace. 'Christina *schatz*,' Bärbel's voice calls out. 'Are you guys getting ready? Frauke just called and was wondering if you and Andy could come over and help her a little bit.'

'I knew it,' Christina whispers to Andalip and lets her mother in.

Bärbel winks at her daughter. Christina blushes like a teenager caught making out. 'Sorry to interrupt you children but it's getting late.'

'We are just deciding what to wear, Mama. You are not interrupting at all.' Christina picks up the clothes next to her bed and holds them up for her mother to decide. Andy pulls out some clothes from his suitcase and heads off to take a shower. 'I'll be done in 10 minutes, Bärbel. Let us know what we need to do and we will be at your service all night.'

Bärbel beams. 'What a lucky girl you are, Christina. Andy is always so thoughtful. Your father is out riding his bike right now not bothered about me or his daughter's birthday party.' She takes the clothes from Christina and hangs them back in her closet. 'Please wear something nice tonight. Everybody will be dressed up. Frauke wants this to be a fancy cocktail party. You cannot wear some tribal outfit or come in your college look. I don't know about India, but I am sure people dress up nicely in New York. You don't want Andy to look at some other woman—you know Frauke has some pretty good-looking girls amongst her friends.'

Christina rolls her eyes at her mother who is busy rummaging through her closet.

'Here, wear this,' says Bärbel pulling out a dress and a skirt. Then she puts them back and shrugs. 'Better still, try one of mine. I will get something that might fit you.'

Christina closes the door behind her mother and this time, locks it. 'Unbelievable, just like I said, nothing has changed,' she mutters to herself. She chooses a dress from her closet, one that Bärbel would definitely classify as 'tribal,' a long brown and orange one with a large Kashmiri pattern on it that Christina had gotten tailored in India from the fabric that future mother-in-law had gifted her. She is pretty sure that would defiantly clash with the typical black and grey party dress code of her sister's friends. Pure evil, she smiles. She throws it on the bed and decides to join Andy in the shower after all.

Chapter 8

The birthday party turns out to be a big hit. Close to 50 people are gathered at Frauke and Berndt's house. For Germany that is considered a big party, Christina muses, but in India the number doesn't even cover close family. Christina recognizes many of her sister's friends from school, most of them are married with kids now. She happily notices that everybody including her brother-in-law is being really welcoming to Andy and most people are making an effort to speak English with him. Christina is surprised to find out that at least two of her sister's friends have been to India. She overhears a conversation with a tall guy that she has never met, talking to Andy, telling him he has been to Mumbai and Delhi on several business trips. 'I work for Volkswagen and go to India twice a year. It's been a great experience. I love your food, man, and your hospitality. I want to take my wife and daughter the next time I go. They have never seen anything like that. I have been telling Berndt that if he is not going for your wedding, I will definitely take his place. You guys are the future, man! What growth and what wealth, unbelievable!' Christina is shocked and looks for Frauke to get more info about the man talking to Andy. Then she suddenly feels all smug about choosing an Indian as a husband and plasters a huge grin on her face.

While working her way through the crowd, she runs into her teenage niece who looks all grown up in her navy blue mini dress and matching ballerina shoes, with her hair pulled back in a tight knot, and wearing her mother's silver earrings. 'Hey, look at you, all dressed up. Looking great, Fiona! I almost thought you were one of your mom's friends. Are you enjoying the party?' Christina hugs her niece. Fiona smiles and says, 'Can I talk to you, Tante Christina?' Christina is surprised. So far her niece has been rather shy while interacting with her. Even though she was always friendly, she seemed to be in her own teenage world, not too interested in her old aunt. Very different from the outgoing girl that she has been following over Facebook. This sounds more like it, she thinks, and asks Fiona what she wants to talk about.

She is not surprised to hear that Berndt doesn't want his daughter to come for the wedding. But she is even happier to discover that Fiona is not at all convinced by her father's horror stories about India. She wants to see for herself what 'Incredible India'—as the travel commercial suggests—is all about, and is not scared about the dangers Berndt had warned her about—from the extreme climate, pollution and chaotic traffic to disrespect towards women, and indifference towards hunger and poverty.

She had even worked out some extra credits with her geography teacher about doing a presentation on her trip. Christina notices Fiona blush with excitement. 'Can't you talk to Papa again and ask him for me? I am sure I would get a good grade in my class if you will help me a bit. Tell him that! My grades in geography have not been that great, maybe I just need a chance like this.' Fiona almost pleads with her. 'Oh, honey, I would love for you to come!' she replies quickly, not knowing what else to say. She dreads talking to Berndt after their fight on the day of her arrival. She doubts her sister has much say in it. Maybe her mother was the most likely to succeed. Then Christina remembers the man who had talked to Andy. She spots him in the crowd and points him out to Fiona. 'Who is that guy over there? A friend of your dad's? He said he likes India and he wants to take his daughter there one day. Maybe he can talk to your father?'

Fiona looks hopeful. Then her smile disappears. 'No, that is Herr Schmidt. His wife works with Mom in the bank. Papa hates him. He says he is always so cheerful and too talkative. The opposite of Dad, you know, who Omi jokes goes into the basement to laugh,' her niece giggles amused. ' Please Tante Christina, you have to talk to him. He might fight with you but I think he respects you too.' Ben comes over and interrupts them, saving Christina from answering. 'I am bored, Fiona, let's go upstairs and watch a movie or something. Or we can just go outside and find some frogs for the fruit punch.' Ben laughs. Fiona gets up. 'No frogs, Ben, let's watch a movie.' Fiona hugs Christina before she follows her 10-year-old brother upstairs reminding her: 'And you will talk to Paps, won't you?'It would be so much fun having her niece and nephew at the wedding, Christina thinks happily. She pictures the gang of cousins playing all kinds of tricks, while hundreds of guests from all over the world dancing the night away. She imagines Ben riding an elephant and Fiona taking photos of cows in the streets for her school project. Fiona could wear matching outfits with Simran's daughter and Ben could ride the horse with Andy and his nephews for the bharat. Full of renewed hope and just a little tipsy, she gets up to look for her brother-in-law to convince him to entrust her with his children in Delhi.

❧

Christina wakes up next to Andy. Her head is spinning. Andy is still snoring. Christina puts on a bathrobe, brushes her teeth and heads down to the kitchen. Michael is already up, reading the paper. 'Good morning, sweetheart. What a party last night, ey? You look like you need a coffee or two…and a glass of schnapps to chase that hangover of yours!' Michael laughs and pours his daughter coffee. Christina grins back at her father as she takes the mug from him. She closes her eyes, smelling the strong coffee and hoping that the headache will go away quickly. She remembers dancing with her sister and her friends. She didn't get a chance to talk to Berndt like she had hoped to, but had chatted with Herr Schmidt and his wife, getting all sentimental about her move to India.

Michael watches her drink the coffee. 'Better?' he grins. 'Much!' Christina smiles back. 'Can I ask you something? How did I get home?' she asks. Michael laughs even louder: 'Good question. I don't know myself. I bet your mother kept a clear head and got us all home safely. Is Andy up there? He looked like he was having the time of his life last night. Especially doing shots with Berndt at 3. 30 in the morning!'

Father and daughter keep laughing, finishing another round of coffee. Bärbel walks in with a bag full of fresh rolls: 'Well, what are you two laughing about?' As always, she sounds a little jealous of her being so close to her dad, Christina thinks, and gets up to hug her mother.

'What a nice birthday party Frauke had last night,' Bärbel says over breakfast. Then she turns to Michael: 'Did you tell her the good news yet?' Christina stops cutting her roll. 'What news? What did I miss?' Michael laughs again: 'Well, if you hadn't drunk so much, you would already know! Berndt is letting Fiona come to the wedding. Frauke called earlier this morning to thank Andy for talking to Berndt last night. She is all excited. She said that Andy turned her party into a special occasion by convincing Berndt to let Fiona go as well. That Andy really knows what he is doing! The way he talked to Berndt, you should have heard him. At the end it seemed as if this had always been Berndt's idea! No wonder you chose to marry him!' Michael lifts his mug and toasts his daughter: 'To the upcoming wedding in Delhi!'

Christina is in shock. How could she have missed that? She is excited that Berndt is letting Fiona go to India. Now she had better not fall sick, she thinks. I will never hear the end of that!

Chapter 9

Staring out of the window in her old room, images of the past few weeks fly past Christina—spending time with family and friends, roaming around her hometown, drinking coffee, riding her bike—the memories of her childhood make her smile. Since Frauke's birthday party, the mood was light. Everybody seemed to be looking forward to the trip, even Berndt seemed to be very supportive about Frauke and Fiona joining them. She never thought that a month in Hamburg would pass so quickly and that at the end of it, she would feel sad to leave. From now on, everything will be different she knows. Her father reminded her of that this morning telling her that even though Christina will always be his little girl, her responsibility will now be to Andalip. 'You are going to be a wife now and you will start your own family. We will be here for you always, supporting you in any way possible, but your life will be in India from now on.' His job was done—he had raised an independent and strong woman who could now take care of herself and her husband. Loving your kids, German style, she laughed to herself and decided not to share this conversation with Andy or his family. After spending time with Andy's family and seeing how several generations live in one house, he would most be upset if he could hear this and think her parents are really mean and literally trying to get rid of her.

Her father's words stuck in her mind. What will it really mean? Being a wife, living in India? A new chapter in her life was beginning. She had realized this on that evening her mom had called her Rotary friends—the two couples who would be joining them for the wedding—for dinner. The entire Von Hoisdorf family had been helping Christina's mom to prepare for 'an evening of first glimpses into Indian culture and wedding etiquette' as her mom had labelled the occasion. Christina knew exactly what was expected of her as the daughter of the house—from helping out with the food, to cleaning and tidying. By afternoon, everything was ready and Christina and her parents had enjoyed coffee and cake, followed by a nap, like so many weekends in the past. She had followed her mother's advice on dress code and appeared in a dark blue suit over a white blouse five minutes after the guests arrived. Her mother's critical look—for being late and wearing a silver necklace instead of the recommended pearls—felt like the last reminder of being the daughter in this house. As soon as she entered the room, she knew everybody saw her as the woman who was about to move to India and therefore an expert on anything related to that country. That's when she knew things will never be the same again! Two couples sitting around the couch table looked at her with great expectations when she walked across the room to greet them. 'So, this must be the famous Christina we have heard so much about!' one of the men said, extending his hand to Christina. 'I am Jürgen Hoffmeister. Please call me Jürgen. I figure that since we will be attending your wedding, first names are more appropriate.' Jürgen laughed arrogantly. Christina had noticed how tall he was, almost towering a head above her father, with broad shoulders and white hair. Christina was amused picturing him in any gathering in Delhi—he would definitely stick out—and almost missed his introduction of his wife. 'My wife Kerstin …' pointing to a petite woman sitting on the sofa, smiling at them. 'Well, as you probably know, we are in your mom's Rotary Club and have known her for many years. It is a pleasure to finally meet you. What a shame, your fiancé is not here!' Jürgen chitchatted and winked at her. Before Christina could respond, the other couple quickly joined in and introduced themselves as Hannelore and Heinz Schwarz. Christina was surprised, unlike her mother's other friends, Hannelore and Heinz were casually dressed in jeans and jackets. Heinz reminded her of a captain of a cruise ship, his face covered with a full brown beard and his hair a little too long over his hairy ears. Hannelore was a little overweight and had coloured her long hair a bright *henna* red. Christina was taken aback when Hannelore folded her hands, bowed her head and greeted her with a loud and clear '*Namaste!*' When she noticed Christina's confusion, she had laughed warmly and told everybody that she had gone to Kerala on a yoga retreat last winter and was in love with Indian culture and people. 'When your mother told us about your wedding, I literally begged her to take us along. This is an opportunity of a lifetime and I am so thankful to you for allowing us to join you on this wonderful journey. Thank you darling!' Christina found herself in a group hug with Hannelore and Heinz and immediately remembered the Hare Krishna groups singing and handing out free food at Union Square in NYC that Andy had watched with amusement. She remembered him saying that at any given day, at any time, at any part of the city, one could find all kinds of people praying and handing out food, with or without music—true religious freedom he had called it.

After another round of hugs and *namastes*, Christina couldn't help but think that this must be the oddest thing that had happened in her mother's living room in a while. But unexpectedly, her mother just smiled and welcomed everybody again before she went into the kitchen to get the first round of appetizers. Watching her mother and friends that night, she had felt like her life had already moved on while she had lived in NYC. She kept wondering how much she even knew her parents. While talking about Delhi to her mother's friends, Christina couldn't help but constantly compare her visits to Delhi with this dinner party. Her mother's baked mushrooms and champagne, discussions on German politics and news suddenly seemed colourless and lacking in spice. When Jürgen started praising her mother's field salad with lemon fish she wasn't sure how he would handle Andalip's favourite tandoori chicken and goat brain curry that was waiting for him in Delhi. Everybody was quizzing her about what to expect. Only Hannelore had been to India, but just to the south and not anywhere close to a big city or Delhi. Everybody else was excited about going to India, but had only read about the country in guidebooks so far. The questions ranged from simple information on what to wear and which vaccinations to take to details and the significance of the wedding ceremonies and her upcoming responsibilities as an Indian bride, wife and later, mother. Her mom was most interested in visiting a school in a slum to find a project for the Rotary members. Even though Christina knew more than the other six people in the room, the questions had made her realize how little she had actually learned about India in the last five years. She felt that she had no idea on how to prepare her family and friends for the trip to Delhi. How could she explain India as a whole when all she has seen so far was a small segment of Delhi's affluent, urban, Sikh population? P is from Delhi, but from a Hindu, government service family that was nothing like Andalip's from the stories that she has heard. Kerstin had brought up the topic of poverty in India and referred to a documentary about street kids in Mumbai that she had seen: '…It was so sad to see these dirty little children begging for food. I was thinking we could maybe collect some clothes to donate. Maybe there is a school like your mother said or an orphanage that we could support. I am looking forward to the wedding but I feel like it is our responsibility to do something good on this trip as well.' Everybody seemed to agree with her statement. Christina had heard this argument about India a lot recently and kind of understood Kerstin's point. But when she had brought this up with Andy, he just asked her in return:

'So when people came for your cousin's wedding in Bremen last year, how many guests do you think considered sponsoring some orphanage in Germany?' She had felt bad bringing it up.

And as so often, her dad had wrapped up the discussion and channelled it back to the essentials. 'I think like other big cities, Delhi won't be much different, and I'm sure the people there enjoy the good times as much as we do! Andy sure can handle a drink and I have seen how much he enjoys Bärbel's pepper steaks, in case you are worried about some ayurvedic vegetarian meals at the wedding. If his family is anything like the maharaja Andy is, I am sure we will find a cold beer somewhere!' Michael had laughed loudly and poured another round of white wine for everybody. For some reason, Christina still hears him even now, days later, joking away: 'Enjoy this one, I am switching over to red after this glass. Bärbel has cooked her creamy pork *Geschnetzeltes* which goes well with this chianti. Although, after eating my wife's delicious shredded pork, I doubt you will develop a taste for the super spicy Indian food that will be served at the wedding!' They had all laughed and she knew then, that the Germans will have a culture shock and be confused when they get to Delhi. No sausages for sure, how will they survive, she chuckled.

When she finally steps away from the window to pack her clothes, she starts questioning everything that she has taken for granted so far. Maybe I shouldn't worry so much about the others and make sure I don't have a culture shock, she panics. Are her clothes too tight and showing too much skin that I might offend somebody by wearing them in India? Do these suits and shoes really look like men's clothes like her father-in-law once jokingly remarked? Will Andy's relatives think she is ugly for having short hair and being too skinny? Was Hannelore right that Christina will have to change her name to a Sikh one so as to not to offend Andy's family and religious beliefs? They have never discussed this but maybe everybody thought she would know. She has told friends and family that it is nonsense to ask about dowry, that in Sikhism men and women are equal, that nobody cares about the gender of her future children and that widows don't burn themselves on their husbands' pier. Her head is spinning. But are these all facts or only prejudices that are making her dizzy? What if Berndt is right and Andy will turn all 'Indian' on her and tell her to quit her job, have children and just serve him and his family once they are in Delhi?

She chooses to have a shower first to clear her head before packing. 'I guess I will find out starting tomorrow,' she thinks and shuts her closet door with a loud bang. '*Achtung* Delhi, here I come!'

Part 3

Namaste!

Chapter 10

Christina steps outside into a busy street. She is looking for something that resembles a sidewalk to sit down for a few minutes to catch her breath. Jazz is still inside the shop behind her, looking at different suits for Fiona to wear during the wedding. After looking at over 100 outfits in the brightest colours in a room that lacks airconditioning with at least five guys staring at her, Christina feels the urge to be outside and alone for a bit. The air in the street feels a little cooler, but it is still at least 30 degrees Celsius, even at 6. 30 on a November evening, and she misses the grey, rainy skies of Germany that she had left two days ago. She spots a few stairs leading up to the store next door and decides to sit down for a while. She rests her head on her knees and reviews the afternoon.

Both women had spent the first half of the afternoon shopping for Andy's mom, Kiran. Christina was getting confused about where they went and felt as if they had sat in the car most of the time, randomly zigzagging through Delhi. Kiran had given them instructions on what to pick up from where and when and both knew better not to question their task on hand. Christina thought she recognized some of the places they passed but felt lost in this mega city overflowing with people. She couldn't help but notice how clean some of the roads looked in comparison to her last visit a couple of years ago. She was looking out for cows and beggars but had not spotted them yet. Still, the wide, tree-lined roads seemed packed with cars, trucks, bikes and auto-rickshaws and traffic moved slowly. The driver was constantly blowing his horn, while Jazz kept telling him to find a better route and avoid the main roads. So far they had been to three markets which seemed to be located at different ends of the city. Christina was still unsure about Delhi's layout and missed the straight-forward, checker board grid of Manhattan.

Before they had set out, almost three hours ago, Kiran had called her meat shop and had placed an order for goat meat that they were supposed to pick up first before collecting the fish from a different market. Aunty, that is how Christina had addressed Kiran until now, had invited some relatives over for dinner tonight. She had explained that during the week before the wedding, close and distant relatives as well as friends would drop by at the house to join the family for a meal. She had hired an extra cook to prepare hot, delicious meals three times a day. Not very unusual, Christina thought who was always struggling to keep up with the amount of food the Singh family kept serving her. But even she had noticed the extra visitors and that each meal was getting more intricate by the day. Tonight, Aunty had invited the families of her sons-in-law, many of whom Christina had not yet met. The meat and fish had to be absolutely fresh and Jazz was in charge of getting everything back to the house in time for the cook to prepare the dinner.

When they had reached the butcher, the order was not ready. They stood in a narrow store with several other people waiting to be served. The chicken and meat products were showcased in a glass counter in front of them, and there were three refrigerated containers offering frozen goods like potato wedges, spring rolls and peas. At the back of the store Christina noticed an elevated platform on which two old men sat. She watched with amazement as they cut what looked to her like ribs, by guiding large pieces of meat with their hands and cutting it with knives clutched between their toes. Jazz noticed Christina's stare, laughed and said: 'That's what we are eating for dinner, my dear!'

Jazz managed to squeeze through the many people in the shop and reach the counter to talk to the shop owner. Christina noticed a stuffy smell but wasn't sure if it came from the street or the meat in the shop. Christina was relieved when Jazz suggested having a cup of coffee at a nearby cafe, since it would take a while for their order to be cut and packed. Christina was sure that if they had stayed much longer, she would have turned vegetarian. She tried to forget the sight of chickens and goats hanging upside down behind the man cutting the meat, and quickly rushed out after Jazz.

They walked across the street to reach a sidewalk lined with shops that Jazz said was Khan Market. 'This is where all the diplomats come to shop,' she explained to Christina. The place looked familiar and Christina was sure Andy had taken her here before. She looked through the windows and noticed how small and narrow most of the stores were. 'If you see anything you want to buy, I will bring you back tomorrow. Let's have a quick drink and go, otherwise we will get late.' Jazz said and led her through a narrow passage into what looked like a backlane to the market. Motorbikes were parked besides trash cans. A street vendor was trying to sell them fruits. Christina was surprised to see more shops and signages for many restaurants. She followed her soon-to-be sister-in-law up two flights of narrow stairs to a surprisingly modern coffee shop. Sun was filtering in through the large front window but the room was chilly because of the air conditioning. A young woman showed them to a table next to the window, overlooking a row of trees, hiding the street and parking lot below. 'A nice change from the meat shop, right?' Jazz teased Christina and told her about the wide coffee selection and awesome cakes that go with it. The minute they had placed the order, Jazz's phone rang. 'Mom!' she said with a smile and covered the phone: 'I bet she is checking on us!' Jazz winked.

Not only was Kiran checking on them, but urging them to be quick. She wanted some chicken added to the order. Dadi had seen the menu and was upset that nobody remembered to serve chicken as well. After her complete check-up at the hospital, she was on a strict diet. She had told the doctors in the hospital about the upcoming wedding and it was agreed that she could make an exception for the wedding of course. Until then she warned her children and grandchildren not to serve her any masalas, overcooked food, *mithai* and especially no meat and fish. She wanted to be in excellent shape and not fall sick again before the festivities. Jazz giggled at their little menu-mess-up and agreed to buy the chicken as soon as Jazz hung up the phone, the promise seemed forgotten and instead of leaving within a few minutes it took half an hour to get their coffee and drink it while Jazz asked Christina lots of questions about her trip to Germany. 'Your parents must be upset that you are getting married in India. You will be so far away,' she remembers Jazz saying. In a way, Jazz reminded Christina of her own sister. Like Frauke, Jazz had just moved a few streets away from her parents' house after her wedding and still sees them every day. She was glad her sister was close to her parents but she would find this really irritating. When Andy and she had agreed to move in with his parents in Golf Links she had made him promise that after a few years they would find a house of their own. Maybe it was the heat or the endless time it took to pick up some meat and chicken, but Christina was feeling antsy and craving her own space to live in she had thought, watching Jazz chatting away over coffee.

After they had picked up the meat, Jazz told the driver to go to another market for the fish. The place, whose name Christina could not remember, lacked sidewalks and looked like one big shack with hundreds of little stalls. As soon as they had gotten out of the car, several men with baskets approached them and offered to help them with their shopping. Christina felt like she was towering over them by at least a head, and kept thinking that most of them looked so skinny—she would feel bad making them carry her shopping bags. She kept saying 'No!' to the ever growing crowd of helpers, but that just made them more interested. Jazz told her to stop smiling, and loudly but clearly, told them to go away which quickly got rid of them. She told Christina to follow and not smile or talk to people as they made their way through the maze of shops. Christina noticed how some guys stuck around just in case they would change their mind. Similar to the meat shop in Khan Market, they reached a narrow store offering all kinds of fish, some stacked on buckets full of ice, some behind glass cases. Again, Christina was overwhelmed by the intense smells in the shop and even after they had left the market she was trying to shake off the images of dead fish staring at her. But she enjoyed watching Jazz getting things done and was taking notes for future shopping trips. Without too much effort, Jazz made herself noticed and was quickly served. Christina watched Jazz explaining her order, haggling with the shopkeeper and getting the fish packed in just a few minutes. Jazz said that she was tempted to do some personal shopping but explained that she prefers to come early in the morning or later in the day for that. This week, her mother had gotten a headstart on the weekly shopping and bought all their vegetables from the even larger *subzi mandi*, she heard Jazz explain.

Christina felt like a small, confused child following her sister-in-law through the maze of shops, working their way back to the car, passing many shopkeepers eagerly offering their goods. 'They can smell good business with you around,' Jazz had joked, stressing the fact that when she comes alone for shopping, people don't approach her as much. Christina knew Jazz was right. She felt too tall, too blonde, too white to blend into the crowd of shoppers and was convinced that it was obvious to the world, that she had no idea about prices and was terrible with bargaining. When they finally reached their car, the driver had disappeared for no apparent reason and Christina felt like they were wasting yet another 20 minutes in the heat, just waiting in a parking lot. Jazz didn't seem to be bothered. While tracking down their driver on the phone, Jazz delegated the boys who carried their shopping bags to search for the driver and also told them to pick up some more things from the market for them that they had forgotten. She continued to be the perfect tour guide, filling in Christina on their location: 'By the way, this market is called INA Market. As you just saw, you get great fish here but also lots of other goodies like your imported cheese and fancy coffees. You will even find *sauerkraut*, canned sausages and baked beans in these cramped stalls. If you bargain, you get some awesome deals here. As long as you don't let them rip you off. As soon as they see a *gori*, they double the price! Like the fish guy, he saw you and gave me some ridiculous price. Well, he was messing with the wrong person!' Jazz had laughed wholeheartedly. Christina wondered if she would ever be able to come here by herself and get her shopping done.

The driver was found. Their shopping trip continued. The traffic and the crowds were making Christina dizzy. Jazz made some phone calls. She had put her baking and catering business on hold for the next few weeks to be fully available for the planning and execution of the wedding. Nobody had asked her to, but she felt that this was the least she could do to help her family, especially her darling brother Andalip. Christina had overheard her tell somebody that she would not be able to take orders for cakes until early December. She wondered if she would ever do the same for anyone in her family. Her thoughts had been interrupted when a dog jumped in front of the car and the driver tried to avoid hitting it. He pulled the car to the left and hit a simply dressed man on a bicycle instead of the dog. Christina screamed. To her surprise the man—and not their driver—looked guilty. He picked up the cycle and quickly disappeared into the traffic. The driver yelled some curses, got back into the car and drove away. Jazz continued with her phone calls like nothing had happened. The driver looked into the rear-view mirror and smiled: 'You OK, madam? Nothing happened. People here just don't look where they are going.'

Christina felt like she was done for the day and decided to wait in the car while Jazz quickly disappeared into a store located along the Ring Road. She felt bad letting the A/C run but the sun was quickly heating up the car. The driver got out and busied himself with something behind the car. She tried to ignore the fact that he must feel terribly hot out there and closed her eyes for a few minutes. She must have dozed off but awoke when Jazz got into the car. 'What a waste of a trip. When I called this morning, they said the jewellery would be fixed and now they have not even started on it. Mom is going to throw a fit!' Jazz vented and looked at Christina for response. She did not even know what jewellery she was talking about and just nodded. When Christina had arrived in Delhi a few days ago, Aunty had told her about the family jewellery that Christina was supposed to wear during the wedding functions. Aunty had worn them and before that Dadi. Now Christina was going to inherit them as the wife of the oldest son from a long line of eldest sons. She had been told that Andy's sisters were given a few pieces at their weddings but the bulk would belong to her until her future son would get married. When she asked to look at them, Aunty had told her that they were usually kept at a bank locker, but were now with the jewellers to be cleaned and for minor repairs. 'The wedding jewels, right?' Christina asked. 'Don't we need that only for the wedding ceremony? So he does have a few more days to finish it. Maybe he will make it on time.'

Jazz looked upset and kept trying to reach her mother. When she did not pick up, Jazz's mood changed. She switched the topic with a brief 'Never mind!' and told Christina that they were close to a market that sold readymade garments. They should stop there to get a *lehenga* or *salwar kameez* for Fiona. Christina was tired but she knew she had no choice but to agree to this since there was less than a week before her family arrived. She had a feeling that each day from now on until the wedding would be packed with action. She might as well cross off things from the long list of what needs to be done before the festivities start! 'Chalo, let's go then!' Christina said with a bright grin, shaking her head from left to right. 'That's the attitude I was looking for. And, spoken like a true Indian!' Jazz replied with a laugh.

The driver dropped them off on a crowded street lined with small shops displaying colourful women's clothing. 'This is Amar Colony. It's going to be hard to find parking here so I will send the driver home to drop off the shopping bags and we can take our time picking out some outfits for Fiona.' Before Christina could reply, she found herself stuck between cycle rickshaws. She watched Jazz scan the shops, then quickly entering the first one at the corner. The bright neon sign read 'Best Clothes Shop'. Christina grinned and mused, 'Of course, this is where we buy the best clothes in town!'

When Christina managed to work her way into the store through parked cars, potholes and sleeping dogs, she found Jazz sitting on the floor with her shoes off. The entire floor was covered with white bedsheets, surrounded by glass-fronted counters filled with colourful fabrics. Behind the counter were several men who all stared at her when she entered. 'She is with me. Come, sit next to me!' Jazz said while waving to her across the room. The men went back to work, and soon one of the older attendants dropped several samples in front of Jazz. He then walked towards Christina, stretching his arms out like he was going to hug her. Christina noticed big circles of sweat under his arms and a big potbelly pushing out under his white kurta. 'Welcome, madam, welcome! You come and sit here next to your friend. I will show the best clothes for you to buy. I have all colours and all styles, best ones in Delhi. Sit, sit and I will show you!' Christina could not help but smile, take off her shoes and sit down.

Jazz explained to the man that they were mainly looking for some partywear for a tall, slim teenage girl from Germany, not for herself. Something comfortable for somebody who was not used to Indian clothes, she said, but fancy enough to keep up with all the aunties at the party.

When the man got busy instructing his helpers to find more samples, Jazz leaned over to Christina and explained that the quality of the fabrics in such stores was OK but not as good as what she herself would wear. But since this outfit would be worn just a couple of times, this was the best place to buy something reasonably priced and somewhat fashionable. Just before Christina could respond, a packet landed on her lap. She shrugged and looked up to find a younger chap, looking apologetic, and telling her to check out the *salwar kameez*. 'Latest style and colour, madam, you will like!' he smiled at her and got busy again. Christina pulled a pink fabric out of the cellophane wrapping and opened it, holding a heavily embroidered shirt up into the air. 'No, the work looks cheap!' Jazz pulled the shirt away from her and threw the packet to the side. The women took turns in rejecting outfit after outfit and Christina was getting antsy. Maybe another store would offer better choices? She suggested moving on but Jazz whispered that all shops will show the same stuff and that it was just the way of doing business. The older man, who turned out to be the owner of the shop, had introduced himself as Harish. He noticed the women whispering and said that he will organize some tea and soft drinks for the ladies, and in the meantime would get some better stock from the store room.

Kiran called while they were waiting for Harish to return. She had received the meat and fish and wanted to know when they would return. Dinner was at 8 so she wanted them to be ready before that. Christina overheard Jazz tell her mom that they were almost done and would be there in half an hour. When she got off the phone, Jazz laughed and told Christina: 'Don't look so shocked. We can always blame it on the traffic if we get late. No one will arrive before 9. 30 anyway so we have plenty of time. Maybe we can even stop at the parlour and get our nails done, what do you think? The kids are taken care of today. I can spend some time with you!' Christina noticed the clock above the door. It was 6 pm now. She knew they would spend at least another half an hour before they could find any clothes for Fiona, then another half an hour in traffic. If they stopped at the parlour it would mean that they would definitely not get home before 8 pm.

A young boy appeared in front of them offering tea and water. Jazz drank some water, put the half empty glass back on the tray and then took the *chai*. When Christina reached for the water, Jazz told her to just drink the tea. She was disappointed since she was really thirsty. She said no to both water and tea. The boy kept standing there and Christina noticed how disappointed he looked as well. He is not much older than Ben, she thought. Harish appeared with a new load of packets. The boy quickly stepped out of his way and Harish kneeled in front of them, spreading out at least 30 different outfits, each brighter than the other. Jazz seemed to like what she was seeing, smiling at Harish and approvingly, 'Now this is looking a lot better, Harish *Bhai*!' Christina felt like she had seen all these before. One dark red packet reminded her of the wedding invitation with the same semi-precious stones on it. 'I am really sorry Jazz, I need to get some air for a minute. I'll be right back. Just select something and I'll make a final decision when I come back.' With that Christina had gotten up and rushed out of the door.

Now sitting with her head in her lap, she feels like she can still see the bright colours in front of her eyes. Better than all that meat and chicken hanging upside down, she thinks. In an attempt to think of something other than suits and smelly meat shops, her mind wanders off and she remembers the bicyclist staring at her through the car window after being hit by their car. Then the boy in the shop comes to her mind and how he stared at her with his large black eyes. Suddenly she feels like laughing hysterically trying to picture Frauke or Bärbel in situations like these. They are going to have a fit! What was I thinking when I invited them here, she thinks and shakes her head. Her thoughts are interrupted by somebody tapping her back. Jazz, she thinks and turns around to find herself staring at a dirty, half-naked man, wearing nothing but an orange cloth around his loins and a bead necklace around his neck, giving her a toothless smile. *'Theek hain, ji?'*

'Theek hu, ji!' she replies. The Hindi comes naturally. She feels truly touched by the man's concern for her and for the first time today, feels like she is actually present in the here and now and not just watching the world around her. She gets up. She pulls out a 50-rupee note from her pocket and puts in into the empty tin cup that he's holding. 'I am absolutely fine, my friend. Thanks for asking! You definitely made my day.' With that Christina walks back into the store, still smiling and shaking her head, and sits down next to Jazz. She picks out two outfits from the pile. 'Let's just stick to the basics. A pink *salwar kameez* and a purple *lehenga*! She will look more like a princess from a Disney film than a Bollywood beauty but I am sure she will love it. What do you think?'

Jazz looks up. 'You look a little stressed. If you are sure, let's take these two and we can always change them later, right Harish?' Jazz stands up and starts discussing prices with the owner. Like at the fish shop, Jazz displays all the emotions from anger to sadness to excitement and finally settles for a price. Jazz folds her hands and says thank you. Christina copies her *namaskar*. Harish hands them the two outfits in a printed cloth bag and offers his hand to Christina. Thank you, sir!' Christina says shaking his hand. 'Please madam, take my business cards and give them to your friends. I promise, you'll come back and I'll make you good price. Good clothes, good price, 100 per cent, I guarantee. You just bring your friends.' Harish hands her a stack of cards. She takes them and gives him a thumbs up: 'Sure, Harish, 100 per cent I will bring my friends.' She rushes out and starts laughing.

She looks at her watch. Ten to seven. 'So the parlour is on the way? Do we still have time for that manicure?' She puts her arm through Jazz's while walking towards the car. 'Sure, let's do that. It will be good for you. And you'll want to look good for all these relatives tonight. Let me call Mom and tell her we are still trying to find some clothes for Fiona.'

Back in the car, they soon get stuck in traffic. Christina listens to Jazz talking to Aunty: 'Mom, we will be there in a bit. Just getting some more shopping done and might stop at the parlour. There is so much traffic, might sit it out for a bit until rush hour is over… Sure, we will be there in time for the guests! Love you, bye!' Jazz smiles: 'When in Rome, do as the Romans do. Let's have some fun at the parlour!'

Chapter 11

Jazz is standing outside the room which she shared with her sister while growing up in their parents' house. She listens to her sisters' giggles and decides to wait a minute before entering. It is 11 in the night and the rest of the family is sleeping. Mom, Dad and Dadi had excused themselves right after dinner to catch up with sleep before Andalip's arrival later tonight, a week later than planned but as promised before the beginning of the official wedding week. In 24 hours the Germans would arrive as well, which would mean the 'party' is about to start. Simran, Jazz and Preets had decided to spend a last night in their parents' house before they shifted to Jazz's house in time for the husbands' arrival tomorrow. The plan is to stay up until 1 am and drive to the airport together and pick up Andalip. Christina had sat with them until an hour ago but wanted to sleep a bit before they left. It has been a hectic week with a lot of last-minute shopping and organizing, dress rehearsals and late-night dinners with friends and family. Jazz had watched her soon-to-be sister-in-law with amazement all week, how she dealt with all the attention and still managed to keep a cool head. All this must be really strange to her, but Christina shows no sign of confusion or culture shock, Jazz thinks.

The laughing has stopped and she enters the room. 'What is so funny?' she tries to sound casual. She watches Simran and Preeti sitting side by side on their queen-sized bed, drinking vodka and orange juice. Jazz feels envious. Even though her sisters are nine years apart in age, they seem to be so close and comfortable with each other. Jazz never seems to fit in when the three of them are together. She sits down at the foot of the bed. Preeti hands her two bottles and Jazz pours herself a drink. 'Cheers to our dear brother Andalip and our new sister Christina!' All three raise their glasses and enjoy their drink.

'I was just telling Preets about what I told Aisha the other day—how we all grew up in this house and what good times we had. Being an only child in Singapore with no cousins around, I think she feels lonely sometimes. It will be awesome to see all the kids get together. I made her try one of my *saris* the other day and the whole thing fell down. She stood there in her underwear, all mad at me, screaming, 'I am not going to wear this for the wedding!' I thought that was just like Preets when I got married and Mom tried to force her into all of her party clothes.' Simran pinches her baby sister in the arm and both start laughing again.

Jazz changes the topic. 'Can you believe that Andalip is arriving just a day before his own wedding celebrations begin? Poor Christina is having to deal with all this by herself. I would be so mad at Vivaan if he did that to me.' Preeti leans over to Jazz and says: 'Poor Vivaan. I don't think he would ever dare to do that to you!' Again, both Preeti and Simran start laughing.

'I think you guys should slow down on the drinks. You're already drunk!' Jazz is annoyed. 'You guys are not much better than Andalip, arriving at the last minute. I thought you are not working these days, Simi, couldn't you have come a little earlier?'

'Come on Jazz, lighten up and have another drink. This is supposed to be fun. And no, I could not leave Singapore earlier. Aisha had exams and I've started writing again. I've got a new job at an online magazine, which is going really well. I didn't want to blow it. I've just joined a few months ago,' Simran replies.

'That's awesome, Sis, good going! What are you working on? Do you have to go to an office or are you working from home? Why didn't you tell us earlier?' Preeti asks excitedly. Preeti is the only one of the sisters who kept her job after getting married. Out of the three, she resembled Andalip the most and ever since she was little, tried to follow in his footsteps. Her parents were happy she chose a college in Delhi and found a job quickly in an advertising agency when she graduated at twenty-three. Work, just like for Andy, was always a priority for her. When she got married to Kabir four years ago, it was given that she would find a new job and continue working once they moved to Mumbai. She had made it very clear that unlike her sisters, she would not give up her career just because she got married. Her response to anyone who asked her about when she was having children is always is the same: 'I can have children later, now I want to make it big in advertising.'

'I go in twice a week but usually work from home. It works out really well with Aisha being in school most of the day now. I can still be around when she needs me and make sure she studies. It is a little scary how grown up she is for her 12 years. Not even a proper teenager yet and she prefers spending her days with the other girls at the mall or chatting with them on her BlackBerry. She gave up ballet last year, telling me that it is for little girls. She was really good at it and could have danced on stages all over Asia. But where do you draw the line between pushing them to be a child star or just letting them enjoy their childhood or teenage years? Since I'm out of the house more, we seem to get a long great and I hope it stays like that. The other day she asked me how she could tell if a boy likes her. How scary is that, *yaar*?' Simran finishes her drink and disappears into the bathroom. When she comes out she continues: 'But to answer your question... I know you hate it when we keep talking 'kids' all the time, Preets... I am writing something like a column for a local edition of Cosmo. It's on being an expat in Singapore. Not very sexy but fun! I get to explore the city and get paid for it. Ha! I even have a press pass now. We can try sneaking into a movie or club opening one day. What do you think? I'll send you the link, read it and let me know if you like it.'

Again, Simran and Preeti seem to be on the same level. Jazz forces herself to show some interest. 'Send it to me too, I want to read it. I should really make a plan to come to Singapore, but I have been really busy with my baking and catering. I still do it out of the house, but it is going really well. Mom does not want me to, but I think I'm baking the cake for the wedding reception. And how is your work going, Preets? Making a name for yourself in Mumbai?'

Preets stretches out on the bed. 'Let's not talk about me tonight,' she replies quickly and closes her eyes. 'That's a new one. Since when don't you want to talk about yourself?' Jazz teases her. She moves around the bed and lies down next to Preeti. The three of them are lying in bed, fully dressed, a little drunk. Simran strokes Preeti's hair and pulls her ear: 'Jazz is right, what happened to you? You always love telling us all about your exciting life in Mumbai. Don't tell me you are drunk. I have seen you drink more than that, party girl!' Preeti keeps quiet.

Simran and Jazz make eye contact and on the count of three, they start tickling their baby sister. 'She just needs a good laugh,' Jazz teases. Preeti sits up, draws her knees up to her chest, puts her arms around them and rests her head: 'Come on you guys, I am not five years old anymore. Stop it!' Simran gets up too. 'What's wrong, Preets? Don't tell me that you are crying?' Jazz pulls Preets around, like she is one of her children. 'Come on Preets, what's the matter? Did you drink too much? You don't look too good!'

Preeti pulls herself free and puts her head back down onto her knees: 'I am fine. Just give me a minute.' Simran and Jazz look at each other. 'I know I had too much to drink. Let's set the alarm and sleep for an hour before we head out!' Simran lies back down next to Preeti. Jazz gets up and goes to the bathroom. In less than a minute she comes back running into the room and jumps onto the bed: 'Don't tell me you are pregnant, Preets? That's why you have been so moody and didn't come earlier, right? Why don't you tell us? Come on, Preeti Singh, admit that I am right!'

Simran gets up and stares at her sisters. 'My God, Preets, is she right? You shouldn't be drinking like this!' Preeti lifts up her head. She stops crying and first looks at Jazz, then at Simran. Jazz wants to ask more questions but tries to keep quiet. Preeti looks upset and not at all in the mood to discuss this. All three sisters just sit quietly for a while before Preeti answers: 'No, Jazz, I am far from being pregnant. I have left Kabir. I want a divorce. I moved out a few months ago, but I don't want anybody to know before the wedding. Kabir will not attend the wedding. Officially his mother is not well, which is true but obviously that's not the reason he's not coming to Delhi. Just don't mention it to anybody, especially Mom or Dad, until after the wedding. Let's not discuss this anymore until Andalip and Christina leave for their honeymoon next week. Promise me?' When Simran and Jasneet don't answer her, she starts walking away but turns around and looks at them one more time. 'Can you please do that for me? I just need to get through this week and I will take it from there!' Her sisters just nod in shock and watch her disappear into the bathroom.

Chapter 12

Andalip's flight arrives almost half an hour early. He makes it through customs quickly. He stops at the duty-free shop before getting his bags. He grabs two bottles of Black Label whiskey. That should last us until Tuesday, he grins and makes a note to himself to tell Michael to pick up some more for the wedding when he arrives with the Germans tomorrow. He notices the wine and champagne on the shelf in front of him and decides to take one Black Label and pick up a bottle of champagne instead for his would-be in-laws. He is sure that Dad would not have gotten either. When Andalip had asked him to get some wine on the phone last week, Dad laughed and said: 'Only girls drink wine! Whiskey is what we need for a real party. Make sure you pick some bottles up at the duty-free shop when you land.' He hopes Dad would not mention this to Michael, who is a big wine and beer drinker. What a way to make a first impression!

When Andalip gets to the luggage belt, he switches on his phone and finds a message from Jazz: 'We are at the airport waiting for you. Come out quick!' A second later there's a message from Christina: 'Counting the seconds until I can hold you in my arms.' He browses through more incoming messages, mainly work and advertising. He puts the phone in his shirt pocket and notices a man waving out to him. Andalip doesn't recognize the person and turns around to see if he might be waving to somebody else. The man smiles, picks up his backpack and walks around the conveyer belt towards him.

'Hello Bhaiya, don't you recognize me?' he says, holding out his hand to greet Andy. The person before him looks like a college kid, dressed in jeans and a frayed striped dress shirt. He looks Indian, Andy thinks, his face tanned by the sun, but his hair is a lighter brown, not too common in these parts of the world. Maybe from Pakistan or Afghanistan, Andy tries to remember where he has seen the young man. 'You have no idea, right?' the guy laughs. Andy feels a little embarrassed.

'I am Raj. Remember, Raj Kumar's son. My dad used to work for your grandfather. When I was little, I used to spent a lot of time in your house, playing in the kitchen or running around the driveway.' Raj smiles at him with friendly light brown eyes, waiting for a reaction. Andalip tries to remember, but cannot recall the face in front of him. Then he remembers a young man who used to work for Dada in the Noida plant. 'It's OK,' Raj continues, 'you had left for the US by then and did not spend much time in the house, I guess. I thought you might remember since my mother was half-German. Your wife is German too, isn't she?'

Then it hits Andy. The man in front of him was the talk of the town almost 25 years ago. His father had shown up with him as a baby at the family's factory. Raj Kumar had told his grandfather he needed some help raising his son. His mother had died giving birth to Raj in Goa, where the couple had met. From what Andy remembers she was a hippie from Israel with some Jewish relatives living in Germany. Raj's mother had run away after school and settled in Goa, working in some guest house where she met Raj Kumar, who was a handyman on the same property. Somehow they had managed to start their own bed and breakfast and things went well until she got pregnant. When she died Raj Kumar could not bear to stay in Goa and returned to his village in the Punjab. When he arrived with the child and no wife, his family wanted to get rid of the boy, hide the past and get him married off to some local girl. Raj Kumar decided to leave his family and look after his son himself and seek new opportunities in the big city. Dada had once told him that he admired this man who worked as a driver during the day and as a guard at night, studying English and hoping for a better future for his son. Dada had helped Raj Kumar to track down his wife's family in Israel and had managed to find a rich Jewish aunt in Germany, who took pity on the child and decided to fund his education. If he remembered rightly, Raj ended up spending some time in Germany after his basic schooling in India. Andalip had not paid much attention to the story after he left for NYC and was not sure how much his family was still involved in the boy's life.

Andy shakes his head. 'I am so sorry, I did not recognize you. I am not sure I even remember seeing you as a kid but, of course, I know your story. What an honour it is to meet you. I am surprised you recognized me!'

Raj laughs. 'Of course I recognize you. I used to admire you from afar as a kid and I remember all the photos of you in your dada and dad's office. You are a star in your family! I am sure you know that. Dad told me that you are getting married to a foreigner. Even though he is not working for your family anymore, he keeps in touch and stops by the factory every few months to pay his respects. If it was not for your grandfather, I wouldn't be standing in front of you today.'

They are interrupted by the arrival of the bags and the crowds pushing pass them to grab their luggage. Andy spots one of his bags and pulls it onto his luggage cart. One more suitcase remains. 'So you're coming from Frankfurt too?' Andy asks Raj. Andy was flying Lufthansa due to his original plan to pick up Christina on the way to India and even though his dates had changed, because of his work commitments, he felt it was too complicated to re-book the ticket to a non-stop flight. He was secretly looking forward to another visit to Germany next year, but this time as Herr and Frau Singh, he smiles while waiting for Raj's answer. 'I was just visiting my aunt in Germany. She's getting old and I try to make it there once a year,' Raj replies. Andy tries to picture him with a German aunt. He imagines a white-skinned old woman walking arm-in-arm with this dark-skinned, good-looking boy through a shopping street in Germany. He could just see people staring at them.

A tall, blonde man bumps into them while trying to get his suitcase from the belt. '*Entschuldigung*…ah, sorry, I mean,' the man apologises with a polite smile. Raj smiles back: '*Kein problem, ziemlich voll hier! Ich helfe Ihnen gerne.*'Both Andy and the man are surprised by Raj's fluent German. Raj laughs: 'What? You have not heard an Indian speak German? Bhaiya, you should know better than to be surprised by that!'

Andy feels embarrassed once again. This is how my children might look a few years down the road, he thinks. The best of both worlds, he hopes. Both Raj and Andy collect their bags. Andy is reluctant to say goodbye. He'd like to ask more questions, but he doesn't want his family to wait around too long. He grips Raj's shoulder. 'Raj, I am very glad we met today. I'm getting married next week and I hope you can make it for the wedding. I assume Dad knows how to reach you, right? Or better, why don't you come by the house tomorrow and I'll give you an invitation with all the details. If you're interested, you can help the Germans feel a little more at home in India.'

'Sure thing, Bhaiya! I will be there tomorrow. *Pakka!*' Raj's eyes seem to light up. He hugs Andy, says his goodbye and heads in the direction of the duty-free shops, while Andy walks towards the exit. He searches for his family and smiles when he spots Christina's blonde head towering over a large crowd of Indians waiting at the gate. When she sees Andy, she jumps up and waves. Andalip is scanning the crowd for his relatives, but only sees Jazz. When he reaches his sister and his soon-to-be wife, he hugs both and asks in surprise: '*Oui*, where is everybody? Is this how you greet the oldest son of the oldest son of the oldest son…' Andy laughs.

Jazz gives him a big kiss on the cheek. 'It's not about you anymore. It is about Christina now. She had at least 10 people picking her up from the airport.' Jazz teases him. 'The oldies need to rest and your dear sisters are passed out at home after too many vodka oranges.'

'I see. You started the wedding celebrations without me. I am glad I made it in time!' Andy jokes and the three of them work their way through the crowd to find the car and finally head home. Andy kisses Christina on the cheek and she smiles in return. He feels happy to have Christina back in his arms and finally be close to his family again.

Chapter 13

The next morning, the Singh family residence in Golf Links is very quiet. There are no signs of any activity that would suggest that a wedding was about to begin. Even though it is a Sunday morning, Manpreet is up at sunrise and enjoying a cup of tea by herself on the lawn in front the house, reciting her morning prayer, as she has done all her life since her school days in Lahore. Like many of her close girl friends and peers from well-off families, she attended the Convent of Jesus and Mary school, following a strict routine given by the English nuns. Besides the tea, her love for prayer at sunrise and a seldom slip into British English when forced to communicate in English, Manpreet tries to forget her childhood habits, friends and memories that she had to leave behind due to Partition and her family's escape to Delhi in 1947.

The rest of the family likes to sleep in, especially on a Sunday. The sun is already strong but the temperature is still comfortable, promising cooler weather for Delhi's upcoming winter months. The 83-year-old grandmother does not expect anybody to get up any time soon to disturb her peace and quiet.

Her daughter Manjeet and her grandson Anhad with his family are living with her on the ground floor. Manjeet had lost her husband just a few years after Anhad was born and had moved back in with her parents. She sometimes feels bad that her daughter had not been able to remarry, but Manpreet counts her blessing for having her daughter and her family living with her in the house.

Especially after her own husband Zorawar passed away. Usually, the house is buzzing with activity at this time of the day—getting her great-grandchildren ready for school and seeing off Anhad and his wife, Jasmine, off to work. On the weekends, the entire family likes to catch up on sleep. Her son Bopinder and his wife Kiran usually arise at noon, after enjoying a night out at the Delhi Golf Club. Last night, she knows, was a late one for everybody with her three granddaughters in the house and Andalip's arrival in the middle of the night. She has not seen much of her soon-to-be granddaughter-in-law, Christina, since her arrival 10 days ago. She prefers it that way, since in her days it was unheard of for a bride to move into the husband's house before the wedding.

No one had asked her what she thought about Christina moving into the apartment on the third floor before the wedding. Bopinder had just informed her that she would be staying there before and throughout the wedding. On top of it, Christina's parents, her sister and niece would be staying with her during that week. Manpreet was glad to hear that at least his parents were smart enough to make Andalip stay in his old room on their floor until the festivities were over and the guests had left.

So much has changed since the day I got married, Manpreet muses while sipping her tea. She had met Zorawar for the first time on their wedding day after her family settled down in Delhi 60 years ago. Her parents had made the choice for her life partner and she accepted it. She would not have dared to question their choice—a young Sikh man from a respected family, who like her own, had their roots in what is now Pakistan. She had full faith that her parents would know what is best to make her happy. Until his death, they had not spent a day apart. She grew to love him and thanked God for blessing her with three healthy children, two sons and a daughter. When it was time to marry off her children, there was no question that she and Zorawar would choose their children's life partners. She thought it was very modern of her to have her children meet and approve of Zorawar and her choice for their life partners. Just like her, her children too trusted their parents. She had expected more arguments from her grandchildren, but five out of the seven had arranged marriages. Only her youngest son's daughter, now 29 years old, chose to marry the man she met at college. She now lives in Dubai with her husband, a smart young fellow from a good Bengali family from Kolkata. The other one, of course, who went against the family traditions is her oldest son's firstborn, Andalip.

Manpreet's help comes out with a large tray. She places it on the table and exchanges the empty cup for another cup of hot *chai*. Next to it she places a plate with two slices of toast and a bowl of mixed fruits. She hands Manpreet a glass of water and a small box of pills and watches her finish both. 'Thanks Mary. Now get back to the kitchen and cook us some mouth-watering *aloo puri* and *channas* for breakfast. Our long lost son arrived last night and must be hungry from the long journey.' Mary smiles. Without replying, she takes the tray and disappears into the house. Manpreet looks at her breakfast with disgust and yells after her: 'Cardboard and monkey food. Don't always listen to what my children tell you I should be eating. I am not dead yet, you know. Bring me some eggs. Quick!' She knows that Mary will not respond this time either and she smiles.

Mary has been living with her for as long as she can remember and must be close to 80 herself. She used to tell her husband that she felt Mary was closer to her than any of her own sisters and brothers, who were much older and who by now had already passed away. Manpreet is often surprised how fit Mary is and even at this age, still oversees the housework and is more or less in charge of the kitchen. When Manpreet told her to slow down, retire and let some younger cook take over, Mary had told her that maybe she should just go ahead and shoot herself. 'What else is there for me than to look after you, Bhabi?' she remembers Mary telling her. Manpreet giggles and thinks to herself: 'Maybe I would be in better shape if I had taken over some of Mary's work instead of getting lazy and rusty!'

She used to do yoga in the mornings, but for the last 10 years the only exercising she did was to sit in the garden, close her eyes, listen to the birds and do some breathing exercises. She was still in pretty good shape and could visit her son on the first floor every day and go to the gurudwara at least once a week. Her hearing was deteriorating and for the last five years she could hardly see properly. Leaving the house meant she would have to take a maid along, even if she went with her children. Maybe it was time to join Zorawar in another life and let the children look after the family themselves, she often thinks.

Still, she really wants to see the last of her grandchildren get married. She shakes her head and gets up to take a short walk on the grass. She is starting to feel anxious again and tries to calm down herself by thinking of something other than the upcoming wedding. She used to take great pride in tending to the garden herself but like so many other things, she had to hand this task to someone else. She tries to remember when the row of palms was planted but her mind quickly returns to the wedding. She notices new flower pots lined up along the fence next to the drive way. The gardener has cleaned and decorated the garden and driveway for the arrival of Christina's family. She knows that Andalip has made the decision to marry Christina and that starting tonight, the bride's family would arrive and the festivities would begin tomorrow morning. Not everyone in her family has married within the Sikh faith, but she had always hoped that her eldest grandson would respect the family religion and traditions that come with being the head of the family one day. She still remembers the pride in Zorawar's face when their oldest son had announced the birth of his firstborn son, Andalip. From that day, the Singhs had placed a lot of hope in the first grandson of the family to keep up the family bloodline and take responsibility for the generations to follow. Out of all children, why did he have to make his own choice and not listen to his family? She feels angry at Bopinder for letting Andalip go to the USA to study. Maybe if he had waited a few years, got him married off before sending him abroad, things would have been different. What would Zorawar have done if he was alive and his oldest grandson had announced his marriage to a *firangi*? Maybe he would have been fine, but she thought he would have just simply forbidden such nonsense. Wherever he might be, she was sure he would be cursing her for not trying hard enough to stop Andalip.

She feels tired and decides to sit down on the grass instead of walking back to her chair. Her knees give in and she suddenly lands on her bottom. She lies down and closes her eyes. Suddenly she feels like a young girl in her parents' house in Punjab. She soaks in the smell of the grass and enjoys the sun on her face. She feels calm and her pulse is slowing down. Maybe this is it, she thinks and smiles. 'Don't be mad at me Zorawar!' she whispers and then lies quietly.

'Ma? Oh my God, Ma, are you OK?' she hears a voice from a distance. She senses a person standing next to her. She opens her eyes and sees Bopinder looking down at her. He hasn't tied his turban and his hair is hanging down over his shoulders. She is sure he looks pale beneath his facial hair right now. 'Good morning, son!' she greets him. 'Maji, what are you doing here? I saw you from the balcony and thought you were dead. You almost gave me a heart attack!'

'Oh, don't be so dramatic,' Manpreet responds. She lifts her arms: 'Here, pull me up. I think my back is out and I need some help getting up. I don't think I am lucky enough to join your dad wherever he is just yet.' Bopinder lifts her up and helps her walk back to her chair. He pulls another chair and sits next to her. Manpreet watches her son tying his hair. He has always been her favourite. She is proud of him for looking after the family business while her younger son chose a career in medicine. She loves her daughter-in-law and feels at times closer to her than her own daughter. Life has treated me well, she thinks. So why is God testing me now and sending a white granddaughter into the house? She feels angry for having to worry about her oldest grandson at such a late stage in her life instead of being able to enjoy her last years amongst her loved ones.

Bopinder leans over and touches her shoulder. 'Mother, you really have to be careful and take a bit more care of yourself. You are not 25 anymore!' He looks seriously worried and a little scared. She wants to hug him as if he's her little baby again. The moment passes quickly though and she cannot hold back her anger: 'Beta, now is your turn to look after me. Let me be very frank—you are not doing such a good job these days. Look what you have done to this family by letting your son go abroad and running wild. It will be your fault if I end up in the hospital again this week!' With that she gets up and leaves her worried son in the garden and returns into the house.

Chapter 14

Preeti watches her mother's housekeeper, Anita, walking up the stairs in front of her. The young girl is struggling to carry several hangers with Christina's clothes for the wedding without dropping them. Preeti follows her with some shoes and a case with jewellery. She realizes that she has not been up these stairs in years. The third floor was always the servants' quarters and allowed access to a terrace that was mainly used to dry clothes when she was growing up. Just last year, her father had started to renovate the back room and turned it into a family room, properly airconditioned with a nice seating arrangement and a large flat screen TV. The narrow, cast-iron spiral staircase that led up to the roof was replaced by wide wooden stairs under which her father had built a bookshelf. Even though it was one of the nicer and larger rooms in the house, Preeti feels the family rarely spent much time here. Then she figures, she herself did not spend much time in her parents' house and only knew very little about their habits and routines these days. She tried to imagine her father sitting here late at night reading while her mother was already fast asleep in their room.

When Anita opens the door at the end of the stairs, a wonderful terrace appears behind it. Preeti is surprised. She steps out onto what looks like a wooden deck framed by all types of plants, flowers and palm trees. To her left, she can see the neighbourhood park and other houses below. She notices a small seating arrangement covered by a bright yellow awning in one corner of the roof. The area to the right, which used to be just another empty stretch of roof, is walled off. Preeti notices two doors. The one to the far left is fairly plain and narrow, but blends perfectly with the wood and brick design of the wall. This must be the door to the servants' quarters, she thinks as she watches Anita standing in front of the door closer to them. With her arms filled with the clothes, she kicks the door with her bare foot, making a knocking sound. Within seconds Christina sticks her head out. When she sees Anita and Preeti, she smiles and opens the door widely. 'Come on in. What brings you up to this corner of the world?' Christina jokes.

Anita quickly enters. Preeti hugs Christina and looks around. She finds herself walking through some sort of a green house: a little square room totally covered by glass, a little patch of stones and sand, surrounded by a beautifully designed, miniature landscape reminding her of a Buddhist garden, creating a private courtyard before entering Christina and Andalip's living space. Christina seems eager to show her around: 'Here, let me give you the tour. It's just temporary but I think it really came out nice. This is our living and dining room. We have enough space to entertain our own guests if we don't want to go down to your parents' floor.' Preeti puts down the package with the shoes and jewellery onto the wooden table that is standing in the centre of the room, which can easily seat eight for dinner but which looks more like a casual hangout during the day. The newspaper is spread out and some books are lying on one corner of the table. A large sofa lines the opposite wall, but the coffee table is missing. 'We still need more furniture. This sofa turns into a bed, too, so I think my niece and sister will sleep here next week.'

Christina points to the door behind her: 'We've even got our own little kitchen. Right now there's just enough stuff to make my own coffee and toast in the morning, but it's fully equipped with fridge, stove, microwave and—you won't believe it—a dishwasher.

I'll show you later.' She turns around and pulls Preeti behind her and opens another door at the end of the living room. What looks like an oversized walk-in closet turns out to be a hallway converted into storage space. Two of the closet doors are actually bedroom doors. Christina opens the one to the right without knocking: 'Andy, get up. Your sister Preeti is here!' Preeti finds her brother sprawled on the bed, still in pyjamas at 4 in the afternoon, drinking tea and working on his laptop. She hugs him and sits down next to him. She has forgotten about Anita, who is standing at the door waiting for instructions. There is no other furniture in the room, just the bed, so she tells her to just put the clothes on it and then sends her downstairs. Before she disappears, Andalip calls after her to get some *chai* and snacks for everyone from his parents' kitchen.

'What a cool space this has turned into! I am really impressed. You totally have your own little place up here. Dad got all this done?' Preeti asks. The bed is placed against the back wall of the room, with large floor to ceiling windows on either side. The blinds are open and the room is drenched with sunlight. She can see their neighbour's house to the back, but only through a clump of tall bamboo plants standing on the small balcony. 'It's awesome, right?' Christina jumps up from the bed. 'Check out the bathroom. It's small but it can match any fancy hotel.' Christina opens a sliding door. Two steps up Preeti can see a large washbasin with a mirror covering the entire wall above it. 'The room next door is another bedroom with pretty much the same design, which we will use as a guest room and study or something. I borrowed some furniture from your parents so that mine have a place to sleep.' Christina sits down. 'And you will never believe who is our interior designer!' She smiles at Preeti: 'You've got three guesses…'

Andalip laughs too, gets up to use the bathroom and before he closes the door tells his sister: 'If you don't get it right, you'll have to do a dance performance at the wedding. All by yourself! No cheating though!'

Preeti throws a pillow after him. 'I will guess but I am not dancing. Dadi is already planning to do an item number at your reception. I would not want to compete with her!' She leans over to Christina: 'Tell me, who?' The bathroom door opens again. 'No cheating I said. Christina, let her guess. Otherwise you will also have to dance!' Andalip jokes and disappears again. The women giggle.

'I know it wasn't Dad because I have seen what he has done with the TV room downstairs. That turned out great but a totally different design. But it was somebody in the family, right?' Preeti asks and Christina nods. 'Somebody who spends a lot of time in the house because you need to be here constantly to supervise the work. The finishing looks great! So my guesses are Mom, Jazz or Dadi. No wait, she won't be able to climb. Could it be Manjeet?' She knows she's wrong because Christina looks amused.

'All good guesses! I thought pretty much the same. I thought it was Mom and Jazz since those two kept asking me about my likes and dislikes. Like do I prefer marble over wooden flooring, modern over traditional Indian, blinds orcurtains. Turns out that your cousin Anhad is quite the architect and he managed the whole project. Which is really funny, since I've hardly spent any time with him in the past and don't really know him!' Christina tells Preeti.

'Wow, that is a surprise!' Preeti agrees. Anhad and Andalip were born in the same year. At that time Manjeet's husband was still alive and the boys could only get to spend time together during the holidays. When Manjeet moved back into the house Anhad was only six years old. Preeti was not even born then. She remembers Simran telling her stories about the boys teasing her and not letting her play with them, which she hated. As soon as Anhad and Andalip hit puberty though, they developed very differently and spent less and less time together. Andalip was definitely more social. For a long time Preeti had thought that Anhad was her real brother since he was always around. Andalip was pretty much gone by the time she turned eight. While Andalip went off to the US to study finance and business, Anhad stayed behind and became a mechanical engineer and then joined the family business. Preeti likes Anhad, maybe even loves him like an older brother, but she often jokes how predictable and boring he is. She had no idea how creative he was.

Then she remembers why she came up. 'Speaking of surprises! Mom wanted me to come up and have you try these.' She points to the pile of outfits at the end of the bed. She walks over to the living room and gets the shoes and jewellery. 'So these are the final versions of what you tried on last week. Some can still be changed but let's hope they fit, since there won't be any time to redo them.' Preeti is going through the hangers and sorts the outfits in the order of the upcoming ceremonies and events. Christina is still sitting on the bed, the smile wiped off her face and looking a bit frightened, Preeti notices.

'Don't worry, you will be fine,' Preeti tries to cheer her up. 'We are all here for you and will help you get ready. Mom's organized a lady to come over and do your make-up and hair every day. I am hanging the clothes in the order of events in your closet and then you just go with the flow. Or we can make a list too, but I think you will be able to remember 10 outfits, right?'

Christina just stares into space. Preeti worries that her sister-in-law is becoming a little panicky. Just then, Andalip and Anita are back in the room. Anita quickly puts the tray with tea and sandwiches on the bed and excuses herself. Andalip, wearing a towel around his waist, gets his clothes from his suitcase. He is in no hurry to put them on but instead sits on the bed and has his tea and sandwich. 'So, from what I could hear in there, you are doing an item number at my wedding. I will thank Anhad for that later. And you honey, having fun with your dress rehearsal yet?' He kisses Christina on the cheek but does not get a reaction. 'Hey, what's happened to you? Was Preets mean to you?' Andalip jokes.

Christina shakes her head. 'No, just look at all these clothes. How many ceremonies are there? I am not sure I can handle all this, Andy. What will my parents say?' Preeti steps in: 'No worries, there are only seven events. Three of these are back-up outfits and can be used after the wedding too. I better hang those in the other closet. It will be fun. You will feel like a princess. Wait until you see the shoes and all the necklaces and earrings that go with all the outfits. It's a once in a lifetime thing, Christina, it will be lots of fun.' She walks around the bed again and removes three hangers, looking for a place to hang the back-up clothes, and leaving them over a suitcase in the corner. 'See, not so bad. Andalip, why don't you get ready and move your stuff downstairs? Mom said to remind you that you are moving out today until after the wedding. And while you are downstairs, why don't you track down Jazz or Simi… or better both and send them up here.'

Andalip checks with Christina: 'Are you OK with that? You spend some time with the girls and come down to see me later. We will go to the airport after dinner to fetch your family, right? If you need anything else up here I will send Anita up later to get the rooms set up and cleaned. Preets is right, you will enjoy dressing up. Just go with the flow and don't worry about it too much.' Christina leans over and hugs him. 'I love you, but I am scared!' and hugs him even harder.

Preeti watches them. What a great couple they are, she thinks. She starts feeling a bit sad, remembering how happy she was to be getting married to Kabir. 'Why don't I leave the two of you alone for a bit? You can prepare for the week ahead and I will find the girls and maybe some red wine, if we are lucky. Then we can do the dress rehearsal.' Without waiting for a response, she leaves the room, closes the door behind her and rushes outside to find her sisters. Before she climbs down the stairs, she stops on the terrace and looks down into the front yard, then into the distance over the neighbourhood park and the rooftops of Golf Links. She wipes away a tear and lifts up her arms, screaming: 'Thank you God for setting me free. Now give me the strength to conquer the world and find new love!'

Part 4

The Wedding Countdown

Chapter 15
✤

Kiran tries to find her mobile phone on the bedside table to check the time. Midnight has just passed. It is dark and quiet outside. Tomorrow the long awaited wedding week will start. Finally, my oldest will settle down, she thinks. She cannot sleep. Thoughts are spinning through her mind, keeping her awake. Lying in her bed, she thinks she hears someone knocking. The fan above the bed is making a rattling noise. When the knocking stops, she thinks she must be imagining things and tries to go back to sleep. In a few hours the day will start. She counts the hours until she has to get up. I will have to be ready to set up the living room downstairs for the *path* before everybody shows up for breakfast. She knows that her sister-in-law Manjeet, who has offered to hold the ceremony in her living room rather than on Andalip's parents' floor, is very organized. She must have already removed everything small and breakable from the room. Still, her mother-in-law will be around trying to help as well, which usually ends in confusion and arguments. On top of that, Manjeet's grandchildren Karnav and Jasmine will be home from school. It will be a challenge to get organized.

Even though this is a special wedding between her son and a *firangi*, they had all decided that just like the other family weddings, they will follow the Sikh wedding tradition of starting the wedding week with a continuous reading of the Sikh scripture, the Guru Grant Sahib. On Saturday morning, her soon-to-be daughter-in-law sat with everybody on the floor, head covered listening to Piji reading a short prayer to commence the Akhand Path. She had asked Andalip to leave New York in time for this family prayer, but she knew work was often a priority for him over religious occasions. For the last couple of days, two priests have taken turns sitting in Dadi's prayer room on the ground floor to read the Guru Grant Sahib in preparation for the wedding. Her mother-in-law was very upset that Andalip missed the prayer, arriving to Delhi on Saturday evening and not half a day earlier as she had urged him. She kept scolding Bopinder in front of the entire family for not being more strict with Andalip to return from New York in time for the Akhand Path. Bopinder had tried to be funny and replied jokingly: 'At least your daughter-in-law is here for the kick-off-prayer!'Manpreet had slapped him at the back of his turban like he was a 10-year-old boy and scolded him in Punjabi: 'You fool! You should know better than that. The bride has nothing to do here today. It is a ceremony for the groom and his family. You should have told her to remain in her room upstairs if you can't send her to a hotel.' Kiran had busied herself telling everybody to come upstairs for a hearty breakfast, hoping nobody would hear her mother-in-law's comments. She wanted to say something to Manpreet but Bopinder had asked her a few days ago to ignore his mother at moments like these and just enjoy the wedding.

'You know Mom is getting old. She is disappointed that Andalip is not marrying a Sikh girl. You and I know that Andalip has made a fantastic choice for a wife and they are a good match. They will have a wonderful life together, I am sure. Times have changed! We should count our blessings that both of them have decided to move back to India. What good is it if we had pushed him into marrying a Delhi girl and if he had chosen to stay in the US?' Bopinder said.

After that, Kiran had decided to make this wedding a success. Her husband was right. As long as their son was happy and he and his bride would be close to them, it did not matter who Andalip marries. She herself had doubts about Christina ever since Andalip had told her about being in love with a foreigner. Seeing her over the last few days making such an effort, helping out, doing what she was told and getting along so well with her daughters, she chose to forget her concerns and just enjoy her only son's wedding. Maybe Dadi would come to the same conclusion at the end, she was hoping.

In a few hours, at around 10. 30 am, family and friends will gather to finish the reading with a final recitation followed by *kirtan* and serving of *prasad*. This would be the first time that Kiran will be holding this ceremony in her house. During her daughters' weddings, the prayers were more informal and the grooms' families had held the ceremony for their sons in their homes or at the gurudwara. For his wedding, Andalip had suggested involving everybody and having the German family and foreign guests be part of the entire ceremony, not just his future father-in-law and close relatives. He envisioned a wedding following the traditions of his faith but also educating his new family about it. Andalip had spent a lot of time on the phone with Kiran and his sisters understanding all the ceremonies. He had asked them to translate and summarize the Punjabi verse into English for Christina and her family. Kiran has to admit that at first she thought it was a lot of work. Now she actually realized that trying to explain the Sikh rituals and wedding traditions to others, she also learned more about the meanings behind traditions and weddings that she has always taking for granted. She only wishes that Christina's relatives would have arrived a few days earlier to get acclimatized before the celebrations started. Arriving on the same flight from Frankfurt that her son arrived with the night before at 2 in the morning and getting up early, totally jet-lagged, she wondered how much they would really enjoy the prayers. She rolls around in bed to hug her husband. His back is towards her and she can still hear him snoring. She puts one arm across his broad shoulders. My bear, she smiles to herself. Unlike her son, she did not know her husband well when she married him and their friendship grew slowly. Tonight, she truly loves him, trying to remember the number of years she has felt so close to him. Life is close to perfect, she thinks, all my four children are happily married. What more do I want? She questions herself, closing her eyes with her head buried into her husband's back. She suddenly feels happy and excited about her son's long awaited wedding.

Again she thinks she hears something. She looks up, over Bopinder's shoulder and notices that the door to the bedroom is opening quietly. The dim light from the hallway comes in. Kiran sits up in bed and sees Andalip's outline in the door. 'Mom?Dad? Are you up?' Andalip whispers into the dark room. Bopinder keeps snoring. Kiran gets out of bed, pulling her *kaftan* into place and fixing her hair as she walks around the bed. She pushes her son back into the hallway. She closes the door behind her: 'Let at least one of us sleep and be fresh for tomorrow, shall we?' She notices Andalip dressed in his jeans and T-shirt. He must be ready to head out for the airport. 'Everything OK, Beta? Are you leaving now? Should I wake up Anita to tell her to make some food for you? Or Christina's family?' She hesitates, 'Or should I make you something myself?' It's been a long time since one of her children has been living in the house. A memory of Andalip as a teenager flashes before her eyes. What a handsome and popular chap he was, always busy running around with his friends, she remembers fondly. How many times had she gotten up in the middle of the night to make eggs and *paranthas* for her son's hungry friends, who he brought home after a Saturday night out, not willing yet to say goodbye to his friends for the weekend but still too young to be roaming around the local market hunting for a late night snack.

Andalip smiles at her. She wonders if he knows what she's thinking. He is over a head taller than her now. He still looks like he did as a young boy. Back then he was still wearing a *patka*. She tries to picture him in a turban. She cannot remember when he told her that he had cut his hair, but it must have been before he started work. She was disappointed at the time and agreed with her mother-in-law that it was a big mistake on Andalip's part to disrespect his religion just because he lived abroad. Bopinder seemed shocked at first and she remembers him spending an entire afternoon at the gurudwara. Finally somebody sent him back to the house and made him announce over dinner, that he had accepted his son's decision and that it had nothing to do with his love towards his family or country whether he wore the turban or not. He is a grown man and he has to live with his own decisions, he had said that night, no matter if it was related to work, religion or love. She did not understand her husband then and was disappointed at him for not even trying to talk to Andalip. Over the years she realized that her husband was right and that one cannot control one's children's life. One can guide them but they have to make their own decisions. Only God will judge if they are right or wrong. Having her son standing in front of her now makes her thankful to Bopinder for letting Andalip grow to be the person he is today. We must have done something right as parents to have him come back to us after all these years abroad, she wonders. The short hair suits him, she looks at him and smiles, reaching up and stroking his head. Andalip wiggles away, giggling like a boy: 'No Mom, didn't' we just eat dinner? I still have to fit into my suit tomorrow morning. Anyway, I'm off to bed now. Christina and I are not going to the airport right now. Some minor change in plans! Christina's family won't be arriving until tomorrow morning. Michael called and said that the flight had got delayed due to some problem with the plane. They only boarded a new plane a couple of hours ago. Now they are scheduled to land at 7 am instead of 2 am. I've already told Jazz to tell the taxis to stay put and wait for them. There should be enough time to drive everybody to their guesthouses, have them change quickly and then join the *path*.'

'Beta, this is awful!' She grabs her son's hand and pulls him out of the hallway to sit down in the bedroom next to hers. The room that once used to be the kids' room, now served as a guestroom. Andalip was going to use this room until after the wedding. 'There is no way they will make it in time for the *path*. You are talking about 20-odd people getting their bags, finding their way out of the airport, going to different guesthouses, etc. They will be exhausted. And they are all on their own, since you obviously cannot go to pick them up now. Maybe we should send somebody else to fetch them? Unfortunately, we cannot wait for them to start the reading because it has to be completed by noon. Somebody should make sure that your father-in-law knows we need him here in time to put the *tika* on your forehead. And maybe we can have one of the cousins come here directly to put the *kara* on your hand, since Christina does not have a brother to do that.' She takes a deep breath. This is going to be the fourth wedding where she will see one of her children getting married. It has worked out so far, it will work out this time too, she tries to calm herself down. 'I hope they make it at least for lunch. We are getting all this food catered, what a waste!' Kiran shakes her head in disbelief. Maybe Dadi's wish of keeping this a small affair just for the groom's family will come true after all.

Andalip and Kiran are sitting side by side on the edge of the bed. Kiran is still holding her son's hand. He leans over and hugs her. 'Mom, it will be fine. I did not want to freak you out, just to give you a heads-up. I will take care of the Germans and you take care of the rest, OK?' He kisses his mother on the cheek and looks at her with his large brown eyes. He always knew how to wrap me around his finger, she smiles lovingly. She kisses him back and hugs him tightly. Then she grips him by the shoulders and looks at him firmly: 'Beta, this is your wedding. You just make sure you are ready and prepared for everything and enjoy being the centre of attention! We will take care of the Germans, don't you worry about that. Now we all should get some sleep and be fresh for the week ahead!' They both get up and hug each other. Kiran feels tired but wants to share one last thought: 'Didn't you tell me that Germans are so organized and punctual? Couldn't they have booked a different flight and got here a little bit earlier than a few hours before the *path*?'

Andalip laughs loudly and says: 'Mom, you are the best! Just don't mention this to Christina in the morning. Good night!' With that he heads towards the door. 'Hey, where are you going? Isn't this your bedroom?' Kiran calls after him and expects him to turn around, recognizing his mistake. Instead he quickly turns his head and grins: 'Mom, I have to take care of Christina. How do you think she is feeling right now with her family being late for her wedding?'

Once again, she realizes how different her son's life is to hers. How little she really knows about him since he left for the US. He has already spent a great deal of time with this woman who she still has to learn to love as much as her own daughter. How grateful she is that he at least is back under their roof. 'OK, go on! You are really too much, my dear son! Don't let anybody see you though, and be back here before the maids start their rounds in the morning. There is already enough gossip going around in this house. I don't want Dadi to call off the wedding because of your premarital affairs!' She watches Andalip disappear and decides to sleep here instead of next to her snoring husband. She knows her son will keep his promise and be back before sunrise. She falls asleep exhausted, but ready for whatever that might happen over the next six days.

Chapter 16

A few hours before the *path* is supposed to begin, Christina finds herself alone in her living room. She feels exhausted. She expects to feel nervous, but instead feels numb. She is telling herself that she is ready to face the next few days. Preets once told her that she viewed her wedding day just like another work assignment. She had repeated a little mantra during the wedding to calm herself down. Christina breathes in, holds her head up high and tries to smile. 'All is fine, all is fine, all is fine…' she whispers into the empty room. That had never worked for her in her professional life, she thinks, and stops whispering. 'Be prepared and know your stuff' used to be her sole mantra. Both do not seem to apply in this situation. Unlike her research work, she knows this wedding is not her project alone, but a team effort and with that she is not the one in full control anymore. All her life, Christina thrived on following a plan, working towards a set goal. She loves plans and so far her life seemed easier this way. To every good plan she usually has a sound proof back-up plan but she is horrified to realise that this is not the case today. The wedding has not even started yet and the first fiasco already happened with her parents' flight being delayed and her entire family and friends most likely missing out on the first official ceremony of the wedding. It dawns on her that maybe it's time to let go of plans and back-up plans and just follow Andy's advice: go with the flow! Before she lets go entirely, she can't help but analyze the last few hours again and again to give her some indication on where to go from here.

She hardly slept last night waiting up for her parents to arrive, hoping for a miracle that the delayed flight would somehow make it to Delhi on time. By sunrise she gave up hope that they will reach in time for the prayers. She would have been more worried if Andy had not distracted her. She really wanted to observe traditions and spend the last few nights before their wedding alone without Andalip. When he climbed into her bed in the middle of the night, even after he had moved his things to his old bedroom on his parents' floor, she was more than happy to welcome him into her bed. He had softly kissed her and asked if she was still awake. Without answering she just kissed him back and soaked in his smell. 'I've missed you!' she whispered, which had made him laugh. 'I just saw you a few hours ago!' he said, but held her tightly. 'It's just that I feel so alone when you are not around. Being with my family and with yours is not the same as being just with you. Even when surrounded by people like I was the last few weeks, I kept thinking that I felt lonelier than I ever did with just the two of us in one room.' She traced his face with her fingers and tried to make out his expression, but the room was too dark. 'I missed you too, baby,' Andy had moved even closer, pressing his body against hers, then pulling up her T-shirt searching for her breasts. Maybe it was the sense of doing something forbidden, spending one last night together before the wedding, but she quickly got aroused and craved for Andy's touch all over her body. They had not been intimate since she had left NYC six weeks ago. At her parents' house she felt she was being constantly watched. Unlike Andy, she did not understand the idea of phone sex. For some reason she did not even miss touching Andy since her mind was so distracted by the wedding preparations. But once he had touched her last night, she felt as close to him as their first week of dating in NYC. When his head disappeared under the bed sheet and he started kissing her belly, she remembered how she used to admire his brown fingers caressing her white stomach. When he kissed her breast, she inhaled the light sandalwood scent in his thick hair. Like their first few nights of lovemaking, he quickly took control and guided her body to feel the fullest pleasure that she had never experienced with any other man before. 'Is this *kama sutra?*' she had asked him shyly one night in NYC. He had laughed at her that night and answered her, whispering in her ear: 'No, *meri jaan*, this is true love!'

When Andy's alarm went off this morning at 6 am, they had just fallen asleep in each other's arms. She realized they were not worried about anybody walking in on them. Both their bodies were still naked under the white cotton sheets. 'Ready to kick off our wedding week?' Andy had asked her, pulling her again on top of him. The pleasure that she had felt last night was gone. Instead, panic had crept up her throat and she could not help but cry. Andy had looked at her worried: 'What's the matter, honey?' She tried to stop but couldn't. She just shook her head and gestured for him to leave. She jumped out of bed and put on her pyjama and threw his clothes at him. He followed her lead and got dressed. He had kissed her, held her face in his hands firmly and said: 'You and me baby, it's destiny. You are my life, *tu meri jaan!* And if you get nervous during the wedding, just think of the *kama sutra* that I will teach you—starting right now if you want—from our official honeymoon night onward for as long as I can climb into your bed.' She felt silly and giggled through her tears. The alarm went off again. He apologized for leaving her alone and promised he would take care of everything. He told her not to worry. She was still crying and he wiped her tears away again, kissing her one last time before he left: 'That's better. You are my strong warrior! I know you are worried about your parents but we will get them here in time. I'll see you later. I will be the guy with the red turban in front of the prayer book, looking all serious about getting married!'

He laughed. She smiled back and told him to leave before she changed her mind about letting him go.

When she got out of the shower and walked in to the kitchen in a bathrobe, she found Simran and Aisha sitting at the dining table drinking coffee out of takeaway cups and eating croissants from paper bags. Once again she realized that even though this was her apartment now, her privacy was limited. People just walked in on her any time of the day. And night. It was just about 8 am and both of them were dressed casually but looked like they had been out for a while. 'Good morning! Jazz told me you like cappuccinos from Khan Market so we got you one when we got back from running errands for mom.' What could be possibly open at this time of the day in India, Christina wondered. Aisha got up and handed her a paper cup, holding up a brown paper bag in the air. Simran smiled: 'You better eat quickly. Mom told us to make sure you are getting dressed. The beautician is already with mom. Then it's your turn.'

Christina sat down and the three of them quietly sipped their coffees. Christina did not feel like talking about the wedding yet, so she started chitchatting.

'How old are you now, Aisha?' Christina asked.

'Twelve, but I will be 13 in March,' Aisha replied proudly with a big smile. Christina can't wait for Fiona to arrive and meet her new cousin. With Fiona just being a year older to Aisha, Christina is convinced they will have lots in common. Maybe one day Fiona would come and spend a year of school in Delhi. Or Aisha might study German in school and visit her German relatives in Hamburg. She remembered her own school days and how fast they had passed.

Aisha had pulled Christina away from her dreams about the new Indo-German friendships and family dynamics by tapping on her shoulder. 'Christina Mami, are you nervous about getting married?' Christina just smiled. She wanted to tell Aisha that she and Andy had been together for five years without being married, but she was not sure how much Simran had told her about that. For Christina, getting married was just another step in their relationship. She knew that being husband and wife would not change her relationship with Andy. She was not worried about becoming Andy's wife, she was excited about it. What she was nervous about was her relationship with her parents and the rest of her German family and friends. She was having a hard time keeping up with this wedding business. How would her parents react? They would arrive in a few hours and be thrown into all these functions. They were probably hoping that she would explain what was going on. But she herself had no idea what to expect. She has been a guest at Indian weddings but she had never really observed what was really going on. She always felt that the bride and groom were not really the main focus at these functions. Weddings were great parties with great food, great conversation and lots of dancing. She could have sworn that at some of the functions she had attended, she had not even met the bride or groom. What would people expect from her? What would they expect from her family? It was one thing to explain Indian customs to her family when she was in Germany or explaining Germany to the Indians when she was in India, one step at a time. But how would she switch between the worlds? Between the languages? Between the traditions?

She felt Aisha staring at her, waiting for an answer. 'I am a little bit nervous, Aisha. But I am glad I have you all around to help me through it!' Christina had told her. She felt awkward again. Andy would have at least hugged his niece at this point or teased her a little, she thought, but she could not do it. Instead, she felt the urge to get up. She said: 'Speaking of helping me: Can you two just make sure I've got everything right with my clothes and shoes?'

Aisha seemed excited. She jumped up and was the first in the bedroom. When Christina entered, the teenager was already looking through her closet. The clothes were still hanging in the order in which Preeti had placed them a few days ago. Christina pulled out the first outfit, a light blue *salwar kameez*. Aisha nodded and said that her outfits would match Christina's throughout the week. Jazz had told her that when she had asked about bridesmaids. 'No bridesmaids in India, my dear. The entire family will be on your side, but some of us will try to match your colour schemes.' Now she knew that Aisha will be her little shadow during the week. Christina was about to change in front of Simran and Aisha, then she remembered that she was not in Germany and could not strip in front of people, even if they were related. She took the clothes to the bathroom. Standing in her underwear, she examined the trouser part of the outfit. One size fits all, she mused while putting her legs through the puffy *salwar*, pulling the drawstring tight around her belly to keep them from falling down. Christina struggled to wear the outfit properly and critically examined the front of the *salwar*. The cloth had collected in the front and she struggled to distribute the fabric evenly around her body and align the centre fold down her legs. She then slipped on the shirt, which seemed too long while the trousers looked to short. She was wondering if this is how the outfit looked when she tried it on the other day, but couldn't remember to save her life. She heard Aisha shuffling around outside the bathroom door and decided to let her be the judge of the first official wedding outfit. Hopefully I don't look too silly, she thought warily and stepped out.

Both Simran and Aisha smiled at her when she came through the door: 'You look so beautiful!' Aisha said in awe. She got a pair of *jutties* from the closet, light silver in colour, matching the embroidery on the suit. Christina was surprised to hear her give advice on what jewellery to wear: 'Now just wear a pearl necklace or something and get your hair done and you are ready!' Simran seemed to get impatient. 'Do you need more help? I think we better go down and get ready ourselves. Can you just show Aisha the jewellery that you will be wearing on the wedding day? Preeti said she left them up here.' Simran said.

Someone knocked at the front door just as Christina was trying to figure out in which closet she had locked the wedding jewellery. Aisha jumped up and said she would get it. Christina started looking for her closet keys. 'I locked everything in one of these closets. Then I hid the key. Now, let me think where I put it?' Simran watched silently as she searched through her bags and then the pockets of her jeans. Before she had finished, Aisha returned with a petite Indian woman. 'Christina Mami, this is Mona. She's here to fix your hair!' Simran turned around and told her to wait in the living room for one moment until Christina was ready. Then she asked Christina: 'Do you need any help finding the key? We can look at the jewellery later, but do you have whatever you're going to wear today?'

'Of course,' Christina replied and pulled out a small bag from the closet that has her wedding clothes in it. Going through the pouch for a few seconds, she retrieved a single string of pearls and matching earrings. 'Andy got them for me on my last birthday!' She put them on quickly and inspected herself in the mirror. She thought she looked good. Then she saw Simran's face.

'Nice. I guess this is OK for today. But from tomorrow just wear the jewellery that mom sent you. I can come up later and help you decide what to wear for which function. Remember, you are the bride, and you don't want any of the aunties outdoing you with their bling. Just make sure you don't leave any of your stuff lying around like this. Don't want to lose it, right?' Simran said before coming over, hugging her and wishing her good luck for the day. 'Somebody will call you or come and get you for the ceremony. Remember, the *path* will be held in Manjeet Bua's living room. You can't sit with Andalip, so we've made a little section on the side for you and your mom, sister, and all to sit. Your dad and maybe one of your cousins will sit with Andalip in front for the ceremony. Do you know what time they will get here?'

Christina was getting confused. Simran sounded like a mother, scolding her on how to behave and what to do. She was hoping that Andy would be there to help her, but she figured she was on her own for the next few days. Instead of answering, she started searching for her phone. She checked her messages only to find none. She shook her head and told Simran that maybe her family was in touch with Andy, and that she was right, it was time to get ready. Both of them went to the living room. Aisha was chatting with Mona asking her all kinds of questions on make-up. Mona seemed eager to share her knowledge and had already unpacked her beauty case and spread out some cosmetics and what looked like hair extensions on the dining room table. '*Chalo*, Aisha, let Christina get ready. We have less than an hour to get our butts to Dadi's house.' Christina pulled Aisha towards her. Aisha turned around one last time and smiled: 'You look beautiful, Mamiji! I wish I was as tall as you and had such beautiful fair skin.' Christina and Mona smiled, Simran seemed annoyed: 'Girls will be girls. Can everybody speed up and get ready! Bye Christina, see you downstairs in a bit. Good luck!'

Christina wondered what she should do with Mona. Luckily, she discovered that her English was almost perfect so Christina did not have to try speaking Hindi. She had picked up a lot but wouldn't have been able to talk about hair and make-up. 'Your mother-in-law told me that you are *gori* but she did not mention that you have white hair. I guess we cannot use these.' With that Mona tossed the hair extensions back into her bag. Mona started looking at Christina more closely and inspected her hair and face. She looked critical. Christina interrupted her: 'Mona, I don't usually wear lots of make-up, so maybe we can keep it simple. And the hair, can I just tie it up nicely?' Christina pulled back her hair and tried to fix them into a bun at the back of her head. Even though she had let her hair grow over the last few months for this occasion, it did not seem to match up with any of the beautiful hair of her sisters-in-law. Her wild curls seemed untidy and any effort of hers to tame them into a glamorous wedding hairstyle seemed to fail. Mona smiled at her: 'Your mother-in-law is right. You're very fair and pretty! I will just try to make you look more like an Indian bride, OK? A hint of *kajal*, a touch of lipstick and a *bindi* to match your clothes. Hair we will cover today. Tomorrow, I will get more white hair for you and I will make something nice!' With that Mona kept shaking her head from left to right.

Christina was getting irritated. 'It's not white hair. It is called "blonde" in English.' She decided she needed to sit in front of a mirror to be able to monitor Mona's work. She told Mona to move her equipment and a chair to the bedroom so that they could sit in front of the dressing table. They argued a bit about the definition of what 'little make-up' means and how to cover Christina's hair. Christina had pulled out an old *Cosmopolitan* magazine to show Mona what she wanted. They agreed to focus on the eyes and lips today and increase the make-up every day until the actual wedding. Mona took just a few minutes to apply the black eyeliner and the lipstick. Christina thought it looked just perfect, Mona seemed critical again: 'Something is missing, ma'am.' Mona pulled out a sheet with colourful *bindis* and choose a small, diamond- shaped blue one for Christina's forehead. 'Now, that is better!'

Before Mona could move to the hair, Christina's phone rang, and she checked the time before answering. Ten minutes to ten o'clock. Almost time to go downstairs and no sign of her family yet. Andy was on the line. 'Hi honey, how's it going?' She thought he sounded a little too casual considering the fact that the *path* was about to start. 'Ready for action?'

Christina did not want to share too much with Andy while Mona was standing right next to her. She quickly briefed him on the fact that she was almost ready to come down but wondered where her parents are. 'Have you spoken to my dad yet? What is taking so long? Didn't you say that they were landing at 7am. It's almost 10 now. Where are they?'

Andalip took what seemed to her like a minute to answer. 'Here is the thing. The plane was on time. They actually managed to go through customs and collect their bags fairly quickly. I think Michael called me before 8 to tell me they are out of the terminal looking for the cars. But there was some confusion with the pick-up. Nobody showed up for almost an hour. Dad said he would go and help them figure it out, but Michael insisted they would be fine. I have been on the phone with Jazz and everybody, but that didn't help. Now they've decided to take the airport taxi, so they should get here any minute. But don't forget, we are talking 20-odd people and five different drop-off locations. Plus Monday morning rush hour.' Christina listened. She did not know what to say. She knew that the *path* had to be today and the timings could not be changed. At least somebody should have gone to the airport to help her family. Still, her parents were the ones insisting that it was OK for them to come alone. 'We are not kids Christina, we are able to take a taxi from the airport. Don't worry about us!' Her mother had told her yesterday on the phone. She didn't want to scare her mother by telling her that one never knows what might happen in India. Considering the fact that they were running out of time to get to Golf Links, she thought it would have been sensible to have a 'local' to help them out. If not from the family, maybe they could have sent Jazz or Simran's husband. The fact that they have not arrived yet, just proved her point, she thought annoyed.

She knew it was too late to argue with Andy, but she felt cheated. Her parents would be tired after the flight and stressed about getting here on time, but she still worried about sitting through the ceremony without them. Andy's mom had tried to explain that the ceremony was traditionally only for the groom and that it would be OK for her parents to miss it. Still, she felt as if her family would be missing out on something. 'So now what?' she wanted to know from Andy.

'Well, Piji has come and they are getting ready to start the *kirtan*. You know the singing of the hymns. I will have to sit next to the Guru Granth Sahib and listen to the songs as people start coming in. Mom, Dad and my sisters will be busy greeting everybody, so you are pretty much on your own. I've told Simmi to send Aisha up to get you in case the ceremony starts, so that you can watch. But for that we really need your dad I think, so if they arrive any time soon, get them ready and come down with them. Got to go. Love you!' Andy did not wait for her response. Before hanging up, Christina could hear people in the background telling him to hurry up. She started crying. Mona looked startled. Christina felt embarrassed, tried to wipe her tears and apologized. Instead of consoling her, like Christina expected, Mona yelled: 'Stop crying! You will ruin your make-up.'

Suddenly her anxiousness turned into anger. 'You know what? I think we are done here. I can take it from here. Thanks Mona, I will see you tomorrow!' With that she got up and stood in front of Mona, who suddenly seemed even shorter than before. Mona just stared at her. Instead of waiting for her reaction, Christina took the cosmetics, put them back in the pouch, handed it to Mona and starting pushing her out of the room. 'But, ma'am, we not done here! What about your hair? You're just nervous about wedding. *thik hai*, don't worry. It will be OK, guaranteed.' Mona tried to Christina calm down as she was being hustled out through the living room towards the door.

'I am sorry, Mona. This is not your fault, but I need to be alone for a while. Right now! You take care of the women downstairs and I will get ready myself. That's what I am used to. If aunty asks, you can tell her you tried your best, but that I don't need help today. We'll try again tomorrow for the *mehendi*. Promise!' Christina was friendly but firm. She opened the door and waited for Mona to disappear, then she slammed the door and locked it.

She does not remember how long she has been standing in the living room since then. She can hear people downstairs. She is not sure if it is the music Andy was talking about or workers setting up lunch in the garden. She tries to call her dad's cell phone, then her mother's, but both are switched off. She walks into the bedroom, to the mirror, to see how much damage her tears have done. She looks fine she decides. The mascara is still in place. So is the *bindi* and lipstick. Her hair is curly and wild, and she again considers tying it back into a ponytail or a knot at the back of her head. Instead, she just brushes it and wears a hair band to keep it from falling into her face. She finds the *chunni* on the bed and covers her head. 'This is as Indian as it will get today,' she tells herself in the mirror. She decides not to wait any longer for her family or for anybody to come and tell her what to do, but to take charge of the situation. 'This is my life now, I better figure it out and take control,' she thinks and looks for her camera. 'Since I am not the typical Indian bride anyway and have to sit on the sidelines, I might as well take some good photos!' she smiles to herself and heads downstairs with a beaming smile.

Chapter 17

About the same time as Christina reaches Manjeet Bua's living room and finds a spot on the floor to listen to the *kirtan*, her family reaches Golf Links. The friends, her parents' and hers, had been dropped off at nearby guest houses and told to quickly freshen up and get dressed. The taxi would be back within the hour to collect them. Everybody seemed tired but curious about the events ahead and agreed to be ready on time.

Only Michael, Bärbel, Frauke and Fiona arrive at the Singh residence. They find themselves in a tree-lined residential street. Houses, with white facades, are lined around a large central park. The car stops at a building that Michael seems to recognize from photos. They all know they are at the right location since the facade is decorated. Flowers lead the way to the front gate, which is hidden behind a large light blue tent. A young man in uniform is sitting outside. He jumps up the moment he sees them driving up and runs inside. By the time Michael gets out of the car, the man appears again, followed by a tall man dressed in suit and turban.

The guard stops next to the car. The man in the turban extends his hand towards Michael and greets him with a warm smile. 'Hi, you must be Michael. I am Ranveer. I am Andalip's father's younger brother.' Ranveer shakes hands with everybody. Almost simultaneously, he directs the guard to take the luggage inside and gestures to Michael to enter through an opening in the blue tent. Michael leads the way through a floral gateway and is taken aback by a beautifully decorated large outdoor dining hall with an endless buffet table—what he rightly figures is the transformed driveway—which leads up to a beautifully carved wooden door to the house. Ranveer quickly takes over again and opens the door, calling out for somebody to come over and assist him. A young girl arrives almost immediately next to him. 'I am so sorry to rush you, but the ceremony has started a few minutes ago. I suggest you go upstairs with my niece Aisha here.' With that Ranveer pulls Aisha forward for everybody to see. Then he continues: 'She will show you the rooms where you will be staying. We need Michael back here in 20 minutes to be part of the ceremony.' Ranveer pats Michael's shoulder: 'Don't worry, there is nothing much to do and somebody will guide you through it. Aisha will make sure that you find your way around.' Ranveer excuses himself and disappears deeper into the house.

Frauke is the first to react. She looks at the girl smiling at them, who is dressed in a blue outfit, almost blending in with the decoration of the driveway. She must be about Fiona's age, she wonders. 'Hi Aisha, nice to meet you. I am Frauke, Christina's sister. This is my dad Michael and my mom Bärbel. And this is my daughter Fiona.' She finds Fiona standing a little behind her and gestures her to come forward.

Without many words, Aisha leads them through the house. They can hear some music. Frauke is not sure how many, but she can see people sitting on the floor behind a wide glass door at the end of the hall. Aisha explains: 'This is where the ceremony is being held. This level is where my great-grandmother and my aunt and uncle live. Christina and Andalip will live in the same house now, but on the second floor. That's where you will be staying this week.' They follow her up a flight of stairs and find themselves walking through another apartment. 'This is where my grandparents or Andalip's parents live. Over there is from where we can get up to the second floor.' Frauke is trying to get a glimpse of the apartment but they just pass several closed doors before coming to a small TV room and another set of stairs. Aisha quickly climbs up and leads them into yet another apartment.

'This is a maze!' Michael laughs. 'I hope we find our way back down. So how many families live in this house?' Aisha looks at him, not seeming to understand the question. 'Just one, uncle. All Singhs. If you mean people, once your daughter moves in, there will be 10 people living here. Not counting the servants, of course. That should add another six people, I think. I don't live here. My parents and I live in Singapore. We just visit once or twice a year. My mom is Andalip's sister, you know.'

They all nod. Knowing that the celebrations have started without them and tired from a long flight, nobody seems in the mood to chat. Remembering Ranveer's words to come down quickly, Michael asks for a place to change and immediately starts getting ready, while Aisha shows the women around the rest of the apartment before she brings them to Christina's room, instructing Frauke and Fiona to use the room to get ready as well. Then she asks if anybody wants some water or food before heading down. 'There will be lunch after the prayer ceremony. That's probably going to be after at least an hour.' Frauke is grateful for Aisha's help but feels the need for a few minutes to themselves. 'Thanks Aisha. Maybe water and coffee and some biscuits or fruit. This way we won't interrupt the ceremony with our growling stomachs.' Frauke tries to joke. Aisha seems eager to complete her task. 'Of course! I will let you get ready and will be back in a few minutes.' Frauke and Fiona watch her leave.

Frauke realizes that Fiona has not spoken since they got out of the taxi. 'Are you OK, *schatz*?' she asks her daughter. 'Fine,' she says. 'But I'm really tired. And I don't really understand anything that's going on.' Fiona had started to learn English in school just a few years ago. Frauke strokes her hair. 'You're not missing much yet. We should get ready so we don't miss out on Tante Christina's wedding though. Do you want to use the bathroom first?' she asks out of motherly instinct. Fiona shakes her head 'no' and instead lies down on the bed. 'You go,' she tells her mom.

Happy to have a minute to herself, Frauke looks around the bathroom. She can't stop comparing everything to her life in Hamburg. To her surprise, everything looks very European. She admires the granite counter top and Italian fittings. She remembers Christina telling her about her first trip to Delhi and how she had complained about not being able to take a proper shower. She peeks into the glass-enclosed shower area. Looks good to her and she is tempted to take a shower to freshen up after the flight. Considering the time, she chooses a quick wash instead. She is glad, since the water does not seem warm enough. She notices a geaser hanging in the shower cabinet but can't figure how to switch it on. Her grandparents used to have one in their bathroom, she remembers, and it was a big deal switching it on for the weekly bath. Frauke notices a bucket as well and makes a mental note to ask Christina about the geaser and bucket. Maybe she is missing something, she thinks.

She puts on a long summer dress. Christina had told her not to show too much skin so she picks up a stole to cover her bare shoulders. She hears voices in the room and quickly combs her hair, puts on some lipstick and gathers her old clothes together. When she steps out she finds her mother sitting on the bed next to Fiona. 'I think Fiona is going to skip this ceremony. I tried to wake her up, but with little success. There will be enough going on this week, we should just let her be.' Bärbel whispers to her daughter, while Frauke neatly puts her clothes away. She is surprised how cold the room is and looks for a blanket for her daughter. When she can't find one, she pulls out another shawl from her bag and covers Fiona. She switches off the A/C and puts on the fan. She gestures Bärbel to follow her out to the living room.

They find Michael and Aisha sitting on the sofa. Michael is drinking coffee and tells them to sit down. Frauke checks her watch: 'Shouldn't we go downstairs? It's been definitely more than 20 minutes since we got here. Won't the ceremony finish without us?' Aisha shakes her head: 'No, they can't finish without us since your dad is supposed to give his blessing to Andalip Mama. But you are right, we should go down. Most people have arrived and they have done enough singing for one morning.' Aisha giggles, then asks: 'Is Fiona not coming?'

Frauke shakes her head: 'She fell asleep. We had a long night. We will take photos for her. Maybe I will leave her a note though and tell her to call me when she gets up.' She looks around for paper but Aisha interrupts her. 'Don't worry, I will check on her and bring her down later.'

On their way downstairs they hear the music, interrupted by what sounds to her like a preacher reciting religious verses. 'It sounds nice,' she says more to herself, but her mother answers by nodding. Frauke looks at her and is surprised to see her mother looking scared. She takes her hand and Bärbel holds it tightly, trying to smile back at her. Michael seems calm and collected. Frauke can't help but thinks about Christina and wonders how she must be feeling right now. They all stop for a second in front of the glassdoor before entering Manjeet's living room.

Almost a hundred people are sitting on the floor in front of them, their backs towards the door. Most men are wearing turbans, the women's heads are covered. Everybody seems dressed up in the brightest of colours. Frauke is surprised to see that the rest of her family and friends are already here. Some look like they have not changed. They seem to be eagerly taking in the scenes around them. Some of the Germans look very intensely at the ceremony in front that it seems as if they understand every word the priest is saying. She spots Christina sitting on the side, in a blue outfit similar to Aisha's, with her hair covered. She looks like she is praying, Frauke thinks. Aisha gives them quick instructions on where to sit. 'That is where you will sit, next to Christina,' she says to Bärbel and Frauke. 'Uncle will sit in the first row next to Andalip Mama. Just sit and enjoy. Should be another 15 minutes or so and we will get some lunch.' Aisha again smiles at them. How confident she is, Frauke notices.

When they enter, most people in the room turn around. Frauke automatically smiles but feels that her smiles are not returned. The crowd returns to their positions watching the priest in the front of the room. Christina looks up and waves. Two men in turbans and a woman get up to greet them, but don't introduce themselves. They are told to cover their heads. Michael does not have a scarf or shawl. One of the men hands him something that looks like a handkerchief and helps him tie it around his head. The priest is still reading from the large book in front of him. Next to him are three men dressed in white with turbans sitting behind what looks to Frauke like drums and some string instruments. Andalip is looking down and does not seem to notice them. Michael is told to sit next to Andalip and wait for further instructions.

Frauke feels like people are talking about them but she is not sure. She realizes her mother is still holding her hand. They climb across people's legs until they reach Christina. She tells them to sit. Bärbel suddenly starts crying. Christina gets up and hugs her. She looks over her mother's shoulders and silently asks Frauke whether there is any problem. Frauke feels dizzy and sits down. The music has started again, this time Frauke thinks it's too loud. The room feels hot and too crowded. She closes her eyes and can still hear her mother weeping. Suddenly people all around her start getting up. Her cousin Olaf is being called to the front. Bettina moves over to Frauke. 'Are you OK? Where is Fiona? Why is your mom crying?' she asks. Frauke just shakes her head and remains seated. She can't see what's going on in front but she feels too tired to stand up. She can hear people talking. Hannelore, still wearing the long linen dress she travelled in, is taking photographs. Between shots she tells her husband: 'Isn't this just great? The music reminds me so much of the ashram. It's so beautiful. And look at the women in their *saris*. They look so graceful. We in Europe just don't know how to dress so elegantly.' She can hear her cousins' wives, Ute and Bettina, making fun of Hannelore. They are giggling like schoolgirls, she thinks, and turns around to tell them to be quiet.

When she gets up, she notices her mom has stopped crying. She is smiling at the scene in front of her. Michael is sitting next to Andalip and both men are surrounded by six kneeling men telling the groom and his German father-in-law what to do. She notices a young boy sitting in front of them, holding a tray with flowers and small bowls. Her dad dips his finger in one of the bowls and applies red powder to Andy's forehead. The men start shuffling around and Olaf is pulled next to her dad, blocking Frauke's view of her brother-in-law. Fiona appears next to her, and ask: 'What are they doing, Mom?' Frauke shrugs her shoulders, not even realizing her daughter had joined them. Hannelore moves closer and explains that this is some sort of blessing from the bride's father to the groom. Again they are told to sit down; the priest reads a few more lines and then there's more music. This time she feels that they are nearing the end of the ceremony because the guests have started talking amongst themselves. Andalip is chatting with her dad. Olaf seems amused by something. When he catches Frauke's eye, he gives her a thumps up, indicating 'This is great!'

Again, she can't help but analyze her foreign surroundings. Frauke notices that there's very little separation between men and women, which for some reason she had expected. There seems to be an obvious separation between the Indian guests and the Germans though, she thinks matter-of-factly, like in Germany where guests sit on either the bride or groom's side. There seems to be no order, however, people are sitting in small groups or alone leaning against the wall. Even though the music is still playing, kids are running around and people seem to keep coming and going. This seems more like a rock concert, she muses, not like a religious ceremony. She hears a cell phone ring and someone answer it. Now she wishes she had brought her video camera to record what looks to her like utter chaos. She remembers her church wedding, and thinks that it seemed almost dark and sad in comparison to the level of noise and activity in this room. Again, she feels dizzy and closes her eyes. The music hurts her ears and her nose itches from the incense in the room.

Suddenly everybody seems to be getting up again. When she opens her eyes, she can see people moving towards the front of the row. The boy who had held the tray earlier, is now handing out garlands of flowers. Andy's family and guests are congratulating him, Michael and Olaf. The Indians seem to know what to do, but the Germans are standing in their corner chatting amongst themselves. Jürgen from Bärbel's Rotary Club is entertaining them with stupid comments. When she hears him say: 'If you think you feel hot, try to wear one of those turbans!' she decides to move back against the wall and let the crowd move out before she joins them.

Then, a young Indian man walks up to her. Frauke quickly gets up. 'I am sorry, I was just feeling a bit tired,' she apologizes before the man says anything. He laughs: 'No, don't be sorry. Must be a little loud and hot for you. Can I get you some water?' Frauke nods: 'That would be nice!' The man turns around and asks a woman standing on the side to get something to drink. Then he turns to Frauke: 'I am Raj. You must be related to Christina, right?' Just then Frauke realizes that Raj is speaking in German. 'Wow, you speak German, and fluently, too. What a nice surprise! Now we have somebody who can explain to us what is going on,' she says excitedly. 'Are you related to Andy?'

'Kind of. Our families have been friends over the last few generations. My mother was half-German and I spent a lot of time in Germany growing up. Looks like Andy did not mention that there are other Germans in his family.' Raj smiles. Frauke laughs: 'No, he sure didn't. I'm Frauke, by the way, Christina's sister.' Frauke burns to ask Raj a few more questions but notices that people are leaving the room. Christina is busy introducing her mother to the Indian relatives, while Andy is still sitting in the front, busy talking to Michael and some Indian women. Again, she feels lost.

Raj seems to notice her distraction. 'No worries, we can hang out here in the air-conditioned room for a while before going outside for lunch. People will have drinks and snacks first. The actual lunch won't be served just yet. Since we are looking at about a hundred people, this party will go on for a while.' He tells her. 'So is this your first trip to India?' Frauke nods, 'Yes, unlike my sister, I don't get around much. I am happy just being in Germany. If it wasn't for the wedding, I don't think I would have ever come to this part of the world.' Raj has a sip of his drink and smiles at her: 'I see. But now that you have come this far, what do you think?'

'Honestly, I landed some five hours ago. What do you expect me to say? Well, between you and me, it is pretty much what I expected. Out of those five hours, I spent three hours waiting for the taxi at the airport, one hour in traffic, and less than an hour getting ready and, listening to some guys with turbans and long beards preaching and singing something that I did not understand. In that much time, my sister could easily have gotten married in Hamburg and had a nice party afterwards.' Frauke feels comfortable talking to Raj, he speaks German and hopefully understands what she means. Raj responds with a loud laugh: 'That's what I love about Germans. How do you say it again? 'You don't take a piece of paper in front of your mouth!' You don't cover your thoughts with formal pleasantries and just say it like you see it. I am sure you will like this wedding once you get used to the idea. You will see some beautiful houses, five-star hotels, pretty people and eat some excellent food. You will dance the next few nights away, get drunk on the best wines and champagne in the world. When you return to Germany, you can tell your friends about your glimpses of a thousand and one nights.' Raj finishes his drink and says seriously: 'If by any chance you change your mind about wanting to know about this part of the world, let me know. I will show you the real India.' He takes her hand in his and looks into her eyes: 'It was a great pleasure meeting you Frauke. Now, it is time for you to be with your sister and meet your new family.'

As soon as he walks off, Christina appears by her side. 'Hey, big sis, here you are. I want to introduce you to Andy's family.' Frauke starts to follow Christina, but stops and turns around to look for Raj. The room is almost empty and everyone has left but Andy, Christina and their closest family members. 'Interesting guy,' Frauke thinks, a little disappointed that he is gone.

Chapter 18

Manpreet is one of the first to arrive in the garden. She finds herself a chair in the shade. Most of the front yard is covered with a light blue awning and fans are blowing from all sides. Still, the sun is hot and at least a hundred guests are expected for lunch. She watches her granddaughters, Simran, Jasneet and Preeti, looking after the guests as they emerge from the living room. What a beautiful *kirtan* it was, she thinks to herself. She hardly recognized Andalip in his turban. What a handsome man he could be if he had not cut his hair, she thinks, and shakes her head. Her thoughts are interrupted by Preeti.

'How are you Dadiji? Can I get you something to drink or eat? Why are you sitting all by yourself? Have you met Christina's family yet? They are all really nice. You will like them!' Preeti sounds excited.

'What do you mean, have I met them yet? They should come and meet me. Or don't Germans respect their elders like we do?' Manpreet barks back. 'Speaking of respect, where is your husband?' He still hasn't come to meet me. Or has he skipped the *path*, that Hindu son of a gun?' She looks around the garden, scanning the crowd, but she can't see her granddaughter's husband. She likes Kabir. His grandparents were close friends of Zorawar. Despite belonging to different religions and settling down in Mumbai for business reasons, the families had remained close over the years. Everybody was thrilled when Kabir and Preeti decided to get married.

'Why do you always have to talk like this, Dadiji?' Preeti asks, visibly upset and walks off. Manpreet smiles to herself and thinks: 'Must be pregnant. Finally, about time!' The moment Preeti disappears inside the house, Andalip steps out followed by his parents and Christina's family. He looks around the garden and when he spots her, gestures everyone to follow him across the lawn. 'Here you are, Dadiji. I want to introduce you to Christina's parents.' He touches her feet and then steps around her chair. Manpreet watches at least 10 tall *firangis* line up in front of her. While Andalip recites their names, she notices Christina standing shyly next to them. Manpreet's not really listening and decides their names sound too foreign to remember. When Andalip finishes he walks around to Christina and hugs her: 'And Christina, you know already!' Christina smiles at her and folds her hands: '*Sat Sri Akal*, Dadiji.'

Manpreet is not sure what to think of this little act and hardly acknowledges the people in front of her, focusing on her grandson instead. The corners of Andalip's mouth twitch — good, he should at least know what he is about to do to this family, she thinks and holds her look. '*Jeete raho, puttar*,' Dadiji mutters to Christina, a bit stiffly. The Germans seem awkward. Like Christina some of them fold their hands. One woman even mutters a *namaste*. Christina's father extends his hand to greet her. She takes it and shakes it quickly: 'Welcome to India!' They all smile at her and say Thank you. Andalip tells them to feel at home and get some drinks when his father's voice interrupts him. Everybody turns around. Bopinder is standing on a chair next to the bar with a microphone to his lips. '1, 2, 3, testing, testing…Do I have everybody's attention?' People in the garden start laughing, some clap and Ranveer whistles.

'Good, I am glad this works!' Bopinder continues. 'I just want to welcome everybody to our house again today. You must be thinking, what is this old man doing up on the chair giving a speech? Well, my dear daughters keep teasing me when I tell them how a true Punjabi can give a speech, anytime and anywhere, and be heard across an entire village—even without using a microphone.' Again, people clap. Simran darts across the lawn: 'We believe you Dad. We just wanted you to test the sound system for tomorrow. We are hoping you all will be back for the *mehendi*. Besides the traditional singing and dancing, we will be holding a karaoke competition. The person to beat was the winner of Preeti's *mehendi* karaoke playoff, no other than my dear Dadiji, Manpreet Kaur!' Simran laughs and points to Manpreet still sitting in the corner. Dadi raises her fist and shouts back: 'I will show you young girls how to sing properly!'

Bopinder continues on the microphone: 'Well, that's sorted out, I want to welcome Christina and her family to Delhi. I know it's been a rough morning for all of you, but I am glad you made it in time. Now that we are done with our prayers for the day, I want you all to relax, get to know each other, have a drink or two and enjoy the excellent food that should be ready soon.' He looks around for the waiter and orders himself a drink. Still on top of the chair, he raises his glass and shouts: 'Cheers to a wonderful week ahead! Cheers to Andalip and Christina!'

The crowd roars. People raise their glasses. Manpreet is having a hard time seeing what is going on because everybody seems to be walking towards Bopinder. She decides to go inside and rest for a while. 'My stomach cannot handle this greasy buffet food anyway,' she whispers to herself and gets up. Christina walks over. 'Do you need any help getting up?' she asks.

Manpreet wishes she could refuse and just walk off, but she finds it difficult to walk across the grass, even though most of it is covered by a carpet. 'Thank you, Beta,' she manages to response.

Christina holds out her arm for her to grasp and they slowly walk towards the house. 'What a beautiful *path* it was!' Christina tells her. 'I wish I could have understood a little more of what Piji was saying. But the *kirtan* sounded beautiful, it calmed me down. My family really enjoyed it too.'

They reach the house. Manpreet let's go off Christina: 'No need to come inside. I can take it from here.' She looks at Andalip's bride and notices the pearls she is wearing. Before she can ask her why she is not wearing any of the family jewels that had been given to her, there's loud explosion. They hear screams. Christina mutters 'Oh God' and runs off. When Manpreet steps outside, the tent is filled with smoke and people are running towards the gate. Her grandson, Anhad, is trying to open the tent to let the smoke out. She walks towards where Bopinder had been giving his speech just minutes ago. She hears her daughter-in-law screaming: 'Are you OK? Say something? Say something?' but cannot see her through the crowd. Her granddaughter, Jasneet, appears with her husband, Vivaan: 'Dadi, let's get back inside. There is too much smoke for you here. Let the guys handle it.' Both of them start drawing her back into the house.

'Beta, what happened? Is everybody OK?' Vivaan just looks at her and then bursts into nervous laughter. 'Dad was messing with the sound system and I think his whiskey bottle spilled over it. Something went wrong and the generator caught fire. When Dad tried to use his jacket to stop it, the whole thing just exploded.' Jasneet hits her husband's shoulder: 'Stop it, you idiot. He could be seriously hurt!' She looks seriously worried. The sliding door to the living room opens and Simran and Andalip walk in. Andalip speaks first: 'No worries, Dad is fine. I'm driving him to the hospital to get his hearing checked. He is complaining about constant ringing in his left ear.' Simran heads to the bathroom: 'We'll just clean him up a bit. His face is all black from the smoke. I think his turban caught fire!' Simran starts laughing and this time Jasneet joins in. 'Without his turban, he would probably be deaf now!' Jasneet muses.

More and more people keep coming in, mostly chitchatting and laughing about the incident. Manjeet and Ranveer enter and tell the servants to remove the carpets and bring in some chairs and tables from outside. The room starts to look more like a formal drawing room and the guests seem content. 'I guess we will be serving some smoked goat after all!' Ranveer jokes and everybody laughs. 'And no karaoke for Mom tomorrow. But I guess we still have your item number to look forward to.'

Manpreet gestures for them to be quiet. She gets up to walk to her room. Andalip comes back, dressed in jeans and a shirt. 'Ready, Simmi? Let's take Dad,' he calls out.

'Just let him suffer. The fool had it coming. You mess with God, he will mess with you.' Dadi tells her grandchildren and disappears into her bedroom. She can hear loud laughter again.

'All fools!' She thinks and rings for her maid. Mary appears in the room. *'Thik hai*, Biji?' she inquires. Without answering she orders some lunch: 'Bring me some *daal* and *roti*, but none of that poisoned food from outside. And make sure those fools out there don't trash my house.' With that she lies down on the bed and calls it a day.

Chapter 19
❦

Günther is jolted awake by the sound of a blaring horn from outside his window. Half asleep and annoyed, he turns around to look for his boyfriend Daniel. When he finds the other half of the bed empty, he remembers that he is in India for Christina's wedding and not in his own bed in Hamburg. He climbs out of bed to see what is going on. When he pulls up the blinds he sees that the sun is not out yet. He watches two cars trying to pass each other in the small lane in front of the house. One of the drivers tries to get out but can't because he is stuck between a parked car on one side and a car blowing horn on the other. A bunch of street dogs are barking. A woman, who he recognizes as the owner of the guest house where he is staying comes out of the house and yells at them. What action so early in the morning, he thinks, and searches for his camera to take some pictures.

He hears voices in the hallway. A second later, Christina's cousins, Olaf and Karl Jr, call out: 'Man, are you up yet?' He opens the door and finds the two of them in their pyjamas standing outside. They quickly come in and sit on the bed. Günther feels a little awkward to join them on the bed and pulls up a chair.

The three of them plus Juan, Anna's boyfriend, had spent last night sitting in the small living room of the guest house drinking and reviewing the first day of the wedding. After Andy's dad had left for the hospital, the lunch continued without much delay. Everybody started drinking beer and enjoying themselves. Most of the Indian guests had left right after lunch, but the Germans remained sitting in the living room with Andalip and Christina. A little hungover from the beer and the heat, they finally left for their guest houses at around 5 pm. Andalip had offered to take them out for dinner, but by then, they were all jet-lagged and decided to rest. Günther and Christina's cousins were in the same guest house. He had not met them before, but they were all on the same wavelength and had spent the evening together. The women had excused themselves a little after 11 pm. Günther could not recall what time he finally went to sleep, but a headache reminded him now that it was very late with lots of alcohol involved.

'I assume the horn woke you up too?' Günther asks, pointing out of the window. Olaf shakes his head: 'No, not really. It's the women, man. You are lucky you came alone. They've been up for an hour now discussing what to wear for today's lunch. Bettina felt totally underdressed yesterday and now wants to go shopping before we go over to the house again for the *mehendi* ceremony. I told them 'no way, did you see the traffic yesterday?' but they are threatening to go on their own.' Karl Jr continues: 'Best is, they are already freaked out by the bathroom. Did you see the bugs in there? How will they go shopping alone? I say, let them go and figure it out.' Both laugh. 'Or we send Juan with them. He could pass as Indian. Maybe he wants to take them.' Karl Jr jokes.

Günther gets up to look for the invitation card to check the day's programme. 'Looks like another lunch to me. At 1 pm back at Andy's house.' Then he pulls out his travel guidebook on Delhi and flips through the pages for some shopping advice. He reads through the list of markets under the section 'Fashion' — Khan Market, Greater Kailash I, Santushti Shopping Complex, Meharchand Market, Hauz Khas Village followed by a list of malls. Olaf and Karl Jr watch him opening a Delhi map and circling the markets, then locating the address of the guest house. Then he looks up: 'Actually, I won't mind going shopping myself. According to this book, shops don't open until 10:30. It is 7:30 now, which leaves us enough time to shower, have breakfast, organize a car and head to one of these markets. If we shop for a little less than two hours and aim to be back here by 12. 30, we'll have enough time to change and head over for lunch. What do you say?' Günther asks.

Olaf gets up and says: 'You are the man! I am glad we have you living next door. This sounds like a great plan. I will tell the women. Maybe I will get some more sleep too!' Karl Jr smiles: 'Now I know why you are friends with Christina. You are as organized as she is. Thanks for helping out. See you downstairs for breakfast at around 9 then.'

'Sure thing!' Günther replies, sees them out and locks the door behind them. He is still tired but instead of going back to bed, he sets up his computer. He makes himself some instant coffee that he finds in the corner of the table under the window. The street is quiet again. Günther decides to read up on Delhi before their shopping trip. He feels happy to be in Delhi for his friend's wedding. 'If only Daniel was here!' he thinks before discovering Delhi online.

Chapter 20

At exactly 10. 15 am, Ute, Bettina, Anna, Juan and Günther are standing in the lobby of their guest house. Mrs Gupta had served them a hearty breakfast of scrambled eggs, toast and Indian tea. Everybody was ready for a shopping adventure. They had dressed casually but their backpacks and cameras gave them away as tourists. The room smelled of citronella mosquito spray that Günther had told everybody to apply. Mrs Gupta had promised to give them some maps and tips on where to go. Olaf and Karl had decided to stay back and catch up with more sleep.

Günther once again pulled out his guidebook and suggested some shops that he thought were good options for their shopping needs. 'There seem to be some interesting boutiques in Meharch-and Market which I think we should check out. According to the map, it's pretty close to us too.' Since nobody else seemed to have any other ideas, they agree with Günther's suggestion.

An elderly man walks into the guest house. He smiles at them, nods 'Namaste.' Anna, who is closest to him, extends her hand and asks: 'Good morning. Are you our driver?' The man keeps smiling but does not reply or take Anna's hand. Juan walks up to him and says: 'Namaste. You. Driver?' Anna pokes him with her elbow and tells him to stop it. This time, the man reacts. He shakes hands and introduces himself as Ramesh. 'Yes, yes. Driver. Driver Ramesh. Aap ready hai? Chale?' Bettina and Ute start giggling.

Günther seems upset: 'I thought we asked for somebody who speaks English.'

Ramesh smiles at him. 'No English. *Lekhin*, no problem.' He pats Juan's shoulder. '*Usko Hindi atti hai. He na?*' Now all the women start laughing. Anna teases Juan: 'He thinks you are a native!' Their laughter uninterrupted by Mrs Gupta's entry. 'Good, I see you've met my driver Ramesh. Your cars are not available until noon so I thought I will send you in my car. He knows Delhi really well and will take you wherever you want to go this morning. Let me tell you though, that nothing will be open before 11 if you are planning to go shopping. Maybe have another *chai* with me before you go?' she says.

Günther answers for everyone: 'No, thank you Mrs Gupta. I found a market in my guidebook that opens at 10. 30. We'll just head over there. Let's go people!' With that he gestures everybody to get going. They follow Ramesh outside. Mrs Gupta tells them to call in case they need any help. Then she jokes: 'A German guidebook, is it? Well then, the market must be open at 10. 30! Have fun shopping!' With that she closes the door behind them.

Ramesh walks through the gate. None of the cars parked in front of the house seem big enough for all of them to fit in, Günther thinks. Ramesh stops in front of a mint-green Ambassador. He opens the back door and gestures them to get in. Günther just looks inside. 'But there are no seat belts in there,' he shakes his head and refuses to get in. Bettina and Ute agree. 'Even if one of us sits in the front, how will we fit four people in the back?' Ute asks. Only Anna does not seem concerned and tells them to just get in. 'Did you see the traffic yesterday? I don't think we will be going fast enough to worry about seat belts. Better than going on a rickshaw or motorbike. Don't you remember the bike next to us yesterday? I swear there was a family of five sitting on that scooter!' Anna laughs. With that she climbs in and tells Juan to follow.

Günther walks to the front and buckles up in the front seat. Both Bettina and Ute are still hesitant.

Ramesh looks confused. He is still holding the car door open, waiting for them to get in. '*Kya* problem *hai*?' he asks the women. Bettina looks inside and tells Anna and Juan to tell Ramesh that she is not going in this car unless there are seat belts. 'My English is not good enough. You tell him! If I don't have a seat belt, I am not going!' With that she folds her arms in front of her chest. Anna gets out from the other side of the car. She tells Ramesh: 'One minute, OK?' He looks puzzled. Juan puts his head out of the car, lifts his index figure and yells at Ramesh: 'One. Minute.' Ramesh smiles and sits down in the driver's seat.

Anna tries to cheer up Bettina. 'Just like in Mexico: When a woman talks, they don't understand. When a man yells, no problem! I don't get it.' Bettina doesn't seem to listen. 'Let's just drive to the market quickly. We are in the back of the car and that should be fine. Things just work differently here. I doubt we will find another car with a seat belt now so let's just forget about it. OK?' Anna tries to convince her, but Bettina shakes her head. 'You go! I don't feel like shopping anymore,' Bettina says and walks back to the guest house.

Anna and Ute watch her disappear through the gate. 'What do we do?' Anna asks. From inside the car, Günther tells them not to worry and just get going. 'It's OK. Bettina is right, you go ahead and have fun. I will look after Bettina. We'll go another day when our rental car is here. I am sure that we will get a chance to go shopping again this week. Maybe it is better anyway to ask Christina or somebody to come along, just to be on the safe side.' With that Ute hugs Anna and follows Bettina into the house.

Anna climbs into the Ambassador. 'Well, maybe it is better this way. Let's have some fun shopping!' She kisses Juan on the cheek. 'You just tell your new friend here where we are going!'

Chapter 21

Raj knows that he is early for the *mehendi* ceremony. People are still setting up the new tent and rearranging chairs and sofas on the lawn. He looks around the driveway. He is surprised how little the house has changed since he had played here as a child. When he enters the ground floor, he is greeted by one of the maids. He is not sure where exactly Christina and her family are staying so he asks for directions. Without any questions, she tells him to go up to the second floor apartment. He heads up the stairs to the first floor but can't find the way up. The doors to the rooms are closed. Fortunately, another maid appears. When he asks to see Christina and her family, she tells him to go through the TV room in the back and take the stairs to the second floor. Somebody is calling the girl and she disappears through another door.

Still another hour to go before the lunch is supposed to start. They must be getting ready, he thinks. Frauke had invited him to stop by before lunch. She seemed eager to chat with someone who knew both worlds. When he knocks on the door, a teenage girl opens the door. She sees him, turns around and calls for her mom in German. Frauke appears through a door at the back of the room. She is already dressed up for the function. She calls out to him: 'Raj, you have come! I am glad. Come in and have some coffee with us. I see you have met my daughter, Fiona!'

Raj steps into the room. Fiona look sat him curiously. She holds out her hand: 'Hi, I am Fiona. I don't speak English that well. I never know what to say to people. Sorry for not saying anything earlier. I did not know you speak German.' Raj smiles: 'I get that a lot. Wonder why?' Fiona giggles. The three of them sit down at the table.

'What would you like to have? I've made some coffee but I can make some tea if you like.' She hands him an empty mug and points at the beverages and goodies on the table. He agrees to have the coffee and Frauke pours him a full mug. While they are chitchatting about Raj's summers in Germany, Michael and Bärbel join them in the living room. Both are ready for the party as well. They had briefly met Raj at the lunch yesterday, but still introduce themselves before joining them at the table. Raj enjoys the casual atmosphere and being quizzed about India.

After he had finished school in Delhi, his aunt had arranged for him to start college in Germany. He was always at the top of his class and fluent in German, so any university was happy to take him. He chose to study civil engineering, but regretted his choice when had discovered the endless courses that were on offer in Germany. Back in India, engineering had seemed to be his best option to become successful. Now he wanted to be more than successful. He wanted to learn something new, not only for his own benefit but to contribute to a better future for his beloved India. His aunt was very supportive and let him switch his major. Since it was not easy to transfer college credits in Germany, Raj ended up wasting a year and starting all over. From the day he started at the Faculty of Earth and Environmental Science at the Ludwig Maximilian University of Munich, he knew he had taken the right decision. His goal was always to come back to India. A year after his graduation, he had secured a research project that was a collaboration between his school in Germany and the School of Environmental Sciences at the Jawaharlal Nehru University in Delhi. He hoped this would allow him to travel back and forth between the two countries he loved most. Now, his research is mostly in English and for the last two years that he been in Delhi, he had only been back to Munich twice.

'I sometimes wish I had stayed in Germany. The pay is really bad over here and my work was much more valued in Munich. But it is good to be back in India. I was born and brought up here, this is my home. In Germany, I always felt like a foreigner. I looked different, I spoke differently. Here, I blend in better.' He tells Christina's family.

Bärbel takes his hand in hers. 'Well, we are certainly glad you are here now. It will be a blessing for Christina to know somebody who knows both sides of the coin.'

Christina's voice from the next room interrupts them. Frauke looks concerned. Before she can get up to check on her sister, the door opens and Christina walks out. She is dressed in a similar outfit to what she wore at the *path*. Only this time it is green instead of blue. Raj smiles to himself when he notices that her clothes again match the colour of the tent and decorations in the garden. On top of the *salwar kameez*, Christina has draped a towel around her neck. She pulls it off her shoulders and throws it into the corner of the living room. Raj notices that she is holding a large red box in the one hand, which she slams onto the table where they are sitting. She voices her anger in German: *'Mir reicht es!* I've had it with this woman. Can somebody please tell her to leave me alone. I will do my make-up myself. Honestly, I don't need to look like those brides in the movies. Her main goal seems to be to turn me into an Indian bride. Do I look Indian to you?' With that she sits down at the table and pours herself a mug of coffee. Raj can see a petite Indian woman standing in the bedroom, obviously waiting for Christina to return. Then he realizes that everybody but Christina is staring at him.

Frauke gets up and gestures Raj to follow her. Before they enter the room, she asks him: 'What do you say? Should we tell her to leave? Do you think Christina knows what she is doing?

Maybe you can talk to my sister? Or maybe just ask this lady to come back later?' He feels a little uneasy, wondering if he should really get involved. He wants to help but knows better not to get caught up in family affairs. The Germans want him to help them out, but he is worried about what Andalip's family would say to that. He can hear Bärbel talking to Christina, trying to convince her daughter to give it another shot. Christina insists that she is done with make-up and hair extensions for the day and again tells her family to get rid of the beautician in the room. Frauke pushes Raj into the room: 'Please, you talk to her!'

Mona looks confused when he walks in. She seems to have no idea that Christina is upset with her. She keeps looking past him to see if Christina is coming back. Instead she sees Frauke. 'You want make-up too?' she asks with a big smile. Frauke shakes her head and again pleads with Raj to tell Mona that Christina is getting anxious about the ceremony and would like to be left alone with her family now.

Raj conveys the message and is relieved when Mona quickly packs her things and leaves.

When he returns to the living room, Christina's parents thank him for helping out and Frauke and Fiona give him a big hug. Christina seems to notice his presence for the first time. 'And who are you, if I might ask?' Before he can answer, Fiona speaks up: 'This is the guy Mom was talking about last night. Raj from Germany! Uncle Andy must have told you about him. He is somehow related to you now!' Again he has no time to explain his background. Michael enters the conversation: 'A really nice guy, I tell you. Thanks Raj for handling this!'

Christina seems too distracted to really care. She opens the box in front of her. Everybody stares at the pile of gold jewellery. Rubies, sapphires and diamonds as large as candy fill the box to the rim. 'Are those real?' Bärbel asks with wide open eyes. Fiona wants to touch them, but Frauke tells her to just sit back and watch.

Christina picks up a necklace and earrings and holds them up: 'Yes, they are real. Passed on over generations to the wife of the oldest son of the family! But honestly, I cannot wear this. It is pretty but not me! I am already wearing the clothes. I need to preserve a little bit of myself during all of this. What do you think?' She looks at her family for their opinion. Raj feels totally out of place and tries to excuse himself.

When nobody replies, Christina asks Raj. 'Maybe my family is right and you can help out with this one too. Don't you know other Germans who are married to Indians? Like your parents for example? What did they do? How did they get married? What should I do? Can't I just skip wearing these and stick to my pearls and silver jewellery?' Christina seems to be pleading with him for an answer. While she is still dangling the jewellery in front of him, the door to the terrace opens without a knock.

Anita walks in, followed by Andalip. Christina jumps up excitedly: 'My saviour! How did you get up here? I thought you were to stay away from me until the wedding?' She hugs him. He hugs her back and without caring about the people in the room, kisses her. 'Well, everybody is really busy down there getting ready. I saw the make-up lady come down and figured you must be ready. Mom sent Anita to see if you needed anything, but I thought you guys would be waiting for instructions on what's happening next. I did not realize you already had a party going on!'

He instructs Anita to clear the table. He also tells her to inform his mom that Christina is ready for the *mehendi* ceremony. They should be downstairs in 10 minutes. When he notices the jewellery on the table he turns to Christina again: 'Sorry, baby, no bling for you today. You are supposed to come down without anything around your arms and neck. Keep your hands free for the *henna*. There will be a ceremony later where Dadi, Mom and my sisters will gift you more jewellery that will take care of your neck. Although it is almost shameful to cover such natural beauty with gold and precious stones!' With that he leans over and kisses her neck to underline his point.

Before anyone can ask him another question, Raj quickly gets up. He bids goodbye to Frauke and tells her to catch up with him at the lunch. The others seem busy with the finishing touches for the party. Quietly, he slips out onto the terrace and heads down to the garden.

Chapter 22

⤞⤝

Christina is sitting on a little platform decorated with flowers in one corner of the garden. Simran had left her here about an hour ago, making sure that Christina was comfortable. She got her a low chair and plenty of pillows to rest on while the *henna* was being applied to her. Then she went to organize something to drink and eat for Christina but never returned. A young man is sitting next to her feet, cross-legged and focused on his work. He is taking his time decorating Christina's left foot and lower leg. Even though it is pretty hot, her leg feels cold. The paste tickles her when he draws on her skin. To her right are a couple of chairs and two women are waiting for other guests to apply *mehendi*. So far, nobody has come. People are just arriving and seem to be stuck at the entrance, chatting with Andalip and his family.

Christina is watching the man applying the *henna*. Considering all the other festivities, she enjoys this part the most. She loves how the design and floral patterns appear on her skin. She has gotten *mehendi* done before but usually only one hand. She is looking forward to seeing her hands, arms, feet and legs decorated with the intricate tattoo that only brides receive. Her *salwar* is rolled up and she watches a peacock appear on her leg. She smiles and looks for her mother or Frauke to show them the patterns. She spots them across the lawn, looking through the selection of glass bangles spread out on a table before them. Bärbel seems to be having a hard time finding a colour that matches her dress. Frauke is trying different colours on each arm. Manjeet and Maya look amused and are giving them advice on how to choose the perfect match. Christina is happy to see that unlike the day before, the families are finally starting to mix. Everyone seems to be enjoying themselves. No one seems to notice that the bride is sitting alone.

Still looking for someone to share her excitement about the *mehendi*, she recognizes Dadi sitting with some of her relatives and friends. All the ladies are over 70, yet they are all dressed up in the brightest of patterns and colours. Most of them are wearing sunglasses. All of them are hanging on to their designer handbags relishing the first rounds of snacks served to them. The music starts to play, so Christina finds it difficult to hear their conversations, but she is sure they are busy chatting away in Punjabi. I hope I will have that much fun when I am that age, she thinks. She picks up her camera and takes a quick picture. For my private wedding album, she muses. When the flash goes off, Dadi notices that she is being watched. Christina smiles and waves to her. Strangely, Dadi seems to just stare back, but the moment passes quickly with the ladies drawing her back into the conversation.

Just at the same time as the man finishes the work on her left leg, Simran returns. She's brought some water and snacks for Christina and places them on a small table next to her. Jazz and Preeti appear behind her with a large tray covered with a red clothes. 'Don't eat any of this. We need them later for a little ceremony we've got to do for you,' Jazz tells her. Preets sits next to her: 'How are you feeling? Getting bored yet? I remember my wedding…the guy was so slow. I had to pee so badly that I had to rush to the bathroom before he could finish. I ended up with all the *henna* on my pants instead of my legs. Mom was furious!' Preeti laughs. Jazz puts the tray down and looks at her sister: 'Yeah, like Dadi says, you have to look out for the omens. Now we know why your husband left you. Christina, don't take any advice from Preets here if you want a happy marriage. Sometimes it's just smarter to follow traditions even if you don't believe in them.' Simran and Preeti stare at their sister. Christina is confused. 'What do you mean? Kabir has left you?' she asks. Preeti looks upset and Simran answers for her: 'Don't listen to Jazz. Preeti and Kabir are fine. These are hormones talking. Little Mrs Grumpy here just found out she is pregnant with number three and is hitting out at every body. Can you guys please stop fighting and focus on Christina here. It is her wedding. Just keep your problems to yourself until this is over!' Preets smiles again: 'Yes, that's right. I am fine, Kabir is fine and Jazz, you better cheer up. Sorry for this little drama, Christina. Enjoy your *mehendi*. Let me get you a drink!' With that she gets up and heads over to the bar. Simran tells the *henna* guy to hurry up and finish the second leg so they can do a quick ceremony. She excuses herself and leaves Jazz and Christina alone.

'What's going on Jazz?' Christina asks. Jazz seems to be looking for the right answers. Before she can reply, some of Andy's relatives walk over to get their *henna* done. Christina's cousins have arrived as well and walk over to greet her. Jazz gets up and hugs Christina, whispering: 'Nothing is going on, Christina. Just focus on your wedding. We are all just a little stressed out.'

The music gets louder. The tent is full of people and it's starting to feel like a party. Christina's family and friends take turns sitting with her but their focus is more on the dance floor than on her *henna*. Anna sits by her side and tells her about the early morning shopping trip.

'And this is what I bought for myself.' Anna twirls around, showing off her red silk dress embroidered with little mirrors and silver thread. 'I had no idea one would find something like this in Delhi. Funky!' Christina compliments her. Anna tells her about Günther's research on shopping in Delhi and that Christina should take his advice on where to buy her clothes. She mentions that Ute and Bettina refused to get into the Ambassador and that the car actually did breakdown in the market. 'The driver spoke no English so we had no idea what he was saying when he locked the car and left. We hung around for about 30 minutes and then decided to take an autorickshaw home. Just imagine Ute and Bettina in an autorickshaw: 'Hey, where are the seat belts?"' Anna jokes loud enough for Ute, who was nearby getting her *henna* done, to hear her. 'We squeezed into the rickshaw. Juan warned us to fix the price first but Günther just wanted to leave. It was a real experience—Juan trying not to fall out, I buried under several shopping bags and Günther rummaging in his backpack for the address!' Anna slaps her knee and starts laughing hysterically. 'I don't how but somehow we managed to get back to the guest house!'

While the two women are still giggling, Kiran, her daughters and mother-in-law walk up to her. Kiran tells the *henna* guy to stop for a while and places some plastic bags next to the items that Simran had left earlier. Some more relatives join them. Andy is busy hanging out with his friends and isn't aware of what's going on at Christina's end.

'Shouldn't we wait for Andalip?' Christina asks her mother-in-law.

Kiran shakes her head: 'No, this is just for you. Traditionally, no guys attend the *mehendi*. Let's just go ahead.'

Christina watches Andy's sisters sort through the plastic bags, Dadi is sitting next to her on the podium. Without any explanation, Dadi opens a jewellery case and pulls out a gold necklace. She leans forward and puts it around Christina's neck. Christina smiles at her, while Dadi waves some rupee notes above Christina's head before dropping them on her lap. Simran does the same but with nuts instead of money: 'May you have many babies!' She says and drops the smaller ones and dry fruits in her lap, followed by a big coconut. She hands her a small jewellery case and tells her to wear it later. Kiran follows suit and puts another necklace around her neck, followed by a set of gold bangles. Jazz and Preeti put more things in her lap. All are wrapped up, but Christina assumes they contain clothes and more jewellery. Christina feels overwhelmed. She's searching for words to thank them but is not sure what's appropriate. Dadi mumbles something in Punjabi.

The women take turns hugging Christina and welcoming her into the family.

'Thank you so much!' is all Christina manages to say. Anna, who is still sitting next to her, is admiring the jewellery. People around them are taking photographs. Kiran hugs her and tells her how happy she is to have another daughter. Preeti excuses herself but is back in less than a minute, carrying some blue glass bangles. 'Here! Wear these before he finishes the *henna*.'

Christina looks sceptical: 'Aren't they too small?' Preeti shakes her head, takes Christina's left hand and starts putting the bangles on. 'You always have to squeeze them over the hand a bit but then they fit perfectly.'

Bärbel has joined them, without Christina realizing it. She is stroking her daughter's back. 'You look so beautiful. This place looks festive. Everything is just so wonderful. Everybody is just so nice.' Bärbel wipes away tears. Kiran takes her hand and tells her how happy they are to have Christina and her family in their lives. Christina watches her mother and mother-in-law. Just like a movie, she thinks. Her heart fills with love for both women. She looks around and cannot help but smile at all her relatives. 'It is so unreal!' she hears Anna say. 'I know what you mean. Weird, isn't it?' Christina replies to her cousin.

Preeti, still having a difficult time getting the bangles over Christina's wrist, hears them and looks confused: 'What do you mean? Are you talking to me? Christina lifts her arm to point at Anna, indicating that she was talking to her cousin. Preeti follows her movement and accidently pushes the glass bangles with greater force. Suddenly, one bangle breaks and cuts Christina's wrist.

Drops of blood fall onto her lap. Christina notices a thin red line on her arm. 'It's nothing, just a scratch. Just hand me a tissue and I will be fine.' She says. When she looks up, Preeti is staring at her in horror. 'Preets, I am fine. Just put the other bangles on. Or is this a bad omen that I shouldn't get married?' she jokes, remembering the sisters' earlier comments.

Preeti gets up and hands the rest of the bangles to Jazz. 'Here, you finish. And you are right as always. Just stay away from me if you want a happy marriage!' She storms off and disappears into the crowd. Jazz shakes her head: 'Why does she always have to be so dramatic? Let's take care of your arm first and then finish up your *mehendi*. No such thing as bad omens around here, don't listen to our nonsense. I will get you a drink and when the *henna* is done, we will teach you some Hindi songs and dance moves.' Everybody busies themselves with helping Christina or chitchatting amongst each other.

Suddenly, Dadi gets up and yells at Kiran: 'First Bopinder gets hurt yesterday, today Christina. How many more signs do you need?' With that she walks away.

Before anyone can react, Andalip appears in front of her: 'Here you are my beauty! I hope everybody is treating you well.' Everybody starts to laugh and leaving Andy to wonder what he just missed.

Chapter 23

At 8 sharp the Germans walk into the Delhi Golf Club. A small notice in the lobby welcomes them to the dinner party hosted by Andy's uncle. The club seems empty. Michael looks through the glass doors, only to find an empty bar and dining room. A waiter dressed in black appears behind them. 'May I help you?' he asks. Michael and Günther answer almost simultaneously: 'We are here for the dinner party in honour of Andalip and Christina.' The man nods and leads them through a large door at the back of the hallway.

When they step onto the terrace, they all gasp with wonder. The lawn is decorated with candles, some tables and sofas. A large bar with mirrors and arrangements of flowers stands in one corner, while to their left, a huge golden tent covers the dining tables and chairs and the long buffet counter. In the middle of the lawn is a big dance floor with a disco ball floating on top. There's smell of jasmine in the air. Music quietly plays in the background. Hannelore is the first to speak: 'Atemberaubend! I cannot catch my breath. This looks more than beautiful. Maybe we got the dates wrong and this is the actual wedding.' Günther pulls out the invitation card and shakes his head: 'No, just a dinner. It's not even mentioned in the official invitation card. We just got this from Andy at today's lunch.' While they are trying to figure out what do to next, Bopinder and Andy walk out of the tent to greet them.

Bopinder shouts: 'Welcome! Welcome!' When they get closer, Bärbel thinks she hears Bopinder joke with Andy about the Germans being more than punctual. Both men are dressed up in dark suits. Bopinder's tie matches his dark red turban. Unlike at the last two events, Andy is not wearing a turban today, she notices with a feeling of relief. Today he looks like her daughter's boyfriend again, not as foreign as everyone else. She can't help but return their smiles.

Andy and his father greet Bärbel first before they shake hands with the others. Bopinder invites them to the bar. They pick a seating area overlooking the dance floor. While Andy is helping Christina's cousins and friends to get drinks, Bopinder sits with Michael, Bärbel and their Rotary Club friends. Within seconds a waiter arrives and serves them snacks. Bärbel bites into a piece of chicken and immediately starts coughing.

Bopinder looks concerned: 'Tandoori chicken. I hope it's not too spicy for you?' Bärbel nods her head. Her throat feels dry and tears come to her eyes. 'I am so sorry,' she tries to speak but keeps coughing. Bopinder fetches some water. Hannelore resumes the conversation: 'You know Bob, this is my second visit to India. I am so glad I got this opportunity to come for Christina's wedding. I keep telling my friends in Germany, 'You have to come and see it for yourself. India is the place to visit nowadays!' And this just proves it again. Beautiful, just beautiful!'

Bopinder smiles: 'Thank you. I am glad you like it. But Germany, I believe is beautiful too.' Then he turns to Bärbel again. 'Are you sure you are all right?' Bärbel drinks more water before answering: 'Yes, I am fine. I just did not expect the spice. Very tasty but too chilli for me I'm afraid.' She feels bad about not liking the chicken. Christina had told them to always praise the food to make a good impression. Good thing she missed this little episode, Bärbel thinks. She looks around and tries to change the topic: 'So where is your dear wife?' Besides them, not a single person had arrived yet. She checks her watch. Close to 8.30, time for dinner, she thinks.

Bopinder chuckles: 'You know, people here in Delhi usually don't show up at a party before 8.30 or 9 pm. No one wants to be the first! Andy had told me that you would be arriving sharp at 8, but I figured you guys would have to deal with the same traffic as us. Good thing we came early to check on the place. My brother Ranveer is actually here somewhere, checking on the food and all.' Bopinder looks around. When he cannot see his brother he tells Andy to find his *chacha*. Then he turns back to his guests and winks: 'The women are probably on their way. We always leave in two cars because the ladies always take too long to get ready. I am sure it's the same in Germany.'

Christina had left the house before them to get dressed at the beauty parlour. After dealing with Mona twice, she had decided to get her hair and make-up done by someone else. But with her family in the apartment, there always seemed to be a fight over the two bathrooms. Good that she's finding time to be alone, Bärbel thinks, looking around for her daughter. Instead, she notices another couple entering the garden. She recognizes Andy's uncle and his wife and gets up to meet them.

Ranveer and his wife, Tripat, greet them with hugs and loud hellos. Tripat is wearing a beautiful black and gold *sari*, and carrying a basket filled with white flowers. She hands flower bracelets to Bärbel and her friends, Hannelore and Kerstin. For the men she has a single flower to pin to the lapel of their suits. Ranveer calls the photographer over and they feel like movie stars caught in the flashbulbs of the paparazzi. A videographer follows and lights up the group, telling everybody to smile. More guests arrive, and the cameras move away. Ranveer and Tripat excuse themselves to welcome their guests, wishing Michael and her a wonderful evening. The youngsters are still standing around the bar, so Bopinder beckons some relatives they had met at the *mehendi* today. Bärbel tries to remember their names but is confused about how to pronounce them. Luckily, Andy's relatives seem to have the same problem with hers. They address Michael by name, with handshakes and hugs. She, on the other hand, receives a lot of smiles but people leave out her name and avoid body contact. Bärbel decides to follow Hannelore and starts greeting everybody with a general *namaste*.

A waiter comes over with more snacks. This time Bopinder tells him to send someone from the bar. 'Do you want us to survive on water and *nimbu pani* all night?' Andalip walks across, followed by a waiter from the bar. Bopinder gets up and starts teasing Andy: 'I see you are having fun over there and forgetting about your old parents over here. We are sitting dry and need some proper drinks served. What will you have, Michael? What can I get your friends?'

Michael looks over to the bar. While the Germans discuss what they would like to drink, the Indians start ordering: whiskey on ice, whiskey with soda, whiskey straight followed by gin and tonics and Bloody Marys. 'If you have a chilled bottle of white wine, we would start with that,' Michael addresses the waiter. Bopinder repeats the order and then turns to Michael again: 'White wine for the women. Now what do you men want to drink?' Andy starts laughing. Michael seems confused. 'No, no, we will all have white wine. Is that OK?' He looks at Bopinder and then at Andy. Bopinder leans over to Michael: 'Now Michael, this is a party. Why don't you have a real drink? Can I order you a whiskey?'

Andy steps up. 'Dad, not everybody likes whiskey. We got a great white in the back, let them start with that. OK?'

Now Bopinder looks confused but he listens to his son and tells the waiter to hurry up and get the drinks. 'White for the Whities it is!' he laughs out and raises his glass of water. Bärbel is not sure that she fully understands what is going on, but raises her glass anyway.

She feels like they are finally getting a chance to talk to Andy's family. The last two days were hectic and they never had the opportunity to sit down and get to know each other. She notices that Bopinder has his arm around his son's shoulder. She tries to remember when she held Christina for longer than a quick hug. The bond between parents and their children seemed so strong in India, she thinks. Earlier, she had noticed how unselfconsciously relatives and friends hugged each other and held hands. Yesterday, she saw several men walking down the street holding hands. You would never see that in Germany, she had told Frauke in the car. In many ways people seemed to be so much closer to each other and almost intimate in public. Then on the other hand, she had not seen any husband or wife or her daughter and Andy, for example, hold hands or kiss in public. She had seen a butt naked man standing in the middle of an intersection yesterday afternoon. She saw a woman on a motorcycle breastfeeding her baby. Yet, Christina had warned her not to change in the room but in the bathroom to avoid shocking the maid, in case she walked in on them.

Andy interrupts her thoughts. 'Here Bärbel, have a glass of wine. You look like you might need it. I hope you are enjoying your time in Delhi so far.'

She appreciates his concern and nods: 'Yes, Andy. We are having a great time. Christina is very lucky to have met you. Your family and you are just wonderful and are looking after us so well.' She gets emotional and tries to fight back her tears. They must think I am constantly crying, she muses and takes a large sip of wine. It's too warm for her taste and she puts it down. 'This is such a special evening. We should have something special with it. How about some *sekt?*' she asks the others.

Suddenly, the Indians at the table burst into laughter. The woman beside her looks shocked. One of the men spills his whiskey. Bopinder starts coughing and spitting his drink on the grass. 'Good one Bärbel!' he chuckles and tries to catch his breath. "What about some sex?" she asks. I knew you Germans are a little kinky but I did not expect an orgy at my son's wedding.' Bopinder can't stop laughing. He starts cracking jokes and shaking his head. 'You are too funny, Bärbel!' he keeps saying.

Bärbel does not understand what is so funny. Her friends continue sipping their wine and seem to agree with her. *Sekt*, German sparkling wine, or even better, a bottle of champagne would be a definite improvement to this wine, they figure. Andy is amused. He leans over to Bärbel and whispers: 'My dad thinks you asked for sex instead of *sekt*. Next time you should use the word champagne instead.'

Bärbel feels awful. Then she looks at Michael across the table, who smiles at her. He leans over and hands her a cocktail of some sort. The glass is chilled, but she knocks it back without taking a break and starts laughing. She walks over to Michael and sits beside him. 'Sorry, *schatz*, but I just ordered a round of sex for the entire table! This entire mixed cultural thing is hard to keep up with. Hats off to Christina, I don't know how she does it!' A little tipsy, she leans back, orders another cocktail and decides to enjoy the rest of the party.

Chapter 24
✥

Christina admires herself in the mirror. 'Now this is much better,' she says to the woman behind her. The hairstylist smiles back. She holds up a small mirror for Christina to see the back of her head. From the front the hair is pulled back tightly, but at the back it is held together in a big breaded bun, decorated with some artificial flowers, matching her purple *lehenga*. Christina had decided to do her own make-up. The woman at the Oberoi Hotel beauty parlour had fixed her hair and helped her with the last-minute touches—getting the outfit, jewellery and *bindi* in place. Christina gets up to check out her overall appearance. 'No, this looks great. Thank you!' Christina picks up her small handbag from the counter. Almost simultaneously, her phone starts to ring.

The stylist tells Christina to take her time and heads to the front to get the bill ready. Christina is expecting Andy to call. It is past 8. 30 pm. The first guests must be arriving at the club. She looks at the number but doesn't recognize it. 'Hello,' she answers the phone. 'Chrissi,' the voice at the other end shrieks into the phone. Christina instantly recognizes P's voice. 'P, did you finally make it to Delhi? How are you? Where are you?' Christina asks. While P is telling her all about her awfully long trip between New York and Delhi, another call comes in. The beeping stops, but picks up again after a few seconds. Christina is getting distracted and checks who is calling. It's her mother-in-law, Kiran. Two missed calls. She tries to interrupt, but P is busy nattering about her trip. 'And then after I complained, they upgraded me to Upper Class, 180-degree flat beds, baby, and an awesome entertainment system! You will never guess who was sitting next to me…well, almost next, just separated by a little plastic wall!' P sounds excited. Again, Christina's phone rings in the background. 'Sorry, P, I will have to hear the rest of your story at the party. Kiran Aunty is on the other line. I've really got to get going! You are coming tonight, right?'

P laughs: 'Of course, Chrissi, that's the reason I'm here. Just wanted to check if I can bring a special guest? The guy I sat next to on the plane…You haven't guessed who yet! Or do you want to be surprised?' Christina's not really listening and quickly says bye and answers the other line. '*Hanji*, Aunty,I'm ready. Just settling the bill, I will be at the club in less than 10 minutes!' Christina says without listening to the caller. She is surprised to hear Simran instead of Andy's mom. 'Hi Christina, Simran here. I am glad I caught you before you reached the club. You need to come home first. Something's come up. We need your help. I've already called the driver to bring you back to Golf Links.' Simran explains. Christina nods into the phone: 'Oh, OK, I will be right there.' She is not sure Simran heard her. The line is dead. Christina walks to the reception and settles her bill. Her phone vibrates again, reminding her to hurry up. 'Thanks,' she says and walks off. While waiting for the car to arrive at the entrance she checks the message that she has just received. It's from Andy: 'How much longer? Missing you. Getting drunk with your cousins! Hurry. Luv u, A.' She decides not to answer.

When she reaches the house she sees that it's all lit up and two white Ambassador cars are parked outside. Simran is waiting for her in the driveway, worried. 'Finally,' she says and pulls her into the house. The women of the house are standing in Manjeet's hallway. Christina frowns when she notices Anhad sitting around the coffee table talking to two police officers. Dadi is sitting on the sofa next to her grandson, holding Mary's hand.

Kiran walks over to Christina and Simran and announces: 'Beta, something terrible has happened!' She holds Christina's hands. Christina looks confused. Suddenly she is worried about her parents: 'What happened? Is my family OK?' she asks, her mouth dry. She looks around for an explanation. The policemen stand up and Anhad leads them up the stairs.

Kiran gently tells Christina to sit down. 'There was a robbery in the house. We don't really know when and why it happened. The men had already left and we women were getting ready. Then Anita noticed lights upstairs and your closet doors open. Your jewellery is gone for sure and some of Dadi's things are also missing. All my stuff is in place, but I have been wearing my necklace and bangles since the afternoon. The rest is in the bank. Thank God for that.' Kiran stops to catch her breath.

Anhad's wife Maya appears from the kitchen with a tray of water for everyone. Christina looks around. Everybody is sitting awfully quiet. Even Jazz and Preeti just sip their water and seem to avoid her gaze. She can hear Karnav and Jasmin fight in the other room. Maya leaves the tray and starts shouting at her kids while walking to the back of the apartment. Christina does not know what to say. Kiran looks at her and shakes her head. 'It's really awful. Just awful!' she keeps repeating.

'So what will happen now?' Christina quietly asks into the room.

Simran is the only one who responds: 'The police are handling it. It looks like we've found the thief. Anhad just wants to talk to you and make sure that you can confirm Anita's statement.' Christina still does not understand. She looks at Simran for more explanations. Simran comes over and sits next to her.

Kiran gets up, still mumbling to herself and excuses herself from the room. She asks Jazz to come upstairs with her. Simran says that she will handle the matter, but before the women can leave the room, Anhad and the officers return. Anhad calls out for the guard and tells Mary to make some *chai* for the gentlemen. Mary and the guard disappear with the policemen to the back of the house. Anhad asks all the family members to sit back down and listen. He addresses Christina:

'Here's the deal. The police have inspected the crime scene. They have taken down all the details of what seems to have happened. We've got an inventory of what's missing. Thanks to Anita, we pretty much know who has taken the jewellery and we should have it back within the next 24 hours. Now, Christina, I just need to confirm that you had kept the jewellery upstairs and that besides your family, the only other person who saw you with the jewellery box this morning was that young fellow Raj.'

Though it is less than 12 hours ago, Christina is having a hard time thinking back. She remembers them having coffee before heading downstairs for the party. She remembers bringing out the jewellery to choose what to wear. And, yes, Raj was there, chatting with Frauke. She does not remember when they all left the apartment but she is pretty sure that she had put the jewellery away in the closet. She later came up to place the new jewellery she had received at the ceremony into the closet. She cannot remember if she saw the wedding jewellery box then or not. The whole day, her family has been up and down between the floors of the house. Christina was the first to leave to go to the parlour. She starts feeling queasy, realizing she had forgotten to tell her parents to lock the door behind them. Then again, how often has she locked the apartment behind her in the last two weeks? She notices Anhad waiting for an answer.

'And, was he there?' he asks again.

Christina nods: 'Well, yes, for coffee this morning, but I wouldn't say that he stole the jewellery. Did Anita see him upstairs again?' she asks Anhad. Andy's cousin doesn't seem to have heard her question. He just gets up and says: 'Good, so that is confirmed.' Then he leaves the room and heads for the kitchen.

Christina jumps up to call him. Simran gets up quickly: 'Christina, let him handle it. Things in India work a little differently than in New York. Especially when it comes to dealing with the police. If we ever want to see the jewellery again before the wedding, we have to act quickly and get this sorted out tonight. Otherwise who knows what will happen.'

'But you don't even know if it was Raj. What exactly did Anita say? Anybody could have walked in here today and taken it. The house was filled with people coming in and out all day.' Christina tries to reason with her. While she is trying to sort her arguments, Dadi stands up and walks up to her. She seems even shorter than usual, Christina notices. Dadi seems to be shaking and Simran gets up to hold her. Suddenly, Dadi starts yelling in Punjabi, addressing Christina. She is surprised by the strength of the grandmother's voice and steps back. Kiran and Manjeet jump up to come to her rescue. Dadi keeps on shouting, while Manjeet tries to calm her mother down. A loud altercation between the three generations of Singh women starts and Christina feels totally lost.

While Dadi is still shouting at her, Christina turns to Simran for answers: 'Can you please tell me what she is saying? What does she want? Did I do anything wrong?' Preeti speaks up instead. 'She saying that the theft is just another bad omen and that this wedding is not supposed to happen! Just ignore her!'

Dadi's shouting stops and everyone stares at Preeti.

Kiran gets upset: 'Preeti, please don't talk about your grandmother like that!'

'No, let her.' Dadi switches to English. 'She is the only one who gets it around here, I think. Even if you don't believe it, I have been seeing the signs. Andalip is not supposed to marry this white woman here. Nobody has been listening to me but now you should start listening to a higher power. God has been speaking to us!' She raises her fist in the air to underline her words. 'First he warned us subtly by delaying Christina's family's arrival. Then he was more obvious by blowing up the music system. Didn't you see the blood on Christina's arm at the *mehendi*? What better sign than blood! But you fools don't seem to understand this. With the family jewellery gone, there cannot be a wedding. Don't you understand?' Dadi screams at her relatives.

Christina is shocked. She falls back into a chair. The room is quiet. Kiran seems to avoid her puzzled look. Simran is still standing next to her, but she's staring at her feet. The first to react is Preeti. She walks over to her grandmother and hugs her. Then she folds her hands and bows down to touch her feet. Everybody watches quietly, while Dadi raises Preeti. Then Preeti speaks: 'You know, I respect you and love you very much. I do not intend to hurt you by what I am going to say next. But I feel you have gone too far! If you believe in what God preaches and the signs he might send us, then how do you explain all the injustice in the world? How do you explain Simran not having a second child even though she is married to a Sikh man, has a perfect marriage and goes to the gurudwara every day? How do you explain Jazz, who does not want to be pregnant again, having another baby? How do you explain me and Kabir getting a divorce, even though there were no bad omens at our weddings? How can you hate the woman who finally brought your long lost grandson back to India, even though he always dreamt of settling in the US? Look at the women around you. You should be happy with what you have got and trust in love not omens to get us through this. I love Christina like a sister. Don't you see how good she is for Andalip? How can you blame her for all the madness going on right now? Many bad things happen in India every day. Lights go off, cars get scratched, the water stinks, children go hungry…that's daily life. Not a sign from God! I say we all get ready for the party now and forget what's just happened.' Again, she hugs her grandmother, then walks over to Christina to kiss her on the cheek. Then she hugs her mother and says: 'I am sorry you had to find out about Kabir and me this way, but I am fine and happy with my life and this was getting really ridiculous, don't you think?' Without waiting for a response, Preeti leaves the house.

Anhad returns: 'Did I miss anything? You guys look a little dazed? Maybe it is time we head over to the club and join the others at the party. I've sorted everything out and I am sure everything will look better in the morning!'

Christina watches her new relatives get up. She can hear them talking but everything seems to be in a blur. Anhad is assigning people to their cars. How can they go on like nothing happened? she thinks confused. She sits in the chair until the house is empty. Maybe Dadi is right and the wedding is not supposed to happen, she contemplates as she hears the cars start in the driveway. Oh my God, she really hates me! For a minute she is considers going upstairs to pack her bags and just leave, but she feels too weak. Then the door opens again and Kiran looks inside: 'Christina, Beta, what are you sitting here for?' When she does not answer, Kiran comes over and pulls her up. Christina stares at her, trying to read her mind. For a few seconds she is convinced, Kiran is going to talk to her and tell her that all will be well and to just ignore what has happened. Instead she keeps quiet and takes her to the car. Anhad's car leaves first.

Christina finds herself wedged between Kiran and Preeti. As soon they are seated, the driver follows the other car. Without saying a word, they reach the club. For a minute they remain in the car. Kiran sits up straight and looks at both her daughter and new daughter-in-law: 'Here is a lesson for you on life and what it means to be a woman. I want you to go inside and forget what just happened. People are expecting a beautiful dinner hosted by this family and we will deliver that. I want you two to be perfect hosts. Anhad will take care of the theft. I will deal with dad and Dadi later. Now get out.' Kiran tells them harshly. Like obedient children they listen. Christina thinks she hears her mother-in-law whispering 'I love you both!' when they climb out of the car. It sounds as if she's crying. She wants to look around and check, but feels too hurt to interact with anyone who had witnessed what had happened at the house.

Chapter 25
✵

The party is in full swing when Anhad and the ladies enter. Some people are already on the dance floor. Andalip is still sitting at the bar with Christina's relatives and friends. Some of his school friends had joined them a while ago and had introduced *hukkah* to the Germans. The mood is light and conversations silly. Andalip tries to skip his turn but Karl Jr keeps telling him to relax and enjoy himself. Andalip smiles at how childishly Christina's cousins act; he had never seen them so cheerful. The waiter refills Andalip's glass and he has lost track of how many drinks he's had. When he sees Christina and his sisters enter, he quickly gets up and realizes that he is drunk.

Within seconds, his family and friends fade into the background, only Christina stands out. She's wearing a *lehenga*, and its silver lining and embroidery reflects the light of the disco ball. My proud Teutonic woman, he muses, watching her briskly walk towards him. She is holding her *dupatta* in her hand instead of draping it over her shoulder. He wonders if the other guests are admiring her low-cut top and the silhouette of her breasts as much as he is. A few hours ago he might have been filled with jealousy having to share her beauty with the rest of the world. Now he was filled with pride.

'Here you are my beautiful bride! I was about to come to the parlour and rescue you. You are missing a hell of a party!' He holds out his arms to hug her, but instead she grabs him by the arm and drags him behind her. He stumbles but follows her as she leads him past the bar towards the golf course. Then she stops and waits for him.

Andalip is getting worried. He can't figure out her mood. She looks angry, but also a bit worried. He wonders if she'll start crying again. 'Are you OK?' he asks. Instead of answering his question, Christina takes his hand and asks him to walk with her. Soon they are at a distance away from the party, but they can still see the lights partly hidden by large trees. Andalip can hear the music. He pulls her close and asks her to dance. 'Andy, stop it, we need to talk!' Christina pulls away from him, folds her arms and waits for him to pay attention to her. But Andy is distracted by her looks, her smell and the sparkles on her outfit. He spots a small monument at the end of the path and tells her to follow him. He walks across the grass and around the tomb to find a set of steps on the other side. He sits down and waits for Christina. For a second he's afraid that she won't follow him but then she appears between the trees and joins him. To his surprise she puts her head down on his knees. He sits quietly and strokes her hair, waiting for her to speak.

Even though it's the end of November, it's still warm at night. He feels hot in his suit jacket. He wants to take it off, but doesn't want ruin the moment, so he remains seated, listening to the music in the distance and inhaling the smell of the grass, trees and, once in a while, Christina's perfume. He feels the effect of the alcohol and *hukkah* disappearing, and his head begins to ache. He is thirsty and craves for some cold water. 'So, what did you want to talk about?' he asks quietly. Christina does not move. Maybe she's fallen asleep, he thinks, still stroking her hair. When he starts to rub her back she moves. She lifts her head and looks at him. Then she gets up and sits on his lap, facing him. To his surprise, she takes off his jacket and drops it behind him. She gently pushes him back and leans over him. He closes his eyes. She softly starts kissing him on the neck, working her way up to his face.

Before she kisses him on the lips, she lies on top of him and whispers into his ear: 'Andy, are you sure you love me? Are you sure you want to marry me?' He's instantly reminded of his first few years in New York when he used to bring girls home after parties. He would tell them anything they wanted to hear just to get them into bed with him. He never promised marriage or true love, but he never denied it either. He had been with a lot of women. He enjoyed the rush, but never really felt close to any of them. That had all changed when he met Christina. Often, just holding her hand in a movie theatre would make his imagination run wild. Leaning against her in the subway was too much to bear sometimes and he would count the minutes till they were back at the apartment. He often pictured himself alone with her in a place like this. Just feeling her close to him, away from everyone, he would promise her anything to ravish her right here, just like those girls in New York. He holds her tight and rolls her over next to him. While he's trying to open her blouse, he tells her: 'Of course I love you. Of course I want to marry you!'

Christina starts kissing him. She guides his hand under her blouse. He feels like a teenager, excited by these first touches. Suddenly, his lust turns to binding love for the woman he is marrying in less than 48 hours. Unlike before, he wants this feeling to last and slowly takes his hand out from under her blouse. He pulls her even tighter, kisses her harder than before. 'How can you even ask me this? In my heart I am already married to you. I love you more than my own life! Now let's get out there and show everybody why they are here. And continue this after the wedding…'

He helps her get up. In the light of the moon, they try to settle their clothes. The anger or sadness or whatever it was he noticed on her face earlier, has disappeared. She kisses him one last time and takes his hand as they slowly walk back to the party. No one seems to have noticed their absence. They join an even larger crowd of youngsters at the bar. Andy orders two glasses of champagne. When he takes his first sip, he leans over to Christina and whispers: 'Now let's party like singles. We'll continue our golf course exploration another night!' He winks at her, eager to be a husband.

Chapter 26

Bopinder spent most of the day on the phone. Even though Anhad had handled the situation with the police as best as he could, Bopinder felt more should be done to get the jewellery back before the wedding tomorrow. He had called his politician friends and police officers at the highest levels, including the Police Commissioner. After the initial report given by Anhad and the women last night, the police had inspected the house thoroughly and quickly narrowed down a suspect. Early this morning Raj, the son of their former factory driver, was arrested. The young man claimed to be innocent. His home was searched. So far, the wedding jewellery is still missing.

In less than an hour, the family is supposed to leave for the Pushpanjali Farms in West Delhi, just south of the airport. It was decided that the *milni*, the formal meeting of the relatives from both sides, would take place right before the *sangeet* instead of the wedding. The farmhouse was the ideal place for the drums, loud music and traditional horse for Andalip to officially meet his in-laws since they were not from Delhi. Everyone agreed that the wedding day would be a more formal affair at the gurudwara. Jewellery stolen or not, Andalip told his family this morning, the wedding should continue as planned. The guests should not be informed about last night's incident. He was certain that the situation would be solved quickly. Everybody agreed.

Last night's crime was hardly discussed at breakfast. Everyone had spent the day in their rooms. At lunch time, the house was eerily silent. Bopinder and Kiran had a meal in their bedroom and decided to let everybody rest. When Bopinder tried to find out what exactly had happened last night, Kiran quickly changed the topic. After lunch he went to the ground floor to see if he could talk to Anhad again, but his bedroom was empty. He was in the hallway when he heard the sounds of a television news channel coming from his mother's closed door. He decided to talk to her instead. He knocked first softly then loudly but she did not respond. When the TV fell silent, he knocked again, this time calling out for her. He waited a few minutes and then tried to open the door but it was locked. He heard somebody walk towards the door. He stepped back, waiting for his mom to open the door. Instead she yelled at him through the locked door: 'Whoever it is, leave me alone!'

'*Maji, mai hu*. Bopinder. I want to talk to you. Can you please open the door and let me in?' His mother remained silent and the TV was switched on. The theft must have upset her the most, he figured. She had received the jewellery as a wedding gift from her mother-in-law and then had passed it on to Kiran, when her oldest son got married. His mother had always been moody, but she has definitely outdone herself the last few days, Bopinder thought. It's just missing metal. At least none of us got hurt.

While his wife spent the afternoon sleeping, resting for yet another long evening ahead, he was lying awake on the sofa, watching the ceiling fan turn. Forget about the theft, he thinks, the last two days have been wonderful. Michael seems to be a friendly fellow, very relaxed and open to anything. Funny how he covered his head with a handkerchief, looking a bit like one of the aunties needing waxing for his little stubble of a beard, Bopinder thinks back to the *path*. Andalip should have prepared him better. Still, he handled the *path* quiet well and played it like a pro. Until the party last night, the German seemed to have kept to themselves.

Once the whiskey was flowing, they relaxed a bit and had a good time, Bopinder contemplates. He had liked Christina from the beginning, but always thought she was a little too serious. She reminded him of one of those proper *fräuleins* from the World War II movies he enjoys watching. Clean, punctual, stiff upper-lip but honest and loyal until death, he pictures Christina dressed like Eva Braun spending the last days with Hitler in the bunker. Seeing her mother yesterday, telling jokes and suggesting sex as a party game, Bopinder was sure, once his daughter-in-law began to feel more at home in Delhi, she would be as much fun as her mother. Analip will add some spice to her life, he smiles. He tries to remember the name of the woman who always looks a bit like a hippie from Goa and greets everyone with a *namaste*. As long as Christina does not try to find herself in some ashram, we all should be fine. Now let's just hope that our dear Dadiji relaxes a bit and is able to enjoy the rest of the wedding, he thinks before dozing off.

❦

Both Tripat and Manjeet are dressed and ready for the *milni*. Both are wearing shades of green, their embroidered *salwar kameezes* snugly fitting their full, slightly overweight bodies, their thick, black hair pinned up in buns. They look more like sisters than sisters-in-law. Like young school girls they sit next to window overlooking the driveway, chatting and laughing. The lights had gone off a few minutes ago but the generator has not come on. They are in no hurry to continue their work. They are quite comfortable just sitting there and gossiping—a well-deserved break from the last few hectic days. The light of the large burning torches along the driveway is reflecting in their eyes.

'Just look at these men down there. All dressed up in their suits, so tall and handsome.' Tripat muses. 'Somebody should tell them to sit down again. It might be a while until Andalip arrives on the horse. I hope they don't think that we are still getting ready,' she giggles.

Christina's family had arrived much earlier than planned, all dressed up and ready to start with the celebrations. Tea was served in the garden while Andalip utilized the time to explain what was to happen this evening.

Christina and Andalip had planned to make the wedding not only fun but educational as well. Till now, it had all been very informal. Today the entire group, including Andalip's relatives, were listening intently to his explanations of the *milni* ceremony. Tripat wonders if her children who were settled abroad knew the meaning of any of this week's functions.

Christina and her family sat like schoolchildren listening to Andalip speak, while his family, well aware of what was about to happen, was focused on the food. Tripat was enjoying the Kashmiri tea and hot *jalebis* and only heard half of what her nephew had said, but smiling at how his accent became more Germanic. She heard her husband and his brother tease him from the back: '*Achtung, achtung, herr general!*' The Germans didn't seem to notice the mockery.

'Usually, this event would start in the groom's house where my sisters would place a veil of flowers on my head, blessing me with garlands and prayers, and helping me mount a decorated white horse, before all of us, led by a wedding band and many more dancing and cheering relatives from the groom's family would come to your—the bride's family's home,' he told Christina's father. 'This meeting of the two families is called the *milni* ceremony. Traditionally, the senior men of both families greet each other formally at this point. This usually happens at your house or wedding venue arranged by you' and with that Andalip had put his arm around Michael's shoulder, grinning broadly: 'But, because of the long distance between our houses we thought we'd change things around a bit and hold the ceremony here tonight before the party.' Only Christina seemed to have gotten his joke and winked at him, while the Germans remained serious. He tried again: 'So, in a short while, there will be a band, me on a white horse, lots of flowers and hugs and kisses being exchanged, followed by a wild party!' This time the Germans had cheered and clapped.

The preparations for the *milni* and the following *sangeet* were still in full force when Andalip—still dressed in jeans—excused himself to get ready for the evening. One by one the Singhs followed suit, leaving the Germans behind in the garden, trying to figure out what to do next. While Bopinder and Ranveer were still sitting in the garden enjoying their tea like it was whiskey, Kiran was arguing with one of the guards about the whereabouts of the musicians and horse. Tripat was in no mood to interact with her guests just yet and was glad when she spotted an Indian woman who she met at last night's dinner and recognized her as Christina's friend from NY, sitting amongst Christina's relatives.

Tripat smiled across the lawn to the woman, whose name she couldn't remember, gesturing for her to come over for second. Wasn't she South Indian? A Christian like Christina? 'Sorry to interrupt, Beta, I need to ask you little favour, since you are one of Christina's friends as well as an Indian: please could you look after the Van H… you know, Christina's family, for me and make sure they know what to do later? We thought we'd start the procession outside and bring Andalip in through the gate, walk around the property and end up in front of the house, at the end of the driveway. Maybe you can tell them to wait there for us?'

'Of course, no problem Aunty, I'm on it!' the woman had smiled and rushed back to the Germans and continued her conversation with Christina's family. By the time Tripat had finished her rounds with the caterers, decorators and general staff, she was happy to see that her instructions had been passed on to the Germans and they were lined up—prim and proper—in the driveway. She cannot help but be amused watching the Germans still waiting in the same position that she had left them in before coming upstairs to change at least half an hour ago. There is still no sign of the horse or the musicians. 'Should I arrange some more *chai* for us?' Tripat asks her sister-in-law smirking.

Manjeet shakes her head no. 'Maybe we should send something down for those poor fellows?' When Tripat gets up, she tells her to keep sitting. Tripat watches her sister-in-law smile. Even though she is a widow and had to move back in with her family, Manjeet always seems happy with her life, Tripat thinks. Even though she really enjoys her sister-in-law's company and they are neighbours, they rarely spent much time together. Manjeet's busy with her children and grandchildren, while Tripat had involved herself with volunteer work once her kids moved out.

'You know, I am not surprised that Andalip is getting married to a German. They have been standing there waiting patiently for something to happen, unlike us. Andalip has lived in the US. He would not be able to deal with us on a daily basis. Let's hope his wife can.' She slaps her knee, chuckling. 'A little cold but I like her. Remember us during our wedding week, sobbing like babies because we had to leave our parent's houses. On top of that, no beautiful jewellery to ease the pain! She is the only bride I have ever seen, who actually seems to be enjoying her wedding.'

'Have you talked to your mother again? Is she still convinced this wedding is cursed? She seems very upset. Will she be fine?' Tripat inquires.

'She is too much. Instead of being happy for Andalip, she is making such a fuss. Times have changed. We are not living in the 20th century anymore. She is too old to accept that. I told her...' Manjeet stops mid-sentence as the light come on. She gets up and draws the curtain. 'Let's not rub salt into their wounds. If they figure out, how nice and cool it is in here, they will come back in,' she laughs. 'Let's see what's happened to that horse and start some dancing.'

'Now tell me what you told your mother.' Since Manpreet yelled at everybody last night, cursing the union between Andalip and Christina, Tripat has been worrying if she's right.

Manjeet stops at the door. She turns around and grins at Tripat: 'I told her, 'Maji how can you believe in such nonsense. If there was such a thing as bad *karma* and God truly exists and only parents know who is best for their children to marry, how did I end up back in this house? My marriage was done according to the books, a perfect Punjabi match, all in line with Sikh traditions. In what kind of God do you believe who has done this to your daughter? Or maybe you made a mistake finding the right match, following the wrong traditions? For Andalip's sake, stay away from this marriage and stop talking about religion and bad omens. Or do you want another person's life in this family to be ruined?' I don't know if she got my point though, since after that, she locked herself in the prayer room, reading the Guru Granth Sahib.' With that she opens the door and disappears.

Tripat feels goosebumps on her arms. She hears Manjeet calling out for her to hurry. She obeys, too shocked not to.

Chapter 27

Christina can hear music and people singing. She leans out of her window but she can't see anything.

She had been looking forward to the *milni* and seeing Andy on a horse. She was one of the first ones to get ready. She had even agreed to give Mona the stylist one last shot to get her make-up and hair done for tonight. Her family had spent their time in the garden, since they had all come dressed for the function. Andy's sisters had changed in her room. They were all in a silly mood.

Preets had asked her many questions about marriage and weddings in Germany. All her knowledge seemed to have come from Hollywood movies and television serials. All three seemed most interested in bachelorette parties and how many boyfriends she had before Andy. For a while she played along and told them about her girls' nights out in New York and her flirtations with other men before Andy. Jazz asked her how her wedding would have been if she had gotten married in Germany. Christina stuck to stereotypes, describing a white church wedding. At the back of her mind, she knew she would never have gotten married in a church. At least not in Germany, maybe in a wedding chapel in Las Vegas or barefoot at a beach. Feeling bad enough about not being a virgin before marriage and seeing her sisters-in-law's excitement over what they called 'her wild life before marriage', she decided it was best to end the conversation sooner rather than later.

When Kiran called them to come downstairs for the *milni*, Christina had followed them to the door. Simran had stopped her and explained that traditionally the bride was not part of the *milni*. 'Wait here and somebody will get you when the time is right. Don't want to upset Dadi more than she already is. Right?' Simran said. Christina was disappointed but nodded wordlessly. She told Simran to send P upstairs to get her. She wanted a friend by her side to face another round of celebrations that she did not seem to understand.

When she heard the music start, she expected somebody to call her downstairs. There was no clock in the room but she was sure she had waited at least half an hour. Worrying that she would miss the entire ceremony she decided to see for herself what was happening. Before reaching the front door, she was stopped by Maya. 'Now, where do you think you are heading?' She was smiling but standing in front of the door, determined not to let her pass. 'I want to see Andy on the horse!' Christina replied.

'I am sorry, but you have to wait a bit. You are not supposed to be at the *milni*. Traditionally...' Maya started. Christina interrupted: 'Sorry, Maya. Isn't it obvious that what we are doing is not very traditional?' Maya looked a bit guilty. Still she wouldn't let her pass. Christina felt silly to insist and went back to her room.

The longer she waits, the angrier she gets with Andy. At least he should have explained what was going on tonight, she thinks, pacing up and down the room in her *lehenga*. She is not sure if the music has stopped or just gotten quieter. She can hear people laugh and talk. Suddenly, she can see the bursts of fireworks above the house, followed by loud explosions. 'Great,' she screams into the empty room and throws herself onto the bed. She plays with the silver pendant around her neck that her parents' had gifted her when she received her doctorate. 'I manage to graduate with honours and receive my doctorate but I have no idea what is going on at my own wedding.' Then she hears a knock and jumps up:

'Finally, P, I have been waiting for you to get me!' She opens the door to find her mother standing outside looking at her angrily.

Not P, but Bärbel is standing outside the room and the moment Christina opens the door, yells at her: 'Here you are, hiding. Everyone has been looking for you. Where have you been? Get ready and come downstairs. Fast!'

'Honestly?' Christina asks, while following her mother down the stairs. Besides her family, more people, at least a hundred, have arrived and are standing on the lawn waiting for her. Jazz tells her to sit down in one of two chairs. Her family are standing around the decorated podium and start taking pictures of her. A professional photographer appears and Christina smiles automatically. 'Where is Andy?' she turns around and asks but everyone is busy, talking and laughing.

She is searching the crowd to find Andy when his sisters appear with a tray covered by a red cloth. Without any explanation they put what looks to her like cheap red plastic bangles around her wrists. Simran hands out little golden bells dangling from red strings to the women around them. She asks them to tie these to the bangles. It is loud and hot and the chair besides her is still empty. Christina feels like screaming but is too confused to act. She can hear comments in German on how interesting all this is, mixed with what sounds like jokes and orders in Hindi and Punjabi. She feels suffocated while Preeti takes control of Christina's arm, pulling it up and down: 'Hey, listen, you need to wriggle these over the girls' heads. Whoever ends up with golden bells on her head is getting married next!' Amongst the women lined up in front of her, she notices Fiona and Aisha giggling.

She stops listening to what is going on around her. Her stomach is turning into knots. Dadi keeps appearing in front of her eyes, telling her to be more Indian.

Christina's thoughts are racing: 'You will never fit it. You will never be good enough. You are ruining Andy's life. Run while you still can. It is not too late to go back home and just do what everybody else is telling you. Just marry somebody from Germany. Or better, don't get married at all.'

'Now just sit a little closer and smile into the camera!' she hears a man with a thick Indian accent. She looks up and realizes Andy has finally sat down beside her. He does what the man with the camera tells them, moving his chair a little closer to hers, leaning over to greet her. 'You look sexy tonight!' he whispers, while smiling into the camera. Christina smells alcohol.

'Are you kidding?' she snaps. 'Have you even realized that I was locked up in the house the last hour or so while you were having a blast down here? Is this all a big joke to you? Or did your dear grandmother finally talk sense into you and you are getting married to somebody else while your family is making a big fool out of me?'

She gets up and runs towards the house. With the music in the background and people talking, she is not sure if anyone had heard what she just said to Andy. She waits for a minute for Andy to follow her, but when he doesn't, she decides to pass the house and keeps running down the driveway towards the gate. All of a sudden, she feels like she needs to run away from all this but quickly runs out of breath and has to slow down. Angry at everybody, she kicks the gravel under her sandals and shouts into the dark: 'Good, that settles it. No wedding tomorrow!'

Chapter 28

While the entire wedding party enjoys the festivities at the Singh farmhouse in Pushpanjali, Raj is locked up in a holding room at the police station. At least that is where he thinks he is.

After the *mehendi* lunch, he had returned to his friend's apartment in Shahpur Jat where he has been staying to avoid the commute to Noida. He met Jean from France at the university when he returned from Germany. Both seemed to have lots in common. Jean was eagerly looking for a roommate and was hoping Raj would move in with him and share the rent. But after spending so much time in Germany, Raj was not ready to leave his dad alone in Noida now that he was back in Delhi. Until Jean found a permanent roommate, he had decided to use the place as and when needed to help out with the bills.

Frauke had invited him to the dinner party at the Golf Club, but he decided to stay at home since Andalip did not mention it to him when they met. He had gone to bed early and was already up, drinking a cup of tea on the roof, when the police arrived next morning. He was sure they had come for one of the neighbours. Jean has been complaining about a man screaming at and maybe beating his wife. Maybe someone's finally taken action, Raj thought watching the officers finding their way through the narrow lanes of the village. Ten minutes later Jean appeared on the roof. 'Man, you better come down. The police are looking for you. They won't say what the problem is. Maybe something with your dad?' Jean sounded concerned.

Raj had rushed down to the small flat, worried. Three men dressed in khaki were waiting for him. Before he was able to enquire why they have come, Raj found himself on the floor with a black boot on his back. A baton was pressing against his ear. Jean started arguing with the men but they just yelled at him. Raj was too scared to argue with the police. This was not Germany. From all he knew, these men might be more corrupt than the criminals they are looking for. Before he was pulled out of the house, he managed to exchange a few words with Jean. 'My phone is in my room. Call my dad and tell him what has happened. If he does not answer, try to find the number for Andy Singh. He might be able to help.' Raj had told Jean in broken French before the police dragged him along.

He was not sure where he was being taken. He was pushed into the back of a small van and told to sit on the floor. The three officers who arrested him, sat with him in the back but on the seats. The car was hot and smelled of sweat. Even with his crumbled jeans and the T-shirt he had slept in, he felt he was the cleanest thing in the van. He could not see where he was going. After a while, he built up the courage to ask why and where they were taking him. The largest of them, who had earlier pushed him to the ground raised his baton again and yelled at him to shut up. When the car finally stopped and they pulled him out, he did not understand where he was. Raj has never been to a police station in India, but this did not look like what he had expected. A large, wired fence surrounded the parking lot and a small white bungalow. Men with rifles stood outside. As soon as he was pulled out of the van, another officer came up to him and quickly led him through a side door into the building. Raj was pushed into a small room and the door was bolted.

Since then he had been left alone, even though he tried banging on to door to get attention. He wonders if Jean has called his dad or Andy. He wonders if anybody else knew he was here. Then he notices a mat on the floor that probably is a bed. He has to pee but can't force himself to urinate into a little hole in the ground which seems to be there for exactly that purpose. He is thirsty but the water left for him smells. Or is it just the room, he is not sure.

Raj is also not sure how many hours have passed since he was brought here. He feels exhausted but cannot sleep. The fear of being hit by the police officers now gives way panic that he is lost to the world. He is about to fall asleep when the door opens and a tray with food and water is pushed in. Before he can react, the door is locked again. Uncertain about how long he will be kept in here or when he will get more food, he decides to eat. The *daal* is watery and the *chapattis* burned but he finishes the meal. The water seems fresh and he drinks it quickly before it starts smelling like the room. Before returning to the mat, he has to relieve himself, so he squats in front of the hole in the corner of the room.

'Look at you now, Herr Raj Kumar. Born to a poor man, always a poor man. Doesn't matter what schools you went to…' he whispers into the room and starts to cry.

Chapter 29

The dance party is in full swing. After the *milni*, snacks were served. The waiters were told to include champagne and whiskey on their trays to get the party started. Even though it is still early, Germans and Indians, the young and the old, are grooving away on the dance floor. Only a few guests are sitting around, watching and chatting. Andalip returns from a quick bathroom run, watches for a while and then joins in the fun.

He is trying to spot Christina but he can't find her in the crowd. He watches his sisters teaching the German women some Bollywood dance steps. Brown and white arms sway in the air, hips covered in all imaginable colours sway back and forth. Andalip's uncles are rocking away, trying to outdo each other by shaking their chests like peacocks. The Germans seem a little stiff in comparison, but they have big smiles on their faces as they attempt to pick up the bhangra moves.

The music switches from a popular Indian song to a slower German tune. Andalip recognizes it as a popular party song played at every German event he has ever been too. As soon as the first words are sung, the Germans form a big circle on the dance floor, wrapping their arms around each other's shoulders. Andalip notices Günther standing on a chair next to the DJ, raising a glass of wine and screaming: '*Ich war noch niemals in New York. Ich war noch niemals auf Hawai…*' The Germans pick up the lines and scream back at him. Andalip remembers that in the song, the singer laments that he has never been to New York or Hawaii or San Francisco, but now the Germans have added their own words, including New Delhi. His family and friends look stunned watching the loud and overexcited Germans. Some are watching, some leave the dance floor. Andalip wonders if this will put an end to the harmony that he witnessed during the Bollywood number. But the Germans themselves seem to realize what is happening and open up the circle to welcome more dancers. Frauke pulls Simran on to the floor. One by one Andalip's friends and family join in and the circle on the dance floor becomes huge. Andalip feels light. Definitely a combination of alcohol and all that love on the dance floor, he muses.

Still searching for Christina, he notices his dad talking to Michael. Like long lost friends, they are sharing a small sofa, almost hugging each other. Andalip moves closer and realizes they are already discussing grandchildren. 'I hope your daughter knows what the honeymoon is for?' He hears his dad ask Michael. Without waiting for his reply, Bopinder continues: 'I know Christina is educated and we value that but you'll have to admit that she's getting a little old for kids. You should talk to her and tell her to get on with it. So, if all goes well, by next summer we should be grandfathers, you and I. I have to tell you though, if it is a boy… which I am sure it will be…. did I tell you that Andalip is the oldest son of the oldest son of the oldest son…well, you get my point. So their firstborn, who will be a son, will be called Zorawar after my father.' Bopinder slaps Michael's knee to underline his point. His father-in-law keeps laughing and agreeing with his dad, but Andalip is sure that Michael has not followed a word of what his dad was saying or thinks he's too drunk to be serious. Andalip walks on, leaving the fathers to themselves. The music has switched back to Indian hits and almost everyone seems to be on the dance floor. Even Dadi's chair has moved near the dancers. Andalip watches Aisha teaching Fiona some dance moves, including Dadi in the performance. 'This is great', Andalip thinks. 'This once again proves that the right mix of kebabs, whiskey and beer combined with kickass Punjabi music can bring the most different peoples and cultures together.' He still can't find Christina and decides to wait for her on the dance floor. He grabs a glass of whiskey from the waiter next to him, gulps it down and runs onto the dance floor with his arms in the air, singing loudly. The crowd greets him with loud cries of joy and swallows him for the next few hours.

Chapter 30
❦

As the party reaches its crescendo, Christina and P are hiding behind the house. They are sitting on a small bench outside the kitchen. Drivers usually hang out here during the day, drinking their *chai* and reading the papers. Now, all the cars and drivers have been banned from the property until after the *sangeet*.

P had been taking photos of the *milni* and the bangle ceremony, when she saw Christina running down the driveway towards the gate instead of going into the house. Nobody else seemed to have noticed. P caught up with her just before she reached the end of the property. 'Where are you going? What's wrong?' P asked her. When Christina turned around she saw that she was crying.

'P, I don't think I can go through with this,' she said looking seriously worried.

'What do you mean? The *sangeet*?' P really didn't know what she was talking about, it definitely couldn't be the wedding, she thought. Christina and Andy are the perfect couple. Both have worked hard to prepare for this wedding. Both families seem more or less happy as well.

'No, the wedding! This was all a big mistake. I am not ready for this.' Christina said tearfully. Some of the drivers had heard them approach and were now standing in the gate watching them. P told them to get lost, more rudely then she intended to, finding it all this very confusing. She tells Christina to calm down and asks where they could have a private chat. 'Let's just drive back to the city,' Christina said, but P convinces her to stay and they end up on the bench behind the house.

'Now, tell me what happened? Something must have happened because from what I can tell, this is a dream wedding. This is better than any wedding I have seen. There's usually some big drama going on between the families. So many expectations from both sides! If the couple is from the same community, it is usually about money. If they are Indian from the same city but different religions, it is about traditions. If they are Indian, but God forbid from two different states, it is usually about the colour of the skin. You being *firangi*, all the above is expected but easily avoided since the usual rules can't be applied anymore. Any drama from Andalip's family is just the usual way of making sure that people know the elders are still in charge. I can bet they are enjoying showing off their European daughter-in-law to their friends. Any drama from your family is normal. You are moving to a developing country and might be lost to the world. But after seeing this week-long party, you being treated like a queen and enjoying tea in bed, I bet your mother is envious of you, never having to cook, clean or work again in your life. Honestly, Chrissie, I am!' P speaks while Christina just stares into the night.

When the music switches from Punjabi to German, Christina starts crying again. 'Did I say anything wrong just now?' P worries.

Christina wipes her face with her *duppata* and P realizes that the hair stylist had finally managed to find some blonde hair extensions. If it was not for the colour, Christina's hair looks as full and as decorated as any Punjabi bride's. Her eyes are outlined with black *kajal*. A perfect line of semi-precious *bindis* follows her eyebrows. Her jewellery is simple. P guesses Christina is happy to wear her own rather than the stolen baubles. Anyway, she has never seen her friend looking more beautiful. In the semi-dark, she looked like the perfect Indian bride.

Christina must have sensed her thoughts. 'Just look at me. This is not me! I know all this is very nice, but I have no idea who this person is.' Christina gets up and swirls around in her *lehenga*. The little bells at the end of her *duppata* make faint tingling sounds. Christina sits down and continues: 'On top of it, this wedding seems to be happening with or without me. I could easily be replaced. I was told to sit on the sidelines during the *path*, which is OK since that is how things are done. The *mehendi* was fun but Dadi thinks my marriage is doomed. Does she seriously believe I cursed my children when my arm got cut and blood dripped on the coconuts in my lap? Andy and I haven't spoken a single word tonight. I was locked in my room while he was getting drunk. I feel like I have no control over my life anymore. I don't know what is going on at this wedding let alone how to deal with any situation in daily life. The driver giggles when I give directions. The maid stares at me whenever I enter the room. Half the conversations in the house I don't understand. Not even if they are in Hindi. Even the conversations in English seem hard to follow. What do I know about Indian cooking? Do I really care where to get the best deals on fabrics? I grew up eating meat. How can it be bad to have a steak once in a while? Do I really disrespect my parents by making my own choices in life after they have educated me and made me independent?'

P realizes Christina has much more to say, but she fears that her friend will have a nervous breakdown any minute. She holds her by the shoulders: 'Stop it Chrissie! You are just panicking right now. Of course you are new here but you will learn. I bet within a year you will speak Hindi better than me. Andy loves you. He will be there to help you. You don't have to be a pro right away. Take it like one of your research papers. Learn something new every day. Now, enjoy your wedding!'

Christina doesn't look convinced. 'But everywhere I go, I will always stick out. I am white and blonde and, on top of that, at least a head taller than everyone in the house. I will never fit in! Maybe Dadi is right and we should listen to all the signs around us. It can't be a coincidence that the jewellery was stolen.'

'Now you are talking nonsense. What can be better place to steal jewellery from than a house where a wedding is taking place? Even better, a rich Punjabi family wedding in Central Delhi. If I were a thief, your in-laws' house would be the first one I would be watching. And please, don't listen to all that talk about *karma*, omens and God's wishes. If your union was not meant to be, how did you even meet and end up living together without any disaster happening. You seemed totally happy. There were no omens!' P tries to convince her friend.

Both women sit in silence for a while. The music has stopped but before long the DJ announces another round of Punjabi dance hits. They can hear people scream in excitement. 'Listen to this. All these people are here for you and Andalip. Shouldn't we join them?' P gets up and gestures to Christina to follow her.

'I can't. They are just having fun because most of them are drunk. Including the groom. I am telling you, once they are sober it will start again. Andalip's family will worry about how I'll fit into their life and society and traditions in Delhi. My family will worry whether I will turn Indian and forget about my family and upbringing. Every step we take will be watched. And what if it doesn't work out? Imagine the 'I-told-you-so' from both sides? I've already had to answer as to what will happen after our divorce. My mom thinks my in-laws will keep the kids and make sure I never see them again. Andy's mom thinks I will run off to Germany with them and never let them set foot on Indian soil again. What if Andy realizes in a few years that he would have been happier with an Indian wife? What if I don't like it here? Where will I go?' Christina's voice is breaking. Tears fill her eyes again.

'Christina, listen to me. No matter where you are from, you cannot plan your life. Nobody knows what will happen to us or where life will leads us. In Germany, you might think you can, but that might only be true for certain aspects of life. Like when you wait for a train, most likely it will arrive on time. People might work in the same job all their lives. When you go to the supermarket, you know what you will be able to buy. But no matter in which part of the world you're getting married in, whether it is for love or your parents' choice, no matter which religion you follow in and no matter what colour of your skin is, you have no idea what life has in store for you. There is no guarantee you will have children. No guarantee you will be healthy or even alive throughout your marriage. There might be natural disasters, family battles, or a big financial crisis. Nobody knows. And it is up to you and Andy how you manoeuvre your path through it. You are in India now, you better start listening to the voice inside you, your heart for all I care, and learn some of the ancient wisdom of life. Learn what is really important. Trust your choices. Trust your choice for a life partner. Marriage is work like so many things in life. But, most important, have fun whenever you can and all will be fine.' For a moment, P feels like one of those preachers she sometimes watches accidently on Sunday morning TV in NYC. What else can she tell Christina to get over her uncertainty?

To her surprise, Christina gets up. She wipes her tears with her *duppata*. For the first time this evening, P sees Christina smile. 'You are absolutely right, P. I am sorry for losing it like this. From New York, this seemed a little easier than I expected. Maybe I am a little nervous about the wedding day. I am so glad you are here. What would I do without you?' Christina hugs her friend. 'Let's go and join the party. And catch up with those drunks out there!' she laughs and takes P's hand.

'Just in time for the item numbers!' Jazz greets Christina and P. 'And Andy has been missing you,' Jazz winks at her. Just then Andalip appears next to her. 'There you are my beautiful bride!' he says, kissing her on the cheek.

'Let's see who can perform better tonight. Your relatives or mine!' Christina giggles and watches how Fiona and Aisha position themselves in the middle of the dance floor. The music starts and both start dancing. Everybody claps.

'I love you, Andalip Singh. Do you want to marry me?' she leans over and whispers into his ear.

'I will. In less than 48 hours you will officially be mine. Until then, let's have some fun.' Andy says and pushes Christina onto the dance floor. The crowd cheers.

Christina copies her niece and swings her hips. Her cousins push Andy right into her arms. 'Let's have some fun baby!' Christina laughs, finally ready to get married!

Chapter 31

The morning after the *sangeet* and a day before the actual wedding, Andalip and Christina are having a late breakfast with their respective parents in Lodi-The Garden Restaurant. The temperature is pleasant with fans and water sprayers cooling the air. Andalip chose a table outside, under a large tree overlooking the garden restaurant. Everybody is sitting back in the low garden chairs enjoying their morning coffee and tea in silence. The restaurant is empty. Besides a handful of waiters, the only other visitors are birds of all colours and sizes.

Last night's party officially ended after dinner was served at around midnight. The music was turned down and the lights became brighter. Guests said their goodbyes, all of them looking forward to the rest of the wedding functions. Only the families and close friends stayed on. Once again the bar opened and the dance floor was full. It was almost close to sunrise when the farmhouse in Pushpanjali fell quiet. Pretty much everybody had too much to drink last night and longed to sleep in.

Still disturbed by the theft, Anhad had woken everyone up at 8 am, calling a family meeting to discuss the still unsolved crime. Even though Raj had been identified as the thief and had been arrested by the police, the jewellery had not yet been found. What if the theft was not as straight-forward as they first thought? How would the wedding proceed? How would the family deal with Dadi who was still convinced that the crime was a sign from God to stop the wedding? Everyone was chatting, turning the recent developments into Bollywood movie scripts. Only a few minutes into the discussion, Andalip had gotten mad at his family to even think of linking the lost jewellery to the outcome of his wedding. He ended the meeting by storming out of the house. Bopinder had told everyone to return to their rooms. He would be handling the situation from now on. 'There's nothing we can do so early in the morning. Go back to bed if you can. Tomorrow will be another long day!' he said to calm everybody down. While he was getting ready for the day, he received a phone call from Andalip. 'Please tell Mom to come and meet me, Christina and her parents for brunch to discuss what's going on!'

Unlike last night, the mood is sombre this morning in the cafe in Lodhi Garden. Michael is the first one to break the silence. 'This is what I always wanted to see for myself.' Michael lifts his arms and gestures all around him: 'Look at the beauty of all of this! I've been reading about India a lot, trust me. Visitors to your country describe its natural beauty, ancient history and incomparable knowledge about life in many ways. Now I am sitting here and seeing it for myself, thanks to you. This place is truly amazing! You have this oasis, almost a jungle with century-old tombs and monuments, palm trees, birds and flowers from paradise in the middle of one of the largest metropolises in the world. As kids in school we learned about India being a developing country. Whenever India was in the news they would show these little dirty faces begging for food. But today, you have definitely arrived amongst the world's biggest players. My daughter is moving here at the right time in history. Just look at all those fancy cars out there. I've noticed people reading newspapers from across the world, wearing designer clothes sold along the world's most sophisticated boulevards and avenues. We are sipping cappuccinos, eating French toast, listening to world music while the waiters over there are waiting to fulfil our every need. Hamburg seems like a small village in comparison. Especially now in November, when it's rainy and grey! Like we say in Germany, it is nice to live in a place where other people go on vacation. I absolutely love being here. I could get used to this in a minute.' He smiles at Andy and his family sitting across from him. He feels like he sounds a little shallow. He wants to discuss global business strategies and India's role in IT and medicine. Let them know that he truly admires India's achievements, but instead he chats away about fashion and cars. Maybe that is OK too, he figures. How much of a serious conversation can you have after litres of beer, he smiles.

'Oh, I am so glad you like it here.' Kiran replies happily. 'This is our home and we want you to feel welcome any time. Whenever you want to come and see the children, remember that this is your home too. It is such an honour for us to have the children move back to Delhi and live with us. I know Christina will soon feel very much at home here!' Unlike the previous days, Kiran is dressed much more casual today. Michael notices the beautiful flower print on the long *kurta* that she is wearing over what looks to him like white leggings underneath. The long shawls of her party outfits have been replaced by a smaller scarf around her neck. Her hair is braided instead of being held tightly back, and he realizes how long her black hair reaches down her back. She must have been a stunning young woman, he thinks and he catches himself smiling at her.

A waiter arrives with the first round of breakfast dishes. Everybody sits back quietly again, waiting for him to finish serving. Michael's head is hurting. From the look on the others' faces, he is sure he is not alone. As soon as the waiter leaves, Andalip decides to address the issue of the lost jewellery again.

'I am very sorry that I have to bring this up again, but I just wanted to make sure that all of us agree to continue with the wedding, whether we find the jewellery or not.' Andy says, looking around for some reaction. Michael just nods. Bärbel, Christina and he had discussed this earlier. They were not sure what their proper reaction should be regarding the theft. Of course it was a terrible loss. He was not sure how much the monetary loss would actually amount to, but he was sure that the real problem was more because of personal loss and sentimental value. It didn't matter to him and his wife if Christina inherits these jewels. He had made sure she was educated and able to look after herself. If his daughters were ever in need of money, Michael had invested enough for both of them to be looked after when he was not around to do so himself. He did not believe in bad omens and saw no reason to postpone his daughter's wedding. Honestly, he thought it's nice of Andy to involve them in this discussion but the kids need to solve this problem themselves. They are grown-up and in charge of their lives. Wedding included! If he was in Germany, he would let them handle this alone. But the last three days have been full of new impressions and insights on Indian culture. From what he understood from Christina, his family and their opinion was very important to Andy, so he was willing to help out as much as he was able too. Right now, he thought not saying too much would do the trick.

'Bopinder. Kiran. We are from different cultures and we do not know what the right procedures are. We will do whatever you think is right. But let me tell you one thing. We are very happy about the children's union. We feel that jewellery or not, they should get married!' He takes Bärbel's hand and nods at her: 'Right, *schatz*, that is pretty much what we think.' Christina gets up and hugs them both. '*Danke*, Papa. I knew you would say that!'

'So, Mom, Dad. What do you think? Christina and I want to get married tomorrow and not postpone the wedding until this is solved. Who knows if we will ever find the jewellery again. For all we know it's being sold off somewhere in China right now. I say we just get some temporary replacements from Lajpat Nagar today for the wedding and address the rest later.' Andy gestures Christina to sit next to him. 'I'll take you shopping on our honeymoon. You can choose some new jewellery if you want!'

Michael knows Andy will be a great husband. They are such a good-looking couple, he thinks while starting on his breakfast. So far Kiran and Bopinder have not responded, he notices. Both of them are eating their breakfast with great concentration. Bopinder is the first to empty his plate. He calls the waiter to clear it and bring him some more *chai*. Michael admires Bopinder's appearance, he looks tall and regal with his turban. Even in jeans and polo shirt, he looks polished and very presentable, Michael observes. For a moment Michael wonders if it was OK to show up in shorts this morning. Even though he's attending a wedding, he wants to feel like he is on a vacation, he contemplates while brushing some crumbs off his bare knees.

'Here is the thing, son,' Bopinder starts, then pauses to see if he's got everybody's attention. Michael feels the urge to put his cutlery down, sit up straight and look alert. 'This jewellery has been handed down from generation to generation of our family. With each new daughter in the house, new pieces have been added. I honestly don't know how many generations ago this tradition had started. I don't know who gave what and which pieces are lost. I am not so interested in earrings and necklaces myself.' Bopinder laughs loudly while accepting a fresh cup of *chai*. After taking a few sips he turns serious again and continues.

'All I know is that my mother received these treasures from her mother-in-law, with great formality and many blessings. Kiran here was presented with the jewellery at her wedding in the same way. Now it would have been Christina's turn.' Everybody nods, waiting for Bopinder to continue. 'This wedding is different from the other weddings in our family so far. We broke with traditions in many ways. Having Christina in our house before the official blessing by our priests. Leaving the jewellery in her room instead of presenting it to her the traditional way. I honestly don't know what went wrong and how the jewellery could have gotten lost. I don't know if Dadi is right about worrying about *karma* and omens and bad signs.' He pauses, then looks at Andy: 'I know that I love you my son and I want you to be happy. So if you want to get married tomorrow, we will not be against it.'

Michael is relieved. At least Andy's parents seem to be willing to go on with the wedding. Andy gets up and touches his parents' feet, hugs them both and thanks them for supporting him. Then Michael realizes that his daughter seems upset. She is still sitting on the sofa, her arms crossed in front of her chest, staring at Andy. 'Are you OK?' he whispers to his daughter. But he doesn't receive an answer until Andy sits down again.

'*Nein*, I am not OK, Papa.' Christina replies loudly. Almost simultaneously, Michael and Andy put their arms around her. 'What's wrong?' they ask.

'Christina, don't you understand what Dad just said? They are fine with the wedding being held tomorrow. Jewellery found or not. We focus on our wedding first and deal with this later. Now what is your problem?' Andy asks.

'You really don't know? Maybe we should not discuss this in front of everybody?' Christina says. Andy looks confused. Michael is surprised by his daughter's reaction.

'No, let's discuss it now. We are all family and everybody should be involved in solving this,' Andy responds.

Christina takes her time to reply. She looks flustered, trying to find the right words. She looks at Bopinder. Before addressing him directly, she changes her mind and talks to Andy. 'I am sorry Andy, but it sounds to me like your parents think it is my fault that the jewellery is lost. 'Having Christina in our house before the official blessing by our priests... leaving the jewellery in her room instead of officially presenting it to her the traditional way...' What does that mean? It sounds to me like they are just agreeing to the wedding tomorrow because they love you. Not because they love the idea of you getting married to me. If I am getting blamed for things going wrong at the wedding, what will I be blamed for the next time something else goes amiss? And you told me yourself, Dadi got stressed out preparing for the wedding and that is why she fell ill last month. What if she falls sick again? Maybe it will be my fault for not producing an heir quickly enough or not quitting my job and learning to be a good Indian wife? How can you act like nothing has happened when obviously some people are not happy about this and blame me for every little screw up in their lives...' Christina stops.

Michael is confused. He is not sure he is able to follow what his daughter is saying. Bärbel definitely does not understand. 'What's going on Christina? Who said you stole the jewellery?' Kiran gets up and walks over. 'No Bärbel, nobody said Christina stole the jewellery. Your daughter is just getting a little upset here and mixing things up. Don't worry, everything will be fine.' Michael is not so sure considering the look on his daughter's face.

'Christina, how can you talk like this?' Andy asks, obviously mad at Christina. 'All my dad said...' he starts but Kiran interrupts him.

'Christina, you are mixing things up here,' says Kiran. 'Everybody is under a lot of stress. This theft is a big tragedy for us and we would like to solve it quickly. But Andy and you are our children and more important to us than anything else. Nobody is blaming anybody. Let's just enjoy the rest of the festivities and get you kids married tomorrow.' Kiran leans down to hug her. Christina hugs her back without saying anything. Instead of her, Andy apologizes to his parents.

They start eating again, and for a while the conversations turns to general small talk. Michael asks a lot of questions about India and Bopinder happily answers them. Bärbel and Kiran are discussing beauty and fashion. Universal to all women in this world, Michael thinks, glad that the conversation on the wedding has ended.

He observes that Andy and Christina are not talking, but decides to leave them alone. He wonders if anybody else has noticed the silence between them. His heart is aching, knowing that in a few days his daughter will be married and officially living in India. How often will he see her now? He will have to share her with all these new family members. He hopes that she will be happy and comfortable with her new life. He hopes that Kiran is right and that it is just nerves that are messing with her mind right now. He hopes Andy is right and his parents will love his chosen wife like a daughter. He knows he likes Andy a lot but men always seem to have a different relationship than women. Life in India is different and he hopes that his daughter will enjoy learning about it. His thoughts are interrupted by his wife speaking loudly on his right. Obviously the conversation has shifted from fashion but he is not sure what the women are talking about. His wife is struggling to find the right words in English.

'Michael, you have to translate this for me. I think I said something wrong.' Bärbel sounds anxious. Andy is getting up and telling his parents to calm down and just go back to the house and rest. Bopinder shakes Michael's hand and apologizes for leaving. Kiran bids goodbye but seems upset about something. She smiles but unlike before she seems stiff and tired. While his parents head towards the exit, Andy sits down again and tells Christina to just back off a bit. 'Maybe I was wrong to involve everybody in this discussion about the jewellery and the wedding. But you should not talk to my parents like this. And maybe you should tell your parents a little bit about India's traditions and culture to make sure nobody fights before the wedding in the morning. I suggest you take them out for dinner tonight or something and we'll talk later.' He kisses her on the cheek. It seems more like a formality than affection and Andy leaves without waiting for anybody else's response.

'What just happened?' Michael asks.

Christina gets up. 'Thanks Mom. This is really not what I need right now. Everybody is already irritated enough without you criticizing Indian society as a whole. I'll see you later at the house…' She runs after Andy and catches up with her soon-to-be-husband just as he exits through the gate.

'Again, Bärbel, what just happened?' Michael asks his wife one more time.

Bärbel looks hurt. 'I am not sure. We were just talking about weddings in general. I said something about all the beauty and wealth in this country. Just like you said earlier. Then I wondered how a country which produces such wealth and beauty could also be so poor. And that it is no wonder that somebody would steal the jewellery since there are so many people who have nothing to eat. Did you see the children this morning running after us begging for food? Barefoot and all! Or even the maids in the house, living in shacks on the roof, eating the leftovers. Did you ask Christina how much these people make in a month? I bet it is less than what Christina's new relatives spend on a good dinner and drinks on any Saturday night. People must get envious seeing the amount of food being consumed and wasted the last three days. New flowers, new decoration, new clothes—sometimes twice a day! One could feed an entire family for a year with all of that. Anybody out there could be a suspect for taking money or anything else from the house. People must be envious of the Singhs' lifestyle being showcased like that during the wedding week. I was just wondering out loud why such a well-educated man like Raj would steal the jewellery. But nobody seems to wonder about that. What traditions are we talking about, whose blessings… I am sure there is enough to be blessed. And then why is it Christina's fault if the jewellery is gone? If you cannot even be safe in your own apartment, worrying all the time that people might steal something out of a locked closet in your bedroom, then maybe it is not safe for our daughter to live in Delhi…'

Michael shakes his head. He is not sure how much of this she had told Kiran. Or how much of what she had said, was clear enough for Andy's mom to understand. Bärbel often mixed up English with German and he hoped that some of her points were lost in translation. From the look on Kiran's face, he is worried that this time his wife had managed quiet well to get her point across. '*Schatz*, how could you? It is one thing to think about this or even discuss it with me or our daughter, but how can you say that to Andy's parents. You don't know much about this culture. Better not say too much until you know his parents better or until you truly understand life over here. Imagine Bopinder and Kiran coming to Hamburg and pointing out the homeless at Hamburg Hauptbahnhof to you and blaming you for walking around in a fur coat and driving a Mercedes instead of feeding the poor. Really Bärbel, I can't blame them for being mad. Let's just go home too and see what we can do to make everybody happy again!'

'Michael, all I am saying is that it is not fair to blame Christina for what has happened when …' Bärbel starts but gets interrupted again. '*Schatz*, please, save this for one of your Rotary meetings. Nobody is blaming anybody. Let's focus on the wedding. And let's try to find some flowers for Kiran to distract her mind from your speech!'

Chapter 32

In the afternoon, Anhad and Andalip decide to drive to the gurudwara to check the arrangements for tomorrow's wedding ceremony. Andy and Christina had chosen the gurudwara in Greater Kailash II, even though it was neither closest to their house nor the most impressive of Delhi's gurudwaras. But it was the one the family enjoyed visiting the most. Manjeet, who is very involved in its activities, had helped to finalize the formalities for tomorrow.

Andy feels a little guilty as they drive up the little hill to the entrance of the gurudwara. He used to spend a lot of time here when his Dada was still alive, but when he passed away, his dad would take him along whenever he was on a visit from New York. In the last few years though he had avoided visiting it, and the closest he came to God was during prayers in the house. When he steps of the car, he is greeted by the aroma of sweet *prasad* and the voice of a *piji* reading from the Guru Granth Sahib. He feels welcome. He takes off his shoes and is about to follow Anhad when he realises that he needs something to cover his head with. After tying an orange piece of cloth around his head, he enters the spacious prayer room. He looks around but can't find his cousin amongst the many turbaned sardars sitting and standing reverently around the Guru Granth Sahib. He decides to pay his respects and bows down, dropping some money before the prayer book. Then he sits down on the floor and instead of looking for Anhad, he listens to the *kirtan* for a while.

He's only been in Delhi for less than a week, but he feels as if he's been home for much longer. He watches the people around him. The men seem fine, but the women are getting a bit out of hand, he smiles to himself. He sees a little girl dressed in a *lehenga* dancing around her father who is sitting with his eyes closed, trying to sing along with the prayer. Andy tries to picture his future children. Would he bring them here to listen to the prayers once in a while? He wants a little girl like that one, obviously loving her dad and not letting go of him for a minute. He pictures a smaller version of Christina, but with darker hair and blue eyes. Then he notices an older woman walking over to the little girl, taking her away from her father and telling her to sit down and listen to the music. She reminds him of Dadi, strict but full of love.

Thinking of his grandmother and how she has aged makes Andy's heart ache. He hopes that she will be around to see the birth of her great-grandchildren. Suddenly he feels the urge to rush home and ask her once again what she thinks about the wedding. He wants her not only to agree to the wedding but truly believe that Andy's choice for a wife is right. He had thought that by just telling his grandmother that he wanted things done in a certain way, she would, over time, put aside her concerns about traditions and culture and accept his choice. Surely she must realize that times are changing, he thinks. But after seeing her demean us over the last few days, he wonders if she will ever change and understand him. He feels that he is right in what he believes. Also, deep in his heart, he understands her concerns as well. Unfortunately, both points of view are too contradictory to reach a common ground. He wants to tell her that if she just gives Christina another chance, she will soon realize that he is right. She, too, must have been young and rebellious at one time, he contemplates while he walks past the little girl now sitting quietly between her father and grandmother.

There's still no sign of Anhad, so he heads out, accepting the *prasad* in the palm of his hands as he steps into the courtyard. While enjoying the hot, very sweet mixture of *ghee*, *atta* and sugar under the shade of a large palm tree, Andy spots Anhad with a *piji* in tow.

'There you are!' Andy calls out and beckons at his cousin to come over. Anhad looks worried and he sits down on a bench next to Andy. Piji catches up with them and greets Andy with his hands folded and a loud '*Sat Sri Akal*'. Andy returns the greeting and waits for one of them to talk, while licking the rest of the delicious *prasad* from his figure tips.

'Beta, good to see you after so long,' Piji says. Andy is not sure if he has met this particular priest before but nods respectfully and thanks him for the warm welcome. Then Piji tells him the bad news: 'I am very sorry, but we cannot hold the wedding at this gurudwara tomorrow morning.'

Andy is confused. 'Why not? I thought Bua had made all the arrangements months ago? Is there a problem with the booking? Do we need to pay anything? Do we need to talk to anybody else for the ceremony, the musicians, the caterers? I hope no one else got our spot.'

'It is not that, Beta. I don't know how to say this without offending anybody. All is fine, but we don't conduct weddings like yours. I am very sorry, I tried to explain this to Anhadji, but he said I should talk to you directly.'

'What do you mean?' Andy asks. 'Weddings like mine?'

'I mean we could probably come to your house and conduct the ceremony. When your Bua did the booking, your family did not mention that you are marrying somebody from outside the country...I assumed...you know...' Piji stutters.

'You mean nobody told you that I am going to marry a foreigner? That shouldn't be a problem. I thought Sikhism is open to other religions. So who has a problem with us getting married here at the gurudwara? You? Tell me who I should speak with to resolve this. I am sure this is a big misunderstanding, right?' Andy tries to be polite.

Piji is standing in front of him, shaking his head. 'No, Beta, I don't have a problem. It is just... this can't be done here. Once we start with you, others will follow as well. I am happy to come over to your house and perform the ceremony. We can work something out, I am sure. You just cannot have the wedding here.'

'What do you mean by "we can work something out"? You want me to pay you for coming to my house to marry me after you have refused to do so here in the house of God. So you can pocket the money and keep it to yourself? All in the name of religion... What religion is this which refuses to marry people from different countries?' Andy is angry. He wants to say much more but stops himself. He wants to shake the man but knows this is not the right place. From the look on his face, Andy knows Anhad must have already tried to talk to Piji and was unable to convince him either.

'Let's go Anhad. We are done here. I can't believe what I've just heard. Let's find another place for the wedding.' Andy turns around to leave, but Anhad holds him back: 'Wait, Bhaiya. Let's sit down again and try to solve this right here. I am sure it is not Piji's fault that we cannot hold the wedding here. It is not Christina's either. Maybe if we avoid the prayer hall and use one of the rooms in the back? Maybe we can convince them that Christina is an American Sikh? Or we can donate something to the gurudwara to save their face over this issue?' Anhad looks back and forth between Andalip and Piji.

'Enough Anhad. Listen to yourself. I've heard enough from both of you to know that this is not where we are getting married tomorrow.' With that Andy leaves without listening to further arguments. When Anhad catches up with him at the car, Andy tells the driver to go back to the house.

'Do me a favour and don't discuss this with anybody until I have spoken to my parents. We are shifting the wedding to Golf Links. I will handle it…' Andy says. Without another word, they drive back to the house.

❦

Andy storms up the stairs right into his parents' bedroom. Instead of finding his parents taking an afternoon nap as usual, the room is crowded with his sisters, their husbands and kids, and Dadi sitting there drinking tea. 'Come join the party,' Simran calls out when he enters.

'Oh, teatime, I forgot,' he says and sits next to his father on the bed. The conversation resumes and laughter fills the room. 'I need to talk to you. Now and if possible alone! I don't want to discuss this with everybody.' Andy tells Bopinder and gets up to walk to the other bedroom. A few seconds later both his mother and father walk into the room. 'Close the door,' he tells them and gestures that they sit down while he paces up and down in front of them. Both do as they are told.

'What happened? I hope it is not because of this morning? Like I said, I honestly believe everybody is a little tense and whatever anybody said, it is OK. Let's just get you guys married,' Kiran says looking at her son worried.

'It's not that Mom. I just got back from the gurudwara. It turns out that we cannot get married there.'

'What?' Bopinder gets up.'What are you talking about? Let me talk to Piji. Don't listen to …'

'No, Dad, it's OK. I've made up my mind. I have done enough talking and I don't want to hear anything else about it. I've decided that we will just shift the wedding here. I will find another *piji*. I will organize it and you just show up. I am sorry but there is just too much going on and I don't want anything else to mess up this wedding,' Andy says firmly.

'But, Beta, where will we fit everybody? Have you thought about the logistics? What about the ceremony, the lunch afterwards? Who will inform the guests about the change in venue? Hundreds of guests have been invited to attend your wedding in GKII, not here. What happened at the gurudwara? Let me just talk to them again, or better still, ask your *bua* to talk to them,' Bopinder tries to convince his son.

'I am sorry Dad. It's too late. I will ask Jazz to help me with the logistics. We have the entire afternoon to figure this out. We will be fine. Don't worry!' With that he storms out of the room, leaving his stunned parents behind. He heads over to the other room and tells his sister to follow him.

'I need your help, Jazz!' Andy pleads with his sister while pulling her down the stairs. 'All will be fine…' he says to her while sitting in the car, more to convince himself than his sister who still has no idea about what is going on.

Chapter 33

Jazz watches her brother talking on the phone. He still looks like the teenager she remembers except that his hair is starting to turn grey and his eyes look tired. She is trying to find out what is going on but cannot make out who he is talking to. When he hangs up, she waits for him to speak, but Andalip just stares out of the window.

'OK. Can you please tell me what is going on? Where are we going?' she asks.

'We are going out for coffee,' he answers without further explanation.

'I was having coffee at home right now. What happened? Why are you like this?' Jazz wants answers, but her brother ignores her. After just a short drive, they stop in front of a small coffee shop in Nizamuddin East. Jazz follows her brother inside. He orders for both of them. She lets him, knowing something must have happened. She has rarely seen her brother acting like this. Only when the coffee arrives, does Andalip start talking.

'I am sorry for dragging you out of the house like this. I just needed to get away from everybody. This whole wedding is getting to me I think. It's only been three days but something or the other seems to go wrong. Was your wedding this stressful?' Andy pauses and looks at his sister. She nods but does not know how to answer him. Without waiting for response, Andy continues: 'Maybe I have been living in New York too long. Maybe people in the West are really smart to just have a one-day wedding. Entertaining so many people for so many days has to end in disaster.' Andy pauses again. Jazz is wondering what exactly he is talking about. When she had spoken to him earlier in the day, he seemed pretty relaxed about the theft. He was getting fed up that Dadi was still not supporting the wedding, but she thought he had handled his grandmother's behaviour rather well. Andy had given his grandmother the respect she was entitled to by listening to her concerns and trying to follow traditions as much as possible, at the same time he did not budge from his decision to marry Christina. She admires her big brother once again for going his own way. Still he remains close to all and loved by his family. Her life is much more dictated by what her family, her husband's family and children demand, she thinks.

'Now, Christina is starting to get nervous about Dadi's talk about omens and bad *karma*. Actually, I don't really know what she is thinking, since I don't get to talk to her much. Which is not really the point... Her family seems tense too.' Andy seems confused. Jazz still doesn't understand what is going on. 'Bhaiya, what are you saying? Is everything OK? Did anything happen this morning at brunch?'

Andy shakes his head: 'No, just the usual cross-cultural misunderstanding between the moms, but that was sorted out right there and then. I think they actually get along great. If they could meet on neutral territory, not during a wedding, they might actually become good friends.' Andy stops and looks at his sister for a while before continuing: 'Jazz, I don't know what is going on with me. I don't think it is Christina who is getting worried about Dadi's talk, it is actually me. Please don't say this to anybody. You know I don't believe in all these superstitious things. I don't want to disrespect Dadi, but I think either she is right or she is manipulating our wedding.'

Jazz can't believe her ears. 'What? Why would you say something like that?'

'I went to the gurudwara today. Anhad came along. We wanted to make sure everything is set for tomorrow morning. And guess what, it is not. Piji told us we cannot get married there. Supposedly they don't do weddings with foreigners. Piji claims he didn't know that Christina was not an Indian until just now. Otherwise he said he would have told us earlier that we can't get married at the gurudwara. How is that possible, Jazz? Bua has organized everything and they know her. They know the family. What is the big deal all of a sudden? Piji tried to make me feel better by telling me he could get me married somewhere else, but it sounded to me like he was looking for some extra money. I just don't know. Maybe Anhad, Bua or Dad could have talked to them again and figured it out, but that comment about not marrying a foreigner at the gurudwara just did it. I lost it! I am not willing to bribe a Piji to do my wedding. I am not willing to let Dadi's talk creep into my head and question my decision about my wedding now. I love Christina. I know she is the right choice. I just feel like I am losing control here… That's why I told him, we are not going to discuss this further. I will find another way to get married tomorrow. I don't need the gurudwara. I want to find somebody else who can bless our marriage without having to bribe a man of God…. Only problem is, I cannot do it alone. Can you help me get this done, Jazz?'

'You did what?' Jazz is shocked. 'Andy, it's 4 pm. How will we organize this in such a short time?' Looking at her brother she knows he is serious and is not going to change his mind. Her head is starting to spin. 'So where are we going to hold the wedding?'

'Let's just do it at home.' Andy replies. She knows he has already made up his mind, but doubts they will be able to pull off the wedding in the house.

'We need a bigger space, Andy.' She has an idea: 'What about the park in front? I have seen parties being held there. I have a contact for the Resident Welfare Association. I can ask them what needs to be done to hold a wedding there. We might have to pay them some money though,' she says. She pulls out her diary and starts taking notes.

'I knew you would be the one to figure this out. Thanks Jazz!' Andy reaches across the table and squeezes her hand.

'Not so fast. There is lots to do. You better start calling all the guests and tell them that the venue has changed. Well, first let me talk to the RWA, the caterer, the tent people. Not to forget a new *piji* for the ceremony.' Jazz smiles. This might actually be fun, she thinks to herself and gets busy looking through her phone and diary for all the contacts that she needed.

Chapter 34

Just a couple of hours later, Andy finds himself standing in the park across from his parents' house. Both his dad and *chacha* have joined him to meet with Mr Gupta from the RWA. Two police officers have arrived as well. The six men look slightly out of place amongst the evening walkers and kids playing in the park before sunset.

Ranveer Chacha does most of the talking, since Andy and Bopinder are too distraught to get the job done. Bopinder had accepted Andy's request to change the wedding venue only because Anhad had told him about the discussion at the gurudwara and how upset Andalip was. He assured Bopinder that they would be able to switch the venue without any problems. Bopinder did not want to fight but he was still upset about the last minute confusion.

Andy had decided it was best to ask Ranveer Chacha for help, since he was very involved in the community and had good contacts with the local politicians and police. Andy preferred to stay on the sidelines for this discussion. Too many things seemed to be out of his hands these days and he wondered, if he had lost his Indian toughness to deal with delicate situations like these. How would he address the man from the RWA? Whom would they need to offer money to? How much was appropriate? What was the right balance between power and obedience?

'So we are expecting between 200 and 300 people to join us for the wedding tomorrow morning. Not all at the same time, but in and out all morning. We will need a tent for the ceremony, big enough for the wedding party to sit and walk around the Guru Granth Sahib and for the *kirtan*. We will need carpets and chairs. Afterwards we will serve lunch, so we will require an area to set up the buffet, tables and chairs for the guests and a small area to conceal all the dirty work.' While Ranveer explains the basic set-up for the wedding, Mr Gupta listens with a smile and underlines each sentence with a 'Theek hai'. The police officers seem to be more interested in the activity in the park than in the wedding planning, walking a few metres ahead of the rest of the group.

When Ranveer finishes, the group stops. 'So, are we all set?' Andy asks, not sure if he followed the entire conversation. Mr Gupta smiles: 'Yes, all set, Beta. Like your *chacha* said, after the wedding, your family will take care of cleaning up and beautifying the park and make sure that it looks better than before. I will arrange for new gardeners, benches, play equipment on your behalf and everybody will be happy about this wedding.'

The men shake hands. Mr Gupta excuses himself and says he will stop by in the morning, wishing Andalip best of luck. Andy smiles and is ready to head to the house, when he notices the two police officers still hanging around. 'Should we go Dad?' Andy asks. Bopinder nods and exchanges a look with Ranveer. 'Why don't you gentlemen have a cup of *chai* at the house before you return to work?' Ranveer says before he starts walking across the grass towards the gate.

Of course, Andy thinks, this would have been too easy if we just had to look after the park to hold the wedding there. He hopes that not too much money will be spent on paying all these people off. He really did not see this coming. Again, he feels a little helpless and wonders if he has been away too long to know how things are done in India. He assumed things might have changed a bit. He feels guilty to have gotten the entire family involved in this. Well, much better to bribe the police than a priest to get married, he tries to comfort himself. The men start walking across the park and Andy follows them. He decides to just go with the flow and let his *chacha* handle the situation. To take his mind of all the details, he starts chatting with the younger officer who is walking beside him.

'Thank you for coming over this evening. And for such a minor issue like a wedding venue. I am sure there are bigger fish to catch out there.' Andy jokes, more to start a conversation than of any real interest. He hates dealing with the police and is happy that enough people in his family don't have the same feeling.

'Sir, this is no trouble at all. Your family is much respected in this neighbourhood. I was just over at your house the other night, solving the jewellery theft. You had already left for your *sangeet*, I believe. Sir, I have to say that your wedding has been a great blessing for all of us. Your family is very generous. First your grandmother's contribution to help find the thief… Now another round of payment for the wedding venue… Like your Dadi, you are a very big-hearted person!' the officer winks at Andy.

Andalip stops in his tracks. 'Excuse me? What? What do you mean by "Dadi's contribution to help find the thief"?' Andy asks.

The officer looks surprised. 'I am sorry, sir. I did not mean anything. I thought you were also handling your family's affairs.'

'Well, I am handling my family's affairs,' Andy replies harshly. 'As you said, I was already at the *sangeet*. Maybe I missed something that evening. Why don't you fill me in?' The young officer tries to walk away but Andy blocks his way.

'No, no sir. I was just talking…' the officer says nervously. The other officer notices that both Andy and his colleague have stopped. He seems impatient and calls out: '*Chalo*, let's go. We have lots to do.'

Andy grabs the policeman's arm. He cannot find a name tag to place him. I should have listened more carefully when they introduced themselves, he thinks. 'Wait, I am sorry. I did not mean to sound rude. Just tell me one thing, why did you mention my Dadi? Did you deal with her directly as well? What happened in the house the other night?' Andy tries to sound friendly. He smiles but still holds the officer's arm tightly.

Bopinder and Ranveer Chacha have left the park and are walking back to the house. Not wanting to attract more attention than necessary, Andalip decides to continue this discussion later and tells the officer to keep walking towards the house. When they catch up with the older men, Ranveer takes over again and quickly tells everybody to join them for tea. Instead of going upstairs to Bopinder's apartment, the men sit in the entrance hall. Bopinder suggests that Andalip go upstairs to rest, but he wants to stay and see what happens next.

The next 10 minutes pass quickly and Andalip is surprised how casual the meeting seems. As soon as they sit down, Mary serves tea. While Bopinder goes over tomorrow's arrangements for the final time, the two officers just listen, sipping their *chai* and eating biscuits. Just for a minute, Ranveer excuses himself. When he returns, the officers get up and bid goodbye. Ranveer hands them a red invitation card and tells them to attend tomorrow's wedding and lunch. 'Just ignore the venue for the wedding mentioned there and come back here in the morning. We don't want you to head over to the gurudwara,' Ranveer jokes. The police officers laugh and leave the house without further comments.

'That's it?' Andy asks bluntly when the men have left the room. Bopinder and Ranveer smile and nod their heads. Bopinder calls out for another round of hot tea and everybody sits down.

'We are all set for tomorrow. Now let's hope your sisters have been able to reach everybody and people don't show up in GKII,' Ranveer says.

Bopinder laughs: 'I should have made sure to take some names off that list. Maybe this way we can avoid some of your mother's relatives.' Both Bopinder and Ranveer chuckle.

'Very funny, Dad! Don't let Mom hear that,' Andy counters. 'Before I go upstairs and mentally prepare for my wedding, I need to ask you something. I know you think that the Americans have brainwashed me and that I should know better than that, but...' He tries to find the right words. He is not sure what he really wants to ask. He is not surprised that his family had to pay off people to get the wedding venue changed at the last minute. He is not surprised about his family's connections to the police. He was not really surprised that these officers were the same as the ones who came to the house on the night of the theft. He was surprised, however, that the young officer mentioned his grandmother. Wasn't Anhad handling the situation that night? Andy knows his dad is too soft to play the tough guy to get things done and that generally Ranveer Chacha likes to handle the 'dirty work'—as he calls it—around the house, having Anhad act as his right-hand man.

'What do you want to know, Beta? How much we had to pay them to get this done? Don't worry about it. We calculated for situations like this when we planned the wedding budget. Now, as I said, don't worry and get some rest. All will be set for tomorrow,' Bopinder says.

'No, it's not that. It's about the theft. The young officer who I was talking to said something about Dadi having been really generous that night...or something like that. Do you know what he meant? Why was she even involved? And why would she pay him money? For what? We still don't have the jewellery,' Andy wonders.

'You must have misunderstood him, Beta. Anhad was dealing with them. And I am pretty sure that we did not have to bribe anybody to work on the case. Solving a theft is very different from getting permission to hold an event in a public place,' Ranveer responds. 'And I thought your maid saw the thief, anyway. It is weird that the jewellery is still missing, but maybe more than one person was involved. Maybe he was able to sell off the pieces before they arrested him in the morning. He had all night to get rid of any evidence. If we had paid them off, wouldn't you assume that they would have done their job a bit faster and gotten our jewellery back in time.'

Andy is not convinced. The way the officer behaved seemed weird, Andy thinks, but does not want to discuss this further with his *chacha*. He busies himself with checking messages on his phone. It's already late. He should probably go upstairs and tell Christina about the big change in plan, he thinks. He is not sure how much she knows already. He had only briefly seen her again after brunch before he went to the gurudwara. The day has gone by too quickly, he contemplates, finishing his cup of tea. 'So I guess we are pretty much all set for tomorrow, right?' he asks his uncle and father. Unlike him, they seem unconcerned about the officer's comment. Maybe I should forget about it too and focus on my wedding.

'I'll talk to Jazz and make sure everything is under control. I will come up later and talk to you again,' Bopinder replies. Andy hugs both men and thanks them for all their help. 'It sure is hard work getting married,' he jokes before heading up the stairs.

'Oh, this is nothing, son. Wait until you're a husband. Your wife will show you the meaning of hard work!' Bopinder calls after him. He can hear the brothers joking and laughing while he walks up the stairs.

Chapter 35

Just a few minutes later, Ranveer's phone rings. Tripat is looking for him. 'That was the wife! Like you said, Bhaiya, these children will learn about hard work after the wedding. Andalip's honeymoon is over. I am sure he will miss his bachelor life very soon.' Ranveer cannot stop laughing. 'I better head back home before my wife beats me.'

'I should do the same. I am sure my better half plus my daughters are sitting in my bedroom, all chatting on the phone, trying to tell people about the new venue. I better make sure I look concerned that all our relatives know about the change in plan,' Bopinder winks at his brother. 'Now is the chance to cross some people off my list.'

'I will call you later and see if there is anything else I can do. And you better be nice to Kiran's relatives. If she finds out what you are thinking, she will break your legs,' Ranveer says before leaving the house.

Bopinder heads upstairs. Halfway up the stairs, he changes his mind. Maybe I should talk to Mom and see if Andalip's concerns are valid. He knocks once on the door and without waiting for her consent, walks in. His mother is sitting in her chair facing the silent TV. At first he thinks she is sleeping but when he walks around to check, she looks at him. 'What do you want? Can't you knock before storming into my room?' she asks in her usual blunt way.

Bopinder ignores her tone, leans down, kisses her on the forehead and quickly touches her feet. He pulls up a chair and sits down next to her. 'How are you, Maji? He tries to sound casual. He knows his mother is unhappy about Andalip's choice for a wife but deep down he feels that she is actually enjoying the wedding. Since his father died, she has been a little difficult to deal with and often very rude, but he always thought she was putting on a show to hide her true feelings. Kiran had told him about Maji's fears that the wedding was under a bad spell. He was sure Kiran had exaggerated and that it was just the way how his mother expressed her love and concern for her grandson.

'Now you are asking me how I am doing? Isn't that a bit late? Everybody is doing what they want in this family. I am the last one to be consulted. I have warned you about this wedding and now see what has happened. Even the gurudwara refuses to marry your son.' Manpreet replies without looking at Bopinder.

'Maji, I thought we had discussed this. Andalip has made his choice. Times have changed. Christina is a very nice girl from a good family, well-educated and very respectful. And she is going to live with us under one roof. Even in Indian families, this is not that common anymore,' Bopinder says. 'And I saw you dancing at the *sangeet*. Don't tell me you are not having a little bit of fun.' he teases.

'Well, that has nothing to do with what is right or wrong. I agree with you, Christina is a very nice person. Everybody is having a great time. Of course, considering the amount of money you are spending on all these functions. I was willing to listen to you and Andalip, even though my heart has been telling me that this is not the right decision for this family. I told you, your father has spoken to me in my dreams. I am sure you think that I am old and confused…' Manpreet pauses and takes her son's hand. Bopinder looks at her and for the first time since her hospital stay last month, he remembers how old and weak his mother has become. Why does she always have to act so tough, he wonders.

'Well, I know you are old. You have to be if your children are older than 60,' he jokes. 'I know you are not confused. Otherwise you would not have been able to keep up with your great-grandchildren on the dance floor, singing to the latest Bollywood hits.'

'Seriously, Beta. I am willing to ignore my dreams but I am not sure how much I can ignore all these other signs. Something is just not right.' Manpreet looks worried.

'Ma, nothing bad has happened. We are living in Delhi. Look at any other day or week in your life and tell me that things don't go wrong. Electricity comes and goes, things blow up. Accidents happen, objects get stolen, plans keep changing. Nothing new! Didn't we just discuss this? Don't blame Christina and Andalip for that. And let me tell you, trying to pull off a week-long wedding with hundreds of guests is a difficult thing. No other country or culture even attempts that. Don't focus on the few mess-ups, see what we managed to do in the last four days. Amazing, I say!' Bopinder tries to cheer her up.

For a moment, Bopinder seems to notice a smile on his mother's face. He feels like he is on the right track to win her over. 'Don't you remember Preeti's wedding? We were all waiting at the house for the *baraat* to arrive. I think there were no cell phones then and we couldn't figure out what took them so long. I will never forget when that young kid walked through the gate… who was it? Kabir's nephew or somebody. All in tears and upset! He told us that it would be a while for his family to arrive, since they needed to find a new horse for Kabir to ride. The one they had hired that morning had collapsed and died of a heart attack before they could even get the groom on it.' Bopinder chuckles just thinking of the confusion around that poor horse. He wipes a tear from his eye, trying to put on a straight face again.

His mother seems not at all amused. 'Come on, mother. You have to admit, that was really funny!' Bopinder keeps chuckling.

'Thanks for reminding me. Did you think I needed more evidence to confirm my belief in bad omens? Out of all weddings, you had to pick that story. Are you really that dumb? Or has your daughter not told you that she is getting a divorce? I wouldn't be surprised if she hadn't. Nobody around here respects their elders anymore. And who did they learn that from other than you? That is why I had to take control of the situation. It is not too late to do something. Or do you want your oldest son to end up like your daughter? Divorced and depressed? Is that what you want?' Manpreet stares at her son.

Bopinder is confused: 'What are you talking about? Divorce? Preeti is not getting divorced.' Bopinder is trying to make sense of what his mother just said. No, she's talking nonsense, he thinks while he watches her holding her chest. 'Why don't you calm down before you get another panic attack?'

'I knew it! She has not told you! It is the talk of town. Your daughter has left Kabir. If you don't believe me, go ask her yourself. And if you don't come to your senses about this wedding tomorrow, I will just handle it myself. Don't underestimate me! Now tell Mary to bring me my heart medication before your stupidity kills me,' she says angrily.

Bopinder is not sure if he should believe his mother. So what if his daughter is getting a divorce and did not tell him about it? She probably has her reasons, like not upsetting everyone during her brother's wedding. Anger grips him. How can she talk about respect if she treats me this way? I am 65 years old and not some dumb teenager, he thinks furiously.

'I will get you your medicine. But first I want you to promise that you won't do anything stupid to ruin your grandson's wedding. That includes dying! We all love and respect you but that does not give you the right to act and talk this way. I came here to talk to you and check on you but not to be insulted. If you want to talk to me about your concerns about the wedding, talk but don't act like this.' Bopinder stands in front of his mother and tries to control his anger as he talks to her.

'Well, bad news. I won't be dying anytime soon. But whatever is going to happen at the wedding is out of my control now,' Manpreet declares while getting up from her chair, pushing past her son towards her bed to lie down.

'What do you mean by "out of your control now"? What did you do?' he asks, suddenly remembering Andalip's questions about his mother's involvement with the police on the night of the theft. He sits next to his mother on the bed and waits for an answer, but Manpreet just stares into space. 'You paid them off, didn't you? To do exactly what, if I may ask? Maybe to invent some new rules about foreigners getting married at the gurudwara? And now we are paying them to allow us to get married in our neighbourhood park. Of course, that police officer is happy. He is making more money from us in a week than he does in a year. That is just fabulous, Maji!' Bopinder's voice trembles. 'I am sorry, but as far as I am concerned, we are all set to get our son married tomorrow. I just wish it did not have to come this far… You definitely have gone mad. I don't need your blessings to feel good about my son's happiness,' Bopinder shouts.

Before he can get up, Manpreet holds his arm and pulls him close. She sits up, speaking calmly but firmly to her son: 'You got it all wrong, Beta. I did not pay money to stop the wedding at the gurudwara. That was God who spoke to us and you ignored it. I paid money to open your eyes. If you don't believe in the little signs that God sends you, I thought you needed something bigger to see what is planned for your children's future. But even the loss of the wedding jewellery, those symbols of traditional values and blessings that have been handed down many generations, did not make you realize what I have been saying all along…'

'Ma? What did you do? Where is the jewellery?' Bopinder panics. He cannot believe what he is hearing. 'I hope it is not with the police? How much money did you give them? Who is involved in all this?' Bopinder's mind is trying to sort all these questions in his head. She has gone mad, he thinks, staring at his mother, sitting on the bed.

The last few days flash by in front of his eyes. He tries to remember every moment of interaction with his mother. He tries to recall his interaction with the police officers. Should he have seen this coming? How is Raj involved in all this? Did Anhad know what is going on?

Bopinder jumps up and leaves the room. 'Mary, where are you? I need you to sit with Mom and make sure she is OK. Don't leave her out of your sight until I am back. Do you understand?' Bopinder yells while running out of the house.

Chapter 36

Tripat decides to call the family next door for an impromptu dinner in her house. Since her nieces had left for Jazz's house and are still busy with last-minute preparations, only Andalip and Christina's parents would come over as well as her sister-in-law, Manjeet, and her children and grandchildren. Nobody picks up on Dadi's landline, so she figures Manjeet will make sure that she was invited as well. Ranveer looks cheerful when he returns from his meeting with his brother and nephews and is willing to help out with last-minute preparations. Tripat sends him to get some dessert and drinks for the evening. While he is out, she makes sure that her cook follows her instructions for the continental meal she has planned. She is sure that after three days of Indian *khana*, Christina's parents would be happy with roast chicken, steamed veggies and maybe a couple of salads.

Just as she finishes laying the table and checking the set-up of the bar and living room, the bell rings. She continues rearranging the snack trays, knowing her maid would let her guests in. After a few minutes, the bell rings again. Tripat walks out to see for herself who has arrived, wondering where her staff is.

Since the theft the other night, they had made it a point to keep the door locked. When she opens the door, she sees her brother-in-law standing outside, looking lost. 'You are the first.' Tripat says and opens the door for him to enter. 'Where is Ranveer? I need to talk to him,' Bopinder says without moving from the driveway. 'He should be back any minute. Getting some more beer and things for dinner. You can wait inside,' she says. Bopinder looks around and then enters the house, heading straight to the living room. 'Just help yourself to a drink. I need to finish something in the kitchen. Where is the rest of your family? You told Christina and her parents, right?' she asks but is not sure if Bopinder hears her. He is standing behind the bar and pouring himself a drink.

In the kitchen, she finds her maid and cook arguing about the finishing touches for the dishes. While Tripat gives them instructions on which plates to use and the recipe for the salad dressing, she hears Ranveer and several others enter the house. She can hear Manjeet teasing her son and daughter-in-law about something and the rest of the family laughing. We don't need a lot of people in this family to make it sound like a party, she muses. If the Germans have come over as well, these guys won't let them get in a word, she smiles. While she is mixing oil and vinegar in a little bowl, she calls out for Ranveer to bring in the things that he has bought and checks on Bopinder in the living room.

Suddenly she hears Bopinder's voice in the hallway, telling everybody to shut up. Tripat tells the cook to take over and leaves the kitchen to see what is going on. 'Listen everybody, I want you to be quiet for a minute before Christina and her family arrive. Better Andy is not here either, so please listen…' Bopinder sounds worried.

'I hope everything is OK?' Tripat asks finding her family standing like school children in a row in the hallway. 'Let's sit in the living room. This is a bit awkward, isn't' it?'

Before anybody gets a chance to move, Bopinder approaches Anhad. 'Beta, you need to tell me what happened the night of the theft. I know you handled the situation with the police while we were out. Who called them? When did they arrive? Was Dadi involved in any way? I need to know.'

Anhad looks surprised. 'Why, what happened, Tayaji?' Anhad asks.

Kiran walks over to her husband. 'Calm down. What happened? Can't we discuss this inside?' Bopinder just shakes his head 'no' while staring at Anhad. 'Please, I need to know. I just spoke to Dadi and something is going on. She has done something to manipulate the wedding but I cannot figure out what it is. The only one who was there with her two nights ago before the party at the Golf Club and dealt with the police was you, right? Did she get a chance to speak to the police alone? Think, Anhad, think!' Bopinder pleads.

Anhad still does not understand. Tripat can tell that he is seriously trying to figure out what is going on. Since she was already at the Golf Club that evening when the crime was discovered, she only knows what was told to her. From what she understands, Anhad dealt with the situation extremely well, talking with the police and getting that boy Raj arrested quickly. God knows what would have happened if her nephew wasn't in the house at that time.

'OK, here's the thing. Dadi said something about taking things into her own hands, making sure that the wedding does not happen. She also said something about the missing jewellery. And from what I can gather after talking to Andalip earlier, the police took some money from her for something. The only problem is that I cannot figure out what exactly happened. Unless we talk to the police and asked them directly, I doubt Dadi will admit to what she has done…' Bopinder says in a trembling voice. Everybody starts talking, voicing disbelief in what they just heard. 'I just don't want anything going wrong tomorrow!' he finishes sadly.

Not knowing what to do, everybody finally moves into the living room and sits down. Anhad tries to remember what happened: 'Dadi had asked me to call the police. She and that maid Anita had noticed that the jewellery was missing. I dealt with them when they arrived and showed them around the house. Anita told me that she had seen Raj coming to the house in the morning and that he had returned later in the afternoon looking for Frauke. Dadi had verified her statement and things were sorted out quickly. We sat in Dadi's room with the officers for a bit while waiting for Christina to confirm where she had kept the jewellery and that Raj had seen the box when he was in the apartment that morning. According to Anita, he was there when Christina showed the jewellery to her family—and I believe Raj—before the *mehendi* ceremony. I don't think Dadi could have talked to the police alone, somebody was always around.'

'Did you pay the police any money?' Bopinder asks.

'No, of course not. For what? Anhad replies. Again, everybody falls silent.

'Sounds like everyone's still recovering from all the partying... I have never seen this family so quiet,' Andalip jokes while entering the room, followed by Christina, her parents, sister and niece. Tripat quickly gets up and greets them. 'Yes, everybody is tired. So let's gets the snacks out and we'll eat dinner soon. We don't want to show up at the wedding half asleep,' she says. The men move over to the bar and prepare drinks. Manjeet tells her daughter-in-law to get the kids over so Fiona has somebody to play with. The conversation starts rolling and laughter once again fills the room.

When Tripat returns to the room with the first tray of snacks, Andalip comes over. 'Thanks Chachi for organizing this. I think we all needed a quiet evening at home. I am not sure about everybody else, but I am really exhausted by all of this already.' Andy then turns to his uncle and says: 'And thanks for helping out with relocating the wedding. I thought I could have done it myself, but I guess I have been away too long to realize what is involved.

And even if I had managed to get it organized, I could never have done it as smoothly as you did.' Andy hugs Ranveer.

'Beta, don't be silly. This is nothing really. And I don't know about smooth… Look at us old Punjabi men, nothing is smooth about us!' Ranveer laughs and slaps his brother's back. Bopinder chuckles: 'No, Bhaiya, Andalip is right. I enjoyed your dealings with the officers, too. Especially the touch with the invitation card! It is so much nicer to hand over money in a red and gold envelope than hiding it in a brown paper bag.' They all laugh.

Anhad suddenly joins them. 'What did you just say about the wedding invitation? Did you hide the money for the cops in that?' he asks his uncles and cousins. Ranveer just waves his hand and tells him to have a drink. 'Let's just move on and not discuss this any longer. As long as we got it all done in time, we should not mention it again.' Ranveer replies.

Anhad's face lights up. He looks at Bopinder. 'That's it, Tayaji. She wasn't alone with the officers but she did hand them a wedding invite before they left and told them to make sure to check out the upcoming events in there. Maybe there was no invitation inside but money and instructions or something like that. What do you think?'

'Who are you talking about?' Andy asks. Bopinder and Ranveer nod their heads. 'Well, I learned from the best!' Ranveer says. 'But what if Anhad is right? What do we do now? How will we find out what she paid them for? And where is the jewellery? We need to talk to her again,' Bopinder wonders. Without waiting for a reply, he rushes out with Ranveer and Anhad in tow. Before Andy gets a chance to follow them, Tripat holds him back.

'Don't worry, Beta. Let them go and take care of it. Let's start with dinner and make sure your in-laws are having a good time. Looks like your mother and mother-in-law are getting a bit emotional over there. Why don't you check on them?' Tripat tells her nephew and guides him back into the living room. To make sure he does not run after the men, she calls Christina over and tells her to help her soon-to-be-husband in dealing with the moms.

Let's hope they know what they are doing, Tripat thinks while making sure her guests are enjoying the evening and having enough to eat.

Chapter 37

Christina wakes up to the sounds of people's voices, blowing horns and hammering noises outside the apartment. For a minute she is confused, the noise reminds her of the construction site next to her apartment in Manhattan. The bare white walls and the suitcases on the floor remind her that she is in her room in Delhi. Today I am finally getting married, she thinks with a smile on her face before jumping out of bed. When she opens the blinds, she notices that the sun is just rising. Still she can hear her family moving around in the living room. 'This is not your quiet Hamburg suburb, where birds wake you up at sunrise. I bet they think the world is coming to an end with that soundtrack outside,' she muses, picturing her parents panicking in the living room. By the time she pokes her head through the door, everybody is gone. She checks her parents' bedroom, which is also empty. She follows the noise and ends up on the terrace outside her front door. Her parents, sister and niece are standing, still in their pyjamas, by the parapet looking at the park below. Unlike the fear she expected to see on their faces, she finds them filled with excitement watching the activity in front of the house.

'What is going on?' she asks but no one responds. Everybody is focused on the hammering and shouts from below. She stands right beside her family. The park is buzzing with people, mainly skinny, shirtless men putting together a wooden structure and moving around rolls of fabric. A large truck with tables and chairs is blocking the narrow lane in front of the house. Christina recognizes one of the neighbours standing in front of his house, yelling at the workers unloading the truck. She quickly steps back, not wanting to be seen by anybody. 'Look at the speed of these people. Looks like a bunch of ants crawling around. See these guys balancing on top of the bamboo poles? Amazing! Is that going to be a tent?' Michael asks excitedly.

'Is that where the wedding will be?' Frauke asks.

Christina shrugs her shoulders. 'I know as much as you do. What was the gossip at the dinner last night?' Christina asks. She is trying to sound casual, not sure herself how this day will turn out. Her only communication with Andy yesterday had been through SMSs, since he was busy with last-minute wedding preparations. At dinner, there was no time to talk to him alone. Fiona giggles: 'Just like you said, Tante Christina. There are always possibilities of last-minute changes in India. This is great, I can take photos from up here while they are setting up the venue and show them for my school presentation.' With that she runs off to get her camera. That's all I need, having this documented for some 7th graders in Germany, Christina shakes her head and follows her niece inside. 'Let's go and have some breakfast. It's too loud to go back to sleep,' Bärbel says, pulling her husband and Frauke with her.

Christina lies down on the pull-out sofa in the living room that her sister and niece have been sleeping on. Fiona has found her camera and runs out again, followed by her grandfather, both eager to be part of the early morning activities outside the house. Her mother and sister disappear into the kitchen to make coffee. Christina feels tired. She closes her eyes. She can hear her mother looking through drawers and cupboards in the kitchen. She calls out, asking if they need help, without opening her eyes, relieved when they say they can manage alone. 'How difficult can it be? Frauke, just look through the drawers and cupboards. There is hardly anything here yet, should be easy to find. Anyway, I think it's nice to have the place to ourselves for a bit. It feels a bit funny having a person around you all the time, catering to your needs. Although, I could get used to the not-cooking-part.' Christina can hear her mother chatting away. Christina cannot help but smile. She can only imagine her mother reporting to her friends back home about her daughter's luxurious life in Delhi with maids and drivers.

Even though the dinner at Tripat and Ranveer's finished early, Christina could not sleep last night. Her mind was filled with too many things. Everybody has been really nice to her yesterday but something was going on in the house, she was certain, but she could not figure out what it was. After Andy dropped her back at the house after brunch, she had been stuck in her apartment for the rest of the day. She had asked Andy if there was anything she could do to help but all he said was for her to rest and look beautiful. When she had asked Kiran what was expected of her for the day, she told her pretty much the same thing. Christina was thankful that her family had decided to spend the day sightseeing and had insisted for her to take the day off. After reading for a while, she had called Andy to see if he wanted to spend some time with her, but he did not pick up. When she went to the first floor to find him it seemed like nobody was home, so she went to her room again and started watching TV.

The afternoon went by with a few phone calls. Her parents kept calling to ask questions about good shopping spots and must-see sights. Christina had suggested that they go to a mall and find everything under one roof but her family wanted a 'true Indian experience' as Michael put it. At one point, Frauke had called asking if it was OK to follow some guy they had met at Janpath market to his house to see Kashmiri carpets. Christina was not sure if her sister was joking. 'What do you mean to go to somebody's house? Would you do that in Hamburg? No? So don't do it here…'

Christina was getting a little worried about them and again told them about the new malls, but her family was determined to explore Delhi like the locals.

P had hooked up with Christina's cousins and Günther to show them around Delhi. After a quick drive by the India Gate the entire group had ended up having cocktails on the terrace at the Imperial Hotel. P called a few times to check whether Christina was sure she didn't want to join them. With every phone call the laughter got louder in the background and P became gigglier. For a moment Christina was tempted to join them and enjoy her last unmarried day with friends, but then she was sure she would get carried away. She chose to listen to the 'rest and look beautiful advice' and promised they would repeat this after the wedding.

Instead of phone calls, she received text messages from Andy. One text said he was on the way to the gurudwara to check out the wedding venue. Another one followed less than an hour later saying that there was a minor change in plan. 'Need to relocate wedding to Golf Links. Will fill you in later, but all good. Don't worry, I've got it all under control. Love u! A.' was all he wrote. When she tried his phone, it was busy. He never called her back. She wasn't worried at first, but now she was. She was itching to find out what happened but did not know what to do.

At some point, Anita came upstairs to tell her to come to Kiran and Bopinder's room for tea. When she asked her if Andalip was there too, she said no. After the argument at breakfast, she felt awkward to go down by herself so she said she wanted to take a nap instead. Anita said that all the children were there too, referring to Andy's sisters and their families, adding that they were all waiting for her. Again, she tried Andy's phone but got no response. She did not want to be rude and had quickly changed. Even while going downstairs, she could hear loud voices coming from the first floor. As she reached the bottom of the stairs she saw Andy in the hallway, storming out of his parents' bedroom into his bedroom across the hall. Christina stopped when she saw his parents following him. She was confused about what was going on and how to react.

Wasn't Andy out somewhere dealing with wedding preparations? Why didn't he answer his phone? Didn't Anita say he was not here? While she was still planning what to do next, Andy came out of the room and headed towards his parents' bedroom. He did not see her. Christina thought he looked stressed and maybe a bit angry. A few seconds later he came out again, this time followed by Jazz. Both of them went down without noticing her. Kiran was the next one back in the hallway. When she saw Christina standing in the TV room, staring down the hallway, she came over to check on her. 'Are you OK, Beta? Did you sleep? Why don't you join us for some tea?' Still frozen in place, Christina asked in return: 'Was that Andy? What's going on?'

Before Kiran could answer, Bopinder appeared in the hallway. Christina watched as he told Kiran to follow him downstairs, saying that he needs to talk to his sister. When he realized Christina was there he stopped talking. Christina thought her in-laws were exchanging strange looks before Bopinder smiled and excused himself. Kiran just shrugged when Christina asked her what was going on and told her to ask Andy. 'Some change of plan. Nothing to worry about! Why don't you get some rest and try to look pretty for tomorrow?' she said and left her standing in the hallway, returning to the room. The conversation inside had stopped and she could hear Kiran say something in Punjabi to everybody. Christina felt totally out of place and rushed back upstairs.

When she couldn't get through to Andy, she tried Jazz's number which was busy too. She was trying to calm herself, thinking this must be normal pre-wedding stress. When somebody knocked at the door she was hoping it was Andy, but instead it was Anita with a plate of *samosas* and chicken sandwiches for her. Christina tried to get some gossip out of her, but she quickly ran out of her Hindi vocabulary. Anita left and promised to return with some *chai*. While settling down in front of the TV again, she went through her phone trying to figure out who would know what was going on right now and would tell her about it. She called Preeti, who picked up after only one ring. 'Hey, what are you doing?' her sister-in-law asked casually. 'Nothing, just resting and trying to look pretty for tomorrow. Just like everybody is telling me to do,' she said. They chatted for a bit before Christina asked her what was going on. 'Nothing, why?' Preeti had replied quickly.

'Because I have been trying to reach Andy and he does not call me back. He only texted me that the wedding venue needs to be changed. Have you heard anything about that? Then I ran into your parents downstairs and they acted a little weird. Just wondering… You know, I am getting a bit nervous here. Maybe it is normal before one's wedding to feel like this. It is just that I don't know how things are done in India and I feel a little lost right now. I wish Andy would take some time to talk to me. Do wedding venues often change at the last minute? Should I be worried?' Christina asked. Before Preeti could answer she had continued: 'Then this thing happened at brunch this morning. I felt like your dad was blaming me for the loss of the jewellery. Again, I don't know if he really did. I just feel like I really don't understand what is going on around me. I speak English, but I still feel like I don't get what people are saying. And then when I say something to people, I think that I might be offending them, but I don't really know why. Like that incident with your grandmother at the *mehendi*… I had no idea how to react to her outburst when my wrist was cut. In Germany, I would know what to say. Well, I doubt anybody would talk about bad *karma* when you get hurt during your wedding…or if they do, I know they would be joking. So I thought she would be fine after the first outburst but then she lost it again at the house the evening when she found out about the jewellery theft. And all Andy says is that I should not worry. You know how often I heard today 'Go rest and look pretty tomorrow'?' Christina stopped, catching her breath.

Preeti took some time to answer her. 'Honestly, Christina, I don't know what's going on, if anything. Must be nerves! I really like you and I know my brother loves you more than anything. You should focus on that right now and you will be fine. It's the wedding blues, that's it.' Preeti had said and quickly ended the conversation. But then to Christina's surprise she had called back. 'I admire you, Christina. You are very brave to go through with this wedding. It takes a lot of courage to stand up against norms and family traditions, especially in India where families are so close-knit and traditions are still strong, unlike the West. Of course things will go wrong and people will say something against your wedding. That won't stop even after the wedding, trust me. But people will get used to you and things will eventually settle down. Just give it some time. You and Andy are a great team, just believe in that and you will have a great wedding. A great marriage!' Then she giggled: 'Now rest and try to look pretty for tomorrow!'

Chapter 38

Christina had spent the rest of the afternoon just sitting on her bed trying to figure out what Preeti had told her. Was it really such a big deal that she was getting married to Andy? Did Andy's family have to get used to her? And vice versa, did her family consider it an effort to like Andy? Wasn't it enough to just love Andy to have a happy marriage in India or was it more important to follow traditions and norms to have a successful married life? Questions were spinning through her head. She tried to calm herself by picturing herself all dressed up as a bride and then Andy's wife. For some reason she kept dreaming of a quiet wedding on a beach; it was hard to get excited about a wedding with 300 relatives whom she didn't even know.

It was almost 8 pm when her parents returned, excited about the treasures they had found at the different markets. They were looking forward to the dinner party next door, that Kiran said they were invited to. She'd also told them to ask Christina as well, since nobody had wanted to disturb her beauty sleep.

Then, Andy appeared in the apartment, all ready to pick them up for dinner. 'Where were you all afternoon?' Christina had asked him as normally as possible. 'I bet in a few weeks you will be happy when you get some time to yourself, without your husband being around constantly,' he said in jest, winking at Michael. Instead of an answer, both her father and Andy got silly, cracking jokes about married life. It was only on their way out that he casually mentioned that he had both bad news and good news. 'I think I texted you that we had to move the wedding venue. Something came up at the gurudwara and we needed to find a new location for the ceremony tomorrow. The good news is that the wedding will be right here in Golf Links, which means everybody will get an extra half an hour of sleep in the morning to look their best for the function.' At that point Christina could not stop herself and hissed back: 'Honestly, how unattractive do I look that everybody is telling me to just rest and try to look beautiful for tomorrow?'

After a cold gin and tonic, Christina had a good time at the dinner. Maybe it was just pre-wedding nerves she felt and enjoyed the evening with her family. She thought it was weird that her father-in-law, Ranveer and Anhad disappeared before dinner, but at that point she had decided that she wouldn't worry about anything unless Andy told her to. He seemed fine so she tried her best to have fun. Her head hurts trying to figure out how many drinks Maya had poured for her last night. So much for resting and looking beautiful, she remembers joking with Andy at some point in the evening.

For a minute she must have dozed off in her living-room, recalling the events of the last few days. Frauke is standing next to her with two cups of coffee in her hand, calling her name several times before she sits up and takes the coffee. 'That's exactly what I need right now,'Christina smiles, enjoying the strong cup of Joe.

For a while the sisters sit quietly on the sofa-cum-bed, watching their mother roam around the living room before disappearing into the bedroom. Michael and Fiona are still outside watching the wedding preparations in the park.

'So, are you ready to get married today?' Frauke asks.

Christina nods: 'Sure thing. More than ready!'

'You know, I wanted to apologize to you. I was not really happy to come to India at first and especially worried about Fiona, but I am really glad we came. I just wish Berndt could have come as well. He really does not know what he is missing. The last three days have been filled with new experiences and impressions that I would never have had just sitting in Germany,' Frauke says, putting her head on Christina's shoulder. Christina smiles. This was how they often sat when they were teenagers in their parents' house, she remembers. Only at that time, Christina was the little one, usually seeking advice from Frauke about boys or trying to get some gossip out of her. For some reason, today she felt like she was the older sister.

'I am glad that you are here. I could not get married without you!' Christina says, wondering when they would get another chance to sit like this again. Our worlds are so different, she thinks.

'But I have to tell you something,' Frauke continues. 'I don't understand most of what is going on around me. India is just too different for me. Not in a bad way, don't get mad at me for saying this, but just nothing like I have ever seen before. Just take the whole story around the jewellery theft. What a big drama that was, almost threatening the entire wedding. I still don't understand how that poor fellow Raj got locked up just to cover up the old grandmother's wicked crime of hiding the jewellery. I bet she is jealous of you getting all the attention and she just wanted to get some too at her old age. It's just like a bad movie. If I try to tell this to any of my friends, I bet they won't believe me.'

Christina is confused. 'What do you mean? They found the jewellery? What about Dadi and Raj? I don't follow you,' Christina stares at her sister. 'Did I miss something?'

Frauke laughs: 'Are you kidding? You were right there last night? Don't you remember when your father-in-law arrived at the house right when we were having dessert? He was telling us how he had confronted his mother who then tearfully admitted that she had the jewellery hidden in her room all the time. And that she was the one who paid the police to arrest Raj to divert attention from her. Don't you remember how your mother-in-law shouted at that maid Anita when she showed up at the end of the party to ask if she was needed any longer for the evening? She had teamed up with Andy's grandmother to help her execute her plan.' Frauke pauses, looking at her sister in disbelief. Christina's head is hurting trying to remember what happened last night after the first conversations at the bar.

'Don't tell me you were that drunk? How can you not remember the drama in the house last night?' Frauke asks. Then she leans over and hugs her sister. 'Oh, baby, I was wondering how you were able to take in all that news without losing it… Maybe you should talk to Andy before you get ready and find out what else happened last night. I don't want to be the bearer of more bad news.'

Christina feels terrible. While she is leaning against her sister's shoulder, listening to her talk, last night's events slowly came back to her. She remembers Bopinder storming into the dining room, looking like he was about to have a heart attack. Andalip had jumped up and helped him to sit down, repeatedly asking him about what had happened. When Kiran suggested discussing this in private after dinner, Bopinder had gotten angry and said that this was a family matter and everybody around the dinner table was family now. He told everybody that Ranveer and Anhad had gone to the police station to pick up Raj and should be back soon. Bopinder's voice was trembling when he told them that a terrible mistake had taken place and that Raj had been arrested without committing the crime. He had held Andy's hand, asked him to sit down and made him promise not to get too upset when he hears about the real culprit. Then, in tears he revealed that his mother was behind the theft and Raj's arrest. Christina remembered how everybody started exclaiming disbelief. Bopinder kept wiping his tears, apologizing for his mother's behaviour, saying how embarrassed he was for what has happened. When Andy reacted with horror, Bopinder had grabbed his hand and said with newfound authority: 'Please, don't confront her right now. I've said what needed to be said, trust me! I believe she regrets what she has done. I did not leave her until she fell asleep. Don't wake her now; she needs to rest. Talk to her in the morning. But remember, I've sorted out and matters I want this wedding to continue without further complications. Sometimes things go wrong in families. The important thing is that at the end, everybody comes together and moves on. I am just sorry that Michael and Bäerbel had to witness all this but I hope they forgive us for this bumpy start.' Like in a trance, Christina had watched her parents and Andy's parents hug each other and shake hands. Andy was just sitting in his chair staring into space. Christina was frozen. Tripat tried to save the evening by keeping the glasses filled and murmuring that things will look better in the morning.

'Chrissie, are you OK?' Frauke asks. 'I did not mean to…' but Christina interrupts her.

'No, don't worry. Of course I remember. I guess I tried to block out last night's events. And I am sure the countless drinks, coupled with the painkiller that I took before sleeping helped me forget.' Christina rubs her head and smiles.

'So what happened after I left to take Fiona upstairs? Did you get a chance to talk to Andy? I take it the wedding is still on, considering the fact that they are building a huge tent out there for the event,' Frauke says.

Christina laughs: 'You didn't miss much. I think everybody was really exhausted and ready to go to bed and digest the evening's drama. There was lots of hugging and teary eyes before everybody headed out. Andy and I talked for a little while but we did not discuss the wedding. I know he is really upset with his grandmother, but I think he will deal with that later,' she tells Frauke.

Christina finishes her coffee and gets up. 'I better get ready before the beautician shows up,' she says to her sister and goes to her bedroom. She sits down on the edge of her bed, one hand rubbing her eyes, the other her head. Panic sets in.

'This is crazy', she thinks,' I cannot get married. I can't believe I just swallowed all this without even saying a word. Some 84-year-old grandmother is acting totally crazy and putting an innocent person into jail, for what? What is she going to do if she does not like the way I raise my children? Hire a head-hunter? And Andy just let's his father handle all this after being impressed by a few tears? What a histrionic performance?' She stands up and stares at herself in the mirror: 'It's not too late to stop this madness, Christina. Don't do it. Don't get married. This mad family is going to eat you alive!' she tells the red-eyed reflection in front of her before she storms out of the room.

Chapter 39

Manpreet is sitting in her bed, still wearing her *kaftan*. Just like every morning, Mary has already brought her tea and tidied the room while she was in the bathroom. While drawing the curtains and opening the door to the garden, Mary reminds her to get ready quickly for the wedding ceremony which is in a few hours. Until then, Manpreet was hoping that last night's events were just a nightmare. Every bone in her body hurts from tossing around restlessly in her sleep. She ignores Mary's advice and lies down, closing her eyes. Maybe Zorawar will come and talk to me again, Manpreet prays while lying still on her side.

Mary switches on the fan before leaving the room. Manpreet can feel the cooler air mix with the warm, heavy breeze from outside. Her hair tickles her cheek and for a moment she wonders if it is her husband lovingly stroking her face. Her heart aches, knowing the next time she will meet him is when she is dead herself.

She curls up like a baby and starts rocking. Until last night, she felt strong and ready to stand up for her beliefs. Today, she is full of pain, shame and anger, convinced that she'd rather die than attend her grandson's wedding. Almost as if someone is pouring salt into her wounds, memories of the previous day come back to her.

Until the afternoon she was convinced that she was doing the right thing in stopping her grandson's wedding, and that she had all the right in the world to use any means to do so. But by early evening, something strange happened while she was sitting alone in her room. She was planning on how to stop Andalip from making a huge mistake by marrying Christina, when her late husband Zorawar appeared in the room. Manpreet was used to seeing him in her dreams but never during the day. She was thrilled to see him and reached out to touch his hand, but he was too far away. She expected him to come closer and say something, but he just stood there, staring at her. She felt awkward talking to him, knowing she must be dreaming or experiencing God's mysterious ways. When he didn't move, she knew she had to address him before he disappeared.

'I am glad you have come today. I promised you that I would take care of your family, and that all the grandchildren would be married before I leave this world to join you. I know I have failed you with Andalip's choice of wife, but I promise I will take care of it. I will stop his wedding tomorrow and see that he marries a suitable girl,' she heard herself speak. Still Zorawar just stood there. When she rubbed her eyes, he was gone.

When her son walked into her room to talk to her, she felt confident enough to stand her ground. She knew she was dealing with the wedding the right way. Seeing him getting agitated just seemed to prove her point that it was up to her to take care of the family. She was certain that her eldest son is weak and unable to make the right choices for his own children. It was up to her to take care of unfinished business. After their fight and when Bopinder left her room, she felt tired and closed her eyes to rest. Zorawar appeared again. This time he spoke. She was afraid to move, in case she lost him again.

To her surprise, he was mad at her. He scolded her like a small child: 'You silly girl. What are you doing? Committing a crime in the name of caring for your family? Ruining innocent people's lives? Talking to your children like that. You are right that I am disappointed in you. But not for letting this wedding happen but for the way you have been acting lately. You talk about respect and family values, but who is not paying any respect and destroying family values? You are absolutely right that I want you to take care of family business. But you should listen to your children more on how to do that.' Before she could answer him he was gone.

Later at night, as expected, her sons had come to talk to her once again. Instead of arguing with them, she let them talk and then handed over the jewellery. How could she have been so wrong? How could she have misunderstood what her husband wanted from her? She felt confused but she could not apologize to her children. Instead of words, she only had tears to speak for her. When Ranveer and Anhad had left the room, Bopinder sat with her in silence. In the badly-lit room, he reminded her of her husband. Before falling asleep she was not sure if it was Bopinder or Zorawar who stroked her head to calm her.

She feels a hand on her back. She turns around and finds her grandson lying next to her on the bed. For a few minutes they just look at each other. She strokes his face like she did when he was a boy, crawling into her bed, spending the night between her and her husband. His hair used to be black and long. In the mornings she would comb his hair and tie it into a neat *patka* before he would go to school in his shorts. She would spoil him with sweets and *paranthas* when he came home, making sure he would spend time with her before heading off to his parents.

To her surprise, Andalip starts crying. She pulls him closer and kisses him on the forehead. '*Mera baccha, mat rona!*' telling him to stop like she did when he used to be unhappy as a child.

He wipes his tears and looks at her seriously: 'Dadi, I am so sorry. I should have listened to you when we talked about Christina the first time. Maybe things would not have come this far.'

'No, Beta.' She says, not knowing what else to tell her grandson. She feels too proud to apologize, guilty to have almost lost him, happy he was here now.

'You know I will marry Christina today, right? I thought about not doing it, just like you wanted, but I just cannot break her heart. Break my heart! I just need you to tell me that it is OK. Or that you will forgive me over time. I need you to be there today!' Andalip looks at her with big eyes.

She just nods. Again, she pictures her grandson as a schoolboy in front of her. She misses the old days and Zorawar more than ever. She knows Andalip still has his entire life ahead of him. She hopes she will live long enough to see him start his own family. She prays that her grandson will get to feel as much love as she did throughout her life.

'Andy? Are you in there? I need to talk to you?' she hears Christina outside her door. Before Andalip replies, Manpreet calls her in. 'He is right here with me!' she says, struggling to sit up. She notices Andalip cleaning his face with his T-shirt before moving to the door. Christina waits for him to open the door. He hugs her before pulling her into the room.

'I should have known this is where you are. Are you OK?' she asks him quietly. He nods and tells her to sit on the bed with him. Manpreet is surprised when she shakes her head and instead walks over to her. She is startled when the blonde woman in front of her, bows down in front of her and touches her feet, then folds her hands and greets her with a 'Sat Sri Akal, Dadiji.' Manpreet watches her sit down next to Andalip, taking a deep breath before addressing both of them.

'Like I said, I need to talk to you. To both of you, actually,' Christina says, looking from one to the other.

'Christina, don't worry. I've spoke to Dadi, and it's OK...' Andalip tells her but Christina gestures him to be quiet.

'Please, let me say this Andy,' Christina stops him, looking at him seriously. 'I have been thinking a lot last night and maybe your grandmother is right. Maybe it is not right for us to get married. I don't believe in bad omens but I do believe in respecting our families. Just look at the amount of tension this wedding has caused and what it has made your grandmother to do. You seem all stressed. My head is spinning. Shouldn't weddings be a bit more fun? I was just wondering, maybe love is not enough for a marriage. I am not sure if I will adapt to life in India. It is just too strange for me. How can we force our families to accept our choice for a life partner when we are not really prepared for all this?'

Andalip looks shocked. 'How can you talk like this? What are you saying? You don't want to get married?'

Manpreet watches her grandson and her soon-to-be-granddaughter sitting next to each other, shoulders drooping, heads hanging. Suddenly, she giggles. 'Spoken like a true Sardarni!'

Andy looks at her startled. 'Stop it, Dadi, this is serious.'

'I know it is. And she is absolutely right. Love is not enough for marriage. But both of you seem mature enough to look after each other, even if love should leave you. And by showing up in my room today, you've just proved how much you care—not only for you and your love for Andy, but also for both of your families…which I guess is more than I can claim for myself.' She hugs both of them, still chuckling away. She is surprised and touched by this blonde woman's respectful behaviour towards her, even though she has been acting so devious during the wedding week. Manpreet is still too proud to apologize for her folly. Her voice catches in her throat. She tries to lighten the mood with a joke: 'Honestly, Beta, if you were not so blonde and fair, I would believe you if you said you came all the way from Punjab. I hope you have not been watching too many Bollywood movies with your silly boyfriend here. Now get out of here. I have to get ready to attend a wedding. I don't know about you, but I don't want to be late or miss it!' she laughs, pushing her grandchildren out of the bed and out of the door.

The aches in Manpreet's body are gone, a burden finally lifted from her shoulders and for a split second she feels like skipping into the bathroom for her bath. A sharp pain in her back tells her otherwise and she calls out for Mary: '*Chalo*, somebody come here and help me get dressed! Don't want the neighbours saying that I look like an old witch.' She chuckles while letting herself fall back onto the bed.

Chapter 40

Raj arrives in Golf Links just before the ceremony is about to being. Just inside the colony, he gets stuck in a traffic jam. In front of him are luxury cars with passengers all dressed up in their finest party outfits. He watches some of the guests getting out of the car, walking towards the end of the street, disappearing behind the next corner. Andalip's father has sent a car to bring him to the wedding, so he doesn't mind the wait; he's enjoying the soft, spacious leather seat of the Mercedes. He runs his fingers down the blue pinstripe of the suit he had borrowed from Jean this morning—a complete contrast from the smelly jeans and T-shirt he had been wearing in prison yesterday.

The night that Raj met Andalip at the airport, his father had warned him about getting too friendly with the Singhs. 'They are not like us, Beta. I might owe them a lot for giving me a job and supporting me with your schooling, but don't mistake this for being accepted as one of them. You might have gone to Germany to study and are well-respected professionally, but in their minds, you are still a driver's son. Things might be changing in India and Andalip might have been educated abroad, but trust me, people's mindsets don't change overnight. Go to the wedding, pay your respects, but please keep a distance. I just don't want you to get disappointed or hurt.' Raj remembers his father telling him. Raj had laughed it off and wondered why his dad had even brought this up. He was old enough to look after himself. He was not looking for new friends. He liked Andalip and was intrigued by the fact that he was marrying a German. He was keen to the see the wedding, because who knew, maybe one day he might marry a German too.

The last 24 hours had shaken him up completely. He felt like he was strapped into a roller coaster taking him up and down the many stages of life in just one day. He had reached the top of the world, mingling with the rich, educated and beautiful people he used to read about in novels. He had inspiring conversations with Christina's family about Indo-German relations, cultures, economics and politics while drinking champagne and eating food served on silver trays at the gracious *mehendi* lunch. In the evening he enjoyed Jean's company, discussed French and Indian philosophy, sipping smooth French wines and eating home-made pasta, while watching the stars from the terrace in Shahpur Jat. All these sweet memories had been quickly driven away by an infinite fear for his life, when he found himself alone in a filthy prison cell somewhere in Delhi, without knowing what or who had brought him there. His sophisticated companions were replaced by bugs and the smell of urine. He had tried to recall the taste of sparkling champagne on his tongue to avoid throwing up the foul water that was given to him. Then, out of nowhere, after God knows how many endless minutes and hours, Andy's cousin picked him up late at night, without any explanations. They had stopped for a quick snack but all he said was, 'This was all a big mistake.'

All night, Anhad's words kept echoing in Raj's head. How could an innocent man just get locked up like this, he wanted to ask but he was busy savouring his meal. Maybe he was not listening carefully. Anhad did not explain why he was arrested. The smell of his clothes distracted him and he was planning to burn them once he got home. He watched Anhad's lips move, but was not sure if his words reached his ears or if his brain could process what was said. He was still confused by the fact that he had been released so suddenly. A prisoner one moment, a free man the next. There was no explanation or formal statement, so he had no idea how this state of being came about.

'I hope you are OK, Raj. Again, the entire family is very sorry this happened to you. But you know how things are in India, the law works in weird ways. The good thing is that your name is cleared and the jewellery has been found. And Christina and Andalip can get married tomorrow. I realize that you have suffered the most in all this and I want you to come and attend the wedding so we can thank you for being there for our family. It would mean a great deal to Andalip if you attend. A car will pick you up and we will have a wonderful day together,' Raj remembers Anhad say. Only at night, lying alone in his bed, Raj regretted not enquiring about the thief and how the police found the jewellery after all.

Realizing that the cars in front of him are not moving at all, he decides to walk to the venue. When he turns the corner into the lane in front of Andalip's house, he sees a large red tent filled with hundreds of wedding guests. He enters the park and instinctively scans the crowd for some familiar faces. He is relieved to find Christina's family sitting at the front, watching the musicians setting up their instruments next to the little throne built for the Guru Granth Sahib, before which Andalip and Christina are sitting. He wonders why, even after growing up in India, he feels closer to the Germans than to anyone in Delhi right now. Still, he hesitates to move closer, not sure how his company would be received. When Frauke notices him, she waves to him with a big smile on her face, gesturing for him to sit with them. He decides that especially after yesterday's madness, he could be of some help to Christina's family by explaining various aspects of the ceremony.

As he walks closer, he realizes that the guests are not what he expected them to be. Besides Christina's family and the foreign guests, Andalip's relatives and Delhi's high society, he notices people from all walks of life sitting in and around the tent. At the side, some kids are playing. At closer look he realizes that they are not very well dressed—like the other party guests around him—and some even barefoot, wondering if they just walked across from the nearest flyover, where homeless families sometimes sleep when they don't find any proper shelter. He spots the help from the house with some people he assumes are her family. 'Isn't this exciting?' Frauke asks when he sits down. He is not sure what she is referring to and just nods.

When Bärbel sees Raj, she gets up and comes over. '*Guten Morgen*, we are so glad to see you here today. Andy told us this morning that the police had falsely arrested you yesterday. I am very happy that things are solved now and you are able to attend the wedding,' she says, smiling warmly at Raj.

'So why are we sitting in this park today and not in the gurudwara or some fancy wedding hall?' Raj wonders.

Bärbel laughs: 'Honestly, I have no idea. I am not sure I really know what has been going on this week. Every day could have been a wedding, considering the number of people who had showed up, the food and drinks that have been served and the beautiful decorations. I don't know how many German weddings you have attended, Raj, but each function so far has outdone most weddings that I have attended in my life.' For a moment they sit quietly next to each other, watching people settling down in front of them. 'But do you want to know what I find most amazing? You have to tell me if this is typical for Indian weddings. When we got to the park this morning, the preparations were still going on, and Bopinder had told every man and woman working on the set-up, the drivers and the people hanging out in the park that this wedding was open to everybody. He said that he wanted to share his happiness with all those who want to attend. He told the guard from the house and those police officers over there, that everybody is welcome to pray, eat, drink, dance and be happy with the Singh family this morning. When I asked him about it, he just told me that after so much confusion this week he was more than thrilled that he was able to get his son married this morning. He was laughing loudly when he told me that he had started to believe in his mother's talk about signs and omens. For him it was a good sign that the wedding is taking place in this park and that he feels that more than his family and friends, the world should witness this wedding,' Bärbel says seriously. Raj watches her wipe a tear from her eye.

He does not get to answer her because Andy's uncle asks everybody to be a quiet for a moment. A microphone is handed around and ends up with Andy's father. Raj watches Andalip get up, calling out to his father: 'Keep it short, Dad, or do you want to blow up this tent as well!' People who attended the *path* giggle in agreement, remembering Bopinder's burning turban. Bopinder grins and starts his speech:

'Dear friends, family, neighbours and people of Delhi. Like my son said, I will try and keep it short to avoid any more disasters in this wedding. I want to welcome you all and thank you for sharing this special moment with us, especially those guests who have joined us from across continents.' Raj looks around to see people listening to every word Bopinder is saying. A little girl who looks like she has not had a bath for ages is sitting next to her parents translating every word he is saying into Hindi. Her parents nod to agree with Sahib.

'Like any father, I want my children's wedding to be special. Andy had asked us to explain our religion and culture to his wife and her family, since they are obviously new to all of this. My first reaction was to gift our new relatives a good book on Sikhism to understand what is happening today.' Bopinder chuckles at his own joke but then turns serious quickly.

'But when I sat down to summarize a few of my thoughts, I realized how little I actually know about our own traditions and rituals and how easily we forget—or worse ignore—the basics of our culture in today's fast-paced world. This wedding to me is a great reminder of what it actually means to be an Indian and not what it means to be Sikh. A reminder to look beyond religion, skin colour and class! So today I want to welcome Christina and her family to be part of this great community and country, and us Indians. I like to quote our great poet Rabindranath Tagore who said that India is a meeting place of all cultures, religions, traditions and beliefs. His vision of "Indianness" was "anyone in the world, who believes in inclusion, tolerance and continuity, is an Indian". Let this be our lesson today! Let us embrace the differences we see in each other's faces today and celebrate them with this wedding!'

With the end of the speech, Raj watches the two families embrace while the wedding guests clap and cheer to underline Bopinder's words. When Andy hugs his father on the small podium above the wedding guests, Raj can't help but wish his own father was here today to witness all of this. The stark contrast between yesterday's brutal reality and today's fairytale wedding still upsets him. 'Only in India is a week like this is possible. Only here can one's senses get challenged to its fullest in only one day. Pain can only be understood after experiencing bliss. Integration only makes sense, when discrimination has been experienced. Love can only exist when hate has been overcome,' Raj thinks to himself, filling the void in his heart with the love for his father, his country and old and new friends in his life—all of which he has felt being an important part of as well as being pulled away from in the most intense ways in less than 24 hours.

&

'So, this is it?' Christina asks Andalip after the ceremony is over and she is covered in garlands that the guests draped around her neck. 'No "You may kiss the bride?" No ring ceremony?' she asks not sure if it appropriate to lean over any further to kiss her husband. Even though they are surrounded by hundreds of people, she feels like she finally has a moment to herself with Andy. The families are busy congratulating each other still, she feels shy; aware that now she has officially become somebody's wife.

Andy looks at her with a serious face: 'Oh no, you better stay on your side. Don't you know it is bad luck if you touch me before we are blessed officially by my grandmother? I thought somebody told you!' Still sitting, he leans back away from her as far as possible. Only the pink *dupattas* that were used to tie them together for life connects them. Christina's happiness is once again marred by a feeling of uncertainty and nervousness of not understanding the world around her. 'Really? Why didn't anybody tell me?' she asks, quickly looking around to see if they are being watched. To her surprise, Dadi is standing right before them.

'Now what is going on?' she asks, balancing herself on a walking stick, looking at them with a stern face. Without a warning, she lets go of the stick and let's herself drop next to the newlyweds. She looks from her grandson to her new granddaughter for a few minutes before bursting into laughter: 'Why so serious? Did you guys realize what you just did? You better get used to it! You are in this marriage-shmarrige thing for the long haul, Christina. Once you marry a Sikh, there is no out. No divorce, to your husband or his family.' Dadi giggles and hugs her newest family member.

Andy joins in the laughter: 'No, I just scared her and told her, no kissing in public. Even at a wedding! And I think she believed me!' Both grandson and grandmother chuckle like naughty school kids, about to get caught by their parents. 'Oh, Beta, he was just kidding!' Dadi says and pushes Christina closer to Andy. Then she calls out for the entire wedding party to hear: 'Andy, can you please kiss the bride now and seal this marriage in front of everybody before she decides to run off with somebody else, realizing how crazy this family really is!' While Andy is pulling Christina towards him, his grandmother covers her eyes and lets herself fall back onto the carpet, calling out from the top of her lungs: 'You go boy, show these youngsters what you have learned in America!'

Listening to the laughter and clapping around her, being cheered on by her family and friends, and feeling the earth move around her from the dancing feet, Mrs Christina Singh kisses her husband for the first time.

Epilogue

Christina: 'So, where should we go for our honeymoon? I think we should go the beach! I can't believe that you have not planned anything yet. We have only a week. We should make sure we know what we are doing, so we are not missing out on anything.'

Andalip: 'Not the beach, definitely the mountains. I love the mountains! Why would you want to plan anything? One never knows what happens and then the best prepared plans don't make sense. And by the way, didn't anybody tell you last week what the honeymoon is for?'

Christina: 'What? Don't tell me to rest and look beautiful. I have done enough of that last week before the wedding. Remember?'

Andalip: 'No, silly. It is for making babies. It's time we produce an heir to the Singh empire. Oh, wait, let me pack that *Kama Sutra* book. I think they tell you how you are supposed to have sex to make a boy. Plus, one should always learn something new every day in life.'

Christina: 'You are kidding, right? Until three days ago, we had to act like we had never done it before and you had to sleep in your own room. And today you want me to get pregnant? And, for the record, we are having a girl first, blonde, blue-eyed and her haircut will a cute little bob like mine.'

Andalip: 'Very funny. You know that I come from a long line of eldest son to eldest son to eldest son. I think according to my

DNA I can only do boys! ... Oh, just talking about making babies gets me all excited. Should we start practising now?'

Christina: 'What, right now? Here at the party? You are creepy! Let's talk about the honeymoon. Where do we go?'

Andalip: 'I think I know the perfect spot. Why don't we drive up to Shimla. We can leave tomorrow and then Mom and Dad, maybe Jazz and the kids can meet us there in a couple of days.'

Christina: 'On our honeymoon? While we are working on producing an heir? Are you even listening to yourself? Seriously, Kerala or Goa? You choose. We can hang out at the beach in the morning and do some sightseeing in the afternoon. I have read that both places have amazing seafood.'

Andalip: 'Oohhh, talking about food. Should we get out of here and grab something to eat? I know this amazing kebab place close by. They have amazing *kulfis* too, plus the best *paan* in town.'

Christina: 'Wasn't this just dinner? We have been eating and drinking for the last two hours, I am kind of full. And tired.'

Andalip: 'Oh, honey, you have so much to learn about Indian weddings. Dinner won't be served until around midnight. This was just snacks. But if you are tired, we can leave now and stop on the way for the kebabs, like I said. I'll just tell my friend Pavan that Dadi is not well and we need to head back. He will understand.'

Christina: 'But that is a lie! Can't we just say we are tired and want to go home? Or that we just got married and want to spend time alone. Or even better, that you need to review Chapter 6 in the *Kama Sutra*?'

Andalip: 'No, that would be rude. You just be quiet and I'll handle it...'

Christina: 'And, what did he say? Was he upset that we have to leave?'

Andalip: 'No, not at all. Anyway, we will be seeing him in Shimla next week.'

Christina: 'Haaa?'

Andalip: 'Yeah, isn't that great? I just figured it out. His family owns a house there which is big enough for all of us. If you want to, why don't you ask P and Günther to join us? They are still travelling around India, right? We are going to be married a long time, baby, there will be enough time to be alone. Let's have some fun with our family and friends now.'

Christina: 'So when your grandmother said, there is no divorce according to Sikh religion, was she serious? I am just wondering, is there still time to get out of this? Or do I really have to take the entire Singh clan on my honeymoon?'

Andalip: 'Sorry, baby. When you kissed me in front of all these people, you signed your destiny right there and then. Now, let's get out of here and work on the next generations of Indians according to the wisdom of Tagore and the *Kama Sutra*!'

Christina: 'Correction, my *patidev*. You mean the next generations of Indo-Germans, of course!'

To be continued…

Acknowledgements

Thank you, *danke* and *dhanyavaad*

Little did I know moving to New York from Germany 15 years ago would lead me to New Delhi. India was a mystery to me—a faraway place I knew little about, a place from my childhood dreams, fuelled by images of maharajas and princesses on elephants and singing animals from *The Jungle Book*.

Love often opens one's eyes and definitely makes learning about a new country more fun. This story grew over many years, enhanced by many interactions, humorous stories, tragic misunderstandings and the daily lives of our many cross-cultural friends and acquaintances who have similar stories full of enthusiasm, wisdom, absurdities, passion, love, tragedies and daily miracles that unfold when people of different cultures or backgrounds share a life together.

Thanks to my move to India and the many special people in my life, this story finally came to life. To them I owe eternal gratitude.

My sincerest thanks to my editor and guide, Kausalya Saptharishi at Rupa Publications, who believed in me and my project from day one. Also, many thanks to Amrita Mukerji at Rupa, who saw this project through till the end.

To my dear friend Christine Mueller Gupta, who saw me as a writer before I even dared to 'go public'.

To my 'Indian sister', Shilpa Khullar Sood, who makes me laugh every day—especially when my German self gets lost in my Indian reality.

To Pavan who 'warned me' about the 'challenges' of marrying an Indian husband before I even knew I would.

To my family in Germany, who always encouraged me to explore the world and do great things with my life, while providing a safety net of love for all my 'stunts'. To my parents—Renate and Eicke—who taught me that I can do anything; without both of you, I literally would have not come this far!

To my family in India—Amrit, Gurpreet, Heena, Amardeep and the extended Salwan family in the country and around the world—who welcomed me with open arms into my new home in New Delhi, taught me love and values, and gave me unlimited support. Without you I would have not been brave enough for such a journey. Most of all, there would have been no time and energy to write this book!

To my children, who add meaning to it all—Angad for your persistence, Mila for your strength and Rohan for your big heart. And to Sushila, my children's nanny, without whose help I would have had no time to write.

And last, but not least, eternal love and thanks to my 'patidev' Harjiv, who dares me to dream big, who shows me how to live life to the fullest and who always pushes me to 'just go for it'!

Namaste!